M000084554

THE
AUTHORITIES

ALSO BY SCOTT MEYER:

Master of Formalities

MAGIC 2.0 SERIES:

Off to Be the Wizard
Spell or High Water
An Unwelcome Quest

BASIC INSTRUCTIONS COLLECTIONS:

Help Is on the Way
Made with 90% Recycled Art
The Curse of the Masking-Tape Mummy
Dignified Hedonism

THE AUTHORITIES

SCOTT MEYER

The characters and events portrayed in this book are fictitious. Any similarity to real persons, living or dead, is coincidental and not intended by the author. Product or service names mentioned in this book may be trademarks, registered trademarks, or service marks of their respective owners.

THE AUTHORITIES

Published by Rocket Hat Industries
Text copyright © 2015 by Scott Meyer
All rights reserved.
Cover design by Missy Meyer

This book is protected under the copyright laws of the United States of America. Any reproduction or other unauthorized use of the material or artwork herein is prohibited without the express written permission of the author.

ISBN-10: 0986239968
ISBN-13: 978-0-9862399-6-0

THE
AUTHORITIES

ONE

Officer Rutherford looked forward to the day that he would finally get used to seeing dead bodies. He had a five-year plan, a rather detailed one, which he had laid out before applying to become a police officer. The first line of the plan said: "Join the Seattle Police Department." The last line was: "Become a plainclothes detective." None of the many bullet points in between said anything about getting used to dead bodies. He now realized that was an oversight.

Of course, he thought, *if I had listed all of the unpleasant things I would need to get used to, the plan would have been three times longer.*

He adjusted his gun belt, which he was also not yet used to, even after a year on the job. The belt had seemed like any other belt to him right up until the first time he actually had to put one on. He discovered that it was too large to go through any belt loop ever made, which was fine, because it wasn't designed to keep your pants up. For that you needed your normal belt.

Wearing two belts at once seemed inelegant to him, and he said so to his instructor at the academy, who agreed with him, but only because he'd misunderstood Rutherford's point.

The instructor went on to explain that the gun belt could slide around the body, becoming misaligned with the officer's pelvis, making it more difficult to draw one's weapon. To prevent this, the gun belt is fastened to the trouser belt with small straps made of leather or nylon, locking them together.

The instructor called them "belt keepers," but Rutherford recognized them for what they were: tiny little belts that belted the big belt to the smaller belt.

Rutherford adjusted all of his belts again.

Shouldn't be surprised, he thought. *Dad always said that when all you have is a hammer, every problem looks like a nail. They went to a belt maker asking him to fix a belt problem. Of course his answer was more belts.*

He was also struck by the bitter irony that while he had an overabundance of belts around his waist, he was required to wear a clip-on tie. The rationale was that in a fight, if some dude who was resisting arrest grabbed you by your standard necktie, he effectively had you on a leash. If he grabbed you by your clip-on tie, it would come off in his hand. You would be free to defend yourself, and your assailant would be paralyzed with laughter. Rutherford sometimes wondered if there was any record of an officer being whipped about the face with his own clip-on tie, but it seemed inadvisable to ask.

Rutherford's goal from day one had been to become a detective, and the overabundance of belts only strengthened his resolve. Plainclothes officers were still supposed to wear either clip-on ties or breakaway ties, which tore off of an officer's neck with a light tug and the slapstick sound of tearing Velcro, and were thus even more efficient at turning an attempted assault into an unexpected moment of physical comedy. But at least plainclothes officers got to carry their weapon in a simple paddle holster that clipped on to a single, relatively normal belt. That seemed much more civilized to Rutherford.

He looked at his surroundings and realized that if what he wanted was a more civilized existence, perhaps becoming a cop had been a poor choice.

Rutherford was working in the seedy part of the University District, a few blocks back from frat row. He was maintaining the perimeter at a crime scene in a dilapidated Victorian house that had been converted into a boarding house for broke students by a determined individual who wasn't willing to let zoning laws, building codes, or public safety get in the way of making a profit.

Rutherford stood in the hallway, trying to exude authority. It was not easy. The house naturally drained the dignity from anyone who came inside. Even the mildew seemed embarrassed to be seen there.

Because he was the lowest-ranking officer present, Rutherford stood in front of the door of the worst room in the house. Perhaps it had not been the worst room before, but it currently had a murder victim in it, so Rutherford was pretty sure it had earned that title now.

The victim appeared to be a college-aged male, and the room showed signs of a violent struggle. The body had been discovered by one of the other tenants, who had noticed through the closed door that the victim was splayed on the floor next to the bed. This sounded fishy at first, but the story was made more plausible by the fact that the door had no knob, only a gaping hole where one could be installed at the tenant's expense. Also, the odor had likely drawn some attention. It certainly had Rutherford's, since he had been ordered to stand right next to the door and make sure that none of the other tenants disturbed the crime scene.

The residents were all outside now. His fellow officers had herded a great many freaked-out college students onto the lawn, but nobody had returned to tell Rutherford that he didn't have to babysit the corpse any longer, so there he stood.

Rutherford tried to distract himself from the odor. He thought about how he would describe the smell later.

Imagine how your hands would smell if you bought fifty pounds of past-due-date ground beef and paid for it entirely with pennies.

Rutherford thought that captured it pretty well. He also thought that trying to distract himself from the odor by describing it in detail had been a stupid idea.

He adjusted his belts again.

He heard the sound of the front door opening and closing, followed by the sound of approaching footsteps. Rutherford hoped that he'd get permission to leave his post, or at least pleasant company to distract him from it, but those hopes were dashed when detectives Stoker and Volz came around the corner.

Seattle was a big city, and the Seattle Police Department had a lot of detectives. Some of them were pleasant to work with. Some were less so. Most were more pleasant than Stoker and Volz. They were sloppy, both professionally and personally. Rutherford might have described them as "scuzzy," but that would be an insult to scuz, and he didn't even know what scuz was.

Stoker's suit looked as if he'd slept in it. His hair looked like he'd styled it hastily after sleeping on it. His coat looked like it had recently been wadded up, possibly for use as a pillow. Despite all this, Stoker looked as if he hadn't slept in quite a while.

Volz was shorter, heavier, and looked like he slept just fine. Indeed, his slow movements and drooping eyelids gave the impression that Stoker had probably had to wake him when their car arrived at the crime scene.

Of course, the thing that really bothered Rutherford was that they had the job he wanted, and they weren't even bothering to do it well.

They smiled at Rutherford. Both men had mastered the art of making a smile feel like both a threat and an insult.

Rutherford knew them, and of course, they both knew him. One of the bullet points on the five-year plan was: "Find a detective to be my mentor." Rutherford had set about this task using the same methods he'd employed to make friends in school—being eager and asking lots of questions. It hadn't worked in school, but he'd hoped it would be a better strategy for a twenty-six-year-old man living in the real world. He'd been horrified to discover that while being a cop was as "real" as the world could get, it was alarmingly similar to being in school. It didn't help that even though he was obviously an adult, he was treated like a kid by most of his fellow cops. His curiosity and enthusiasm were often misconstrued as peskiness. His small physical stature and thin frame didn't improve matters. Sure, he was large enough to join the force, but so were all of the other cops, most of them by a substantially larger margin than he was.

"Hey, look who it is," Stoker said.

Volz spread his arms wide in a mocking gesture of delight. "Officer Sinclair, the future detective!"

"Detective Volz," Rutherford said. "Detective Stoker. You both know that my last name is Rutherford." He knew that by correcting them he was giving them what they wanted, but he also knew that to not correct them would have the same effect. The only way he could win was to endure, eventually become a detective, then be better than them. Better at the job, better dressed, and better company, none of which would be difficult.

Stoker furrowed his brow and shook his head, "No, no, I thought your name was Sinclair."

"My first name is Sinclair. My last name, as you know, is Rutherford."

Volz said, "But Sinclair is a last name. Why would your parents give you two last names?"

Stoker said, "I think I get it. His parents were idiots."

"I am named after my father's favorite writer," Rutherford said through clenched teeth, "Sinclair Lewis."

"So there's one other guy in history with the first name of Sinclair. That doesn't mean it's not a stupid first name."

"Actually, Sinclair was his middle name," Rutherford said, regretting it the instant the words left his mouth.

"Which brings us back to the theory that your old man was a dummy," Volz said. "Look, Sinclair, I'm sure it's a nice distraction for you to stand here and tell us your family history, but we have police work to do." He pointed at the door behind Rutherford. "The stiff's in there?"

Rutherford stepped aside and started to recite the details of how the body had been found. Stoker waved him off.

"Inman told me all that outside. All we need you to do is shut up and stay out of our way."

"Done," Rutherford said. I'll just go and—"

"No," Stoker interrupted. "You'll stay right here at your post in the hall, where you belong. Just stay quiet and let the grownups do their jobs. Maybe, if you listen really close, you might learn something."

Stoker and Volz gave Rutherford the stink eye as they walked into the scene of the crime. He turned to watch them. As much as he hated to admit it, this was a chance to learn from them. Today's lesson was in how to close a door in a younger officer's face, then laugh about it with your partner.

Rutherford turned his back to the door and listened. It was a cheap hollow-core door, and the sound went through it like it was tissue paper. The large hole where the doorknob should have been only made it easier for noises to come through.

"Okay," Stoker said, mechanically, reading from his notebook. "Meet Christopher Swanson, at least that's the name we were given. We were also told that he's a student at The University of Washington, like everyone else who lives in this dump. Major: unknown. Discovered at approximately 0645 hours by another tenant who stopped by so they could go grab some breakfast before class. Upon finding the body and determining that Swanson was deceased, he called the police and alerted the landlord. No known enemies. Some of the other tenants who have been questioned say they heard a brief commotion around 2300 last night, but nothing they found alarming. Officer Inman was first to the scene. He went in, confirmed that the victim was dead, and that it was probably not accidental, then established a perimeter and called us in."

There was a brief silence, then Volz said, "No computer. Kid's a student. He'd have a computer. Maybe the killer stole it."

"Nah," Stoker said. "We know about that. The landlord took it before the first responders arrived. Planned to hock it to recoup the rent he's not going to get paid. We've already confiscated it."

Volz exhaled heavily. "Okay, there's not a lot of blood, considering. What there is came from the nose and ear. Forensics haven't been here yet, but looking at the body, I'd say from the bruises that someone beat this guy to death with his bare hands."

Stoker asked, "What makes you say that?"

"Look for yourself. Tell me that bruise doesn't look like a fist."

Rutherford closed his eyes and tried to picture the bruises. He hadn't actually seen much of the body, standing on the opposite side of the door from it, and the odor hadn't yielded many clues.

"You can even pick out the individual fingers and the thumb," Volz said. "That's obviously a fist."

"Yeah," Stoker agreed. "But it's really weird. For the fist to hit him at that angle, the killer can't have thrown a real punch. My guess is that he swung his arm like, I dunno, a bear paw or something."

Rutherford tried to picture this, and couldn't. He even made a fist, then swiped it palm first through the air in front of him. He couldn't imagine any person strong enough to kill someone with such a blow.

"And whoever the guy was, he made his fist weird too," Stoker said.

There was a silence while the two detectives thought about it, then Volz said, "Well, he don't know how to hit a guy right, why would he know how to make a fist right?"

Stoker said, "True. Still, he did the job well enough on this poor sap."

Rutherford heard a muffled rendition of the iPhone default ringtone. Stoker said, "That's me," then grumbled as he dug his phone out of his pocket.

"Stoker. Yes, sir, we're at the scene now. No, sir. Ugh, sir, is that really . . . No, sir! I understand, sir . . . yes, sir."

There was a heavy silence, then Stoker said, "Come on."

The door behind Rutherford opened, and Stoker emerged, trailed by a confused-looking Volz.

"Sarge says we're to clear and guard the scene," Stoker explained to Volz, as if Rutherford wasn't even there. "We gotta make sure nobody comes in or out of here, not even forensics, until after Capp's people have had the run of the place."

Volz and Rutherford both said, "Capp's people?"

Rutherford said it with excitement. Volz did not.

"Yeah, that's right," Stoker said. "It's your lucky day, Sinclair. The circus is coming to town. Anyway, we're to keep the crime scene pristine for them. Volz and I'll wait at the end of the hall. Sinclair, you just go ahead and stay here. You've been doing such a good job of standing around doing nothing, I'd hate to stop you now."

Stoker and Volz retreated to the end of the hall and came to a halt before it emptied into the house's front room. They were only twenty feet away, so there was no way to keep Rutherford from hearing them talk, but it was clear to Rutherford that he was not included in the conversation.

"Yeah," Stoker muttered. "Captain Weinart is running over. He told the sergeant that he wants to be here to meet them. If he doesn't make it, we're to cooperate, but not enthusiastically. That's what he said."

The detectives were deeply annoyed. Rutherford was ecstatic, partly because he had heard lots of things about *Capp's people* and this was his first chance to actually see them work, but mostly because the detectives were annoyed. Rutherford usually didn't take pleasure in other people's unhappiness, but life was serving Stoker and Volz's unhappiness to him on a silver platter. He felt it would be rude not to accept.

TWO

Vince Capp was a known quantity. His name and face were familiar to anyone who paid attention to technology news, as well as those who just happened to live in the Pacific Northwest. Way back in the mists of time, when few people understood computers, Capp had made a killing by writing a piece of software called *Grink*, which did things few people understood even now. It was just one of the torrents of nonsense words that would cascade down the screen too quickly to read whenever you started a program in MS-DOS. Most just accepted that there were certain technologies baked into every operating system that allowed people to interact with their computers, and Vince Capp owned a patent on one of those technologies. Thus, it was impossible to buy a computer without Capp wetting his beak.

After his success with Grink, he had used his monumental fortune to fund CD-ROMs, ISPs, dot-coms, and a company called *Stephenson Auto*, which made cars equipped with a unique steam-electric hybrid drivetrain called *The Stephenson*

Drive. The company's logo looked like a little chrome rocket. Anybody who paid any attention to cars or technology had heard of Stephenson Auto, but since its least expensive two-door hatchback cost six figures, few people had seen one in person.

Capp's ventures had met with varying levels of success, but all had been well funded and extensively publicized. Two years earlier Capp had announced that he was retiring, but as with most people of his ilk, he seemed to think that retirement meant working just as hard, but on a few less-profitable, more civic-minded projects.

Word was that Capp had turned his attention to law enforcement. Sometime in the last several months he had put together a hand-picked team of specialists to test experimental crime-fighting technologies and techniques. People whispered that he'd made substantial donations to various political campaigns to get the governor, the state crime lab, and the chief of police to treat his group as a sort of consulting CSI and investigation firm. In exchange for sharing their findings and experimental techniques with the department, they would get police cooperation and access to records and crime scenes.

Capp hadn't announced anything publically yet, and any officers who interacted directly with the team were not legally able to discuss it, but that didn't stop people from talking. There was rampant speculation about robots, lasers, and more than one person had mentioned a ninja. Rutherford didn't believe a word of it, but he was excited to get to see "Capp's people" firsthand. It almost made the rest of the morning worth it.

Less than five minutes after word had arrived that Capp's people were on the way, Rutherford heard the front door open. Rutherford thought it might be the Captain, but Stoker and Volz stiffened as if awakened brutally from a nice nap, and an unfamiliar female voice said, "Good morning. If I'm not mistaken you're Detective Stoker, and you're Detective Volz."

"That's right," Stoker said. "And you are?"

"Terri Wells," the woman said. She had stopped short of the end of the hall, so Rutherford couldn't see her. He tried to draw an impression from her voice, and settled on *friendly but crisp.*

She said, "I trust you got the call from the Chief of Police's office."

"We got a call from our boss. He got a call from his boss, who probably got your call from the chief." Stoker grunted. "And neither of them were happy about it. We aren't either, for the record."

"From what I gather, neither was the chief when he got the call from the mayor after he got a call from the governor, but the point is, you're expecting us. Now, if I could just get your signatures on these forms. They say that you won't divulge anything you see or hear about my team and its methods unless compelled to do so in the course of your duties. You know, you can file your reports and testify and all that, but no talking to the press or your friends. Are there any other officers in the building at the moment?"

Stoker looked down the hall at Rutherford and jerked his head slightly, expending the least possible amount of energy to beckon him forward.

Rutherford finally got a look at Terri Wells as he approached the detectives. She was a black woman somewhere in her midforties who was neither particularly tall nor particularly thin. Her attire was extremely professional, like that of a realtor who specializes in properties you will never be able to afford. She looked at Rutherford, said, "Good morning officer," and smiled. She wasn't what you'd call "beautiful," but Rutherford wouldn't have respected the taste of anyone who didn't think she was cute.

She reached into the large leather bag she was carrying and produced a metal clipboard and a disposable pen, both of which she handed to Stoker. The clipboard held several copies of a boilerplate nondisclosure agreement, which laid out the penalties for telling people anything about her team's techniques, methods, and technologies in terms simple enough that even a layman could be haunted by them for life.

When all three had signed their lives away, she thanked them, turned her head slightly downward and away from the officers, and said, "You're clear to enter."

"Who are you talking to?" Volz asked.

Wells said, "The team. So, where is the victim?"

"Second door on the left," Stoker said.

"And are there any witnesses?"

"None that we know of yet, but we just got here. The kid who found him and the landlord are being questioned out front. All the other tenants—"

Wells held up a hand, silencing Stoker midsentence. "Thank you, Detective, that'll do. We'll read the details in your report."

"I don't report to you," Stoker said.

Wells said, "Not directly."

The front door of the house opened, admitting a bearded man in his late fifties. He wore a cardigan, a jaunty cap, and a friendly grin. He nodded quickly to the officers and said, "Good morning, gentlemen," as he stepped lightly around the door and held it open for the rest of the team. Next came a man in his twenties. If forced to guess, Rutherford would have said he was of Korean origin. He wore a tweed three-piece suit and carried a briefcase so large it nearly qualified as a midsized suitcase. Behind him was a tall black man with graying hair who wore black slacks, dress shoes, and a blue nylon windbreaker.

They had been described to Rutherford as a top-secret group of high-tech specialists. He had pictured a cross between a SWAT team and an MIT study group. So far, Wells's team didn't look anything like what Rutherford had expected. But the final member to enter the house looked almost too much like what he'd expected.

The woman was wearing a sleek black pants suit over what appeared to be a dark gray turtleneck. It was an ensemble that was undeniably both feminine and menacing. With her left hand, she was using a cane. Between the thickness of the polished black wood and the knurled silver head that resembled the business end of a very small Polynesian war club, the cane looked as if it had been designed more as a means of defense than support. The cane's shaft boasted a gleaming metal inlay pattern that, while decorative, also undoubtedly added to its heft. Rutherford didn't have the opportunity to develop an impression of her face because he couldn't see it. Her entire head was covered by what appeared to be some sort of high-tech helmet, complete with an opaque, featureless front shield. She entered in silence. She made no sound, and the world seemed to quiet itself in her presence. It was as if reality was trying to keep her from noticing it.

The bearded older man closed the door behind her and continued his thought from earlier. "It's a pleasure to meet you all. Sorry it has to be under such unfortunate circumstances." Rutherford thought he detected some sort of European accent, though he couldn't quite place it.

Wells said, "The person who found the body is out front being questioned. Sloan, Warmenhoven, you know what to do."

The older man clapped. "Yes, certainly we do." After rubbing his hands together as if preparing to chop wood, he opened the door he had only just closed. The woman in the helmet stood motionless for a second or two, then nodded to the detectives and walked out the door, followed by the older man.

Stoker and Volz were apparently too thrown by the woman's appearance to return her silent farewell, but as the door swung shut, Volz managed to spit out a feeble, "Bye-bye." Stoker seemed embarrassed at his partner's behavior, and glared at him. Volz seemed embarrassed at his own behavior, and glared at Rutherford.

She really does dress like a ninja, Rutherford thought. *A ninja from a kid's cartoon. A really unrealistic one that's based on a series of action figures. She might as well be wearing a sandwich board that says: "Trouble Wanted." To even attempt a look like that you'd have to be either stupid or incredibly badass. I doubt a stupid person would keep it up for long.*

When the helmeted woman and the bearded man were gone, Terri Wells turned back to the detectives. "Would one of you gentlemen please show my technicians to the crime scene?"

Stoker glanced at Volz, who shook his head slightly and looked at Rutherford. Stoker too turned his dull gaze toward Rutherford, who got the hint.

"I'd be happy to," Rutherford said, and for the first time that day, he meant it.

Wells turned to the young man with the large case and the three-piece suit. "Albert, please be thorough."

"Always," Albert replied.

"I'll be thorough as well," the older man in the light blue windbreaker said. He lifted his hand. Only then did Rutherford notice he was carrying some sort of device. It resembled a handheld metal detector, but it was smaller, looked lighter, had a small display screen, and was emitting a faint buzz. "But I warn you," he continued, "there may actually be too many scents in there for me to get any clear readings."

Wells's smile strained a bit as she said, "I'm sure you'll do your best."

Rutherford led the two men down the hall, back to the doorjamb he was sad to admit he now thought of as *his territory.*

The man Wells had called Albert glanced at the name tag on Rutherford's uniform, then thanked him by name. Turning to the man in the windbreaker, he said, "Professor Sherwood, you could take a look at the scene while I set up. Just please don't disturb anything."

The older man said, "Of course," then entered the room and started waving his device at everything but the dead body. The buzzing grew uneven as he moved around the area. Rutherford noticed that Professor Sherwood's windbreaker had "B-9" written on the back in bright yellow lettering.

Albert sat his case down on the floor and opened it, revealing a black screen almost the exact internal dimensions of the case. The screen was hinged at the front, and swung forward opposite the case's lid, briefly revealing the interior of the case. Half of the space was taken up with a brushed metal box, perforated with holes. The other half was filled with a dull black jumble of spherical and cylindrical shapes. Albert tilted the screen back at an angle, then swung the suitcase lid forward to meet the upper edges of the screen, propping the case open. The screen lit up and filled with a familiar Windows desktop, complete with a wallpaper image of a classic Aston Martin.

"I've never seen a computer like that," Rutherford said.

"I bet you have," Albert said, unbuttoning his suit jacket and crouching over his computer. "I built it myself, but I got the idea from a prop computer in the first *Avengers* movie. That one was larger, like a small trunk, and had a transparent screen, of course, which is just silly. Still, a good idea's a good idea. The roomy case allows me to build and upgrade it with desktop components. They're cheaper and more powerful, and there's storage room to spare."

Rutherford said, "That's really interesting. Still, it is kinda big."

"Yeah," Albert admitted, grinning up at him. "Design is about compromise. On the plus side, it doesn't have to fit in a laptop case. It's its own case."

Rutherford glanced into the crime scene, gratified to finally get a good look after being stuck outside it for so long.

Unlike Stoker and Volz, Albert and Professor Sherwood didn't seem to mind letting Rutherford watch them. He craned his neck until he could see the bruises on the victim's cheek. Just as Stoker and Volz had discussed, he could make out fingers and a thumb, and also, like they'd said, the direction of the blow and the shape of the fist were all wrong.

Rutherford glanced down at Albert, who was crouched over his computer in his three-piece suit, swiping through submenus on the hinged touch screen. Then Rutherford looked down at his own hand and tried to replicate the fist that caused the bruises. The fingers were skewed with the index finger and the tip of the thumb almost making a point. It was as if the assailant had been holding a stick, or preparing to knock on a door with the second knuckle of his index finger. It was a weird way to knock, and an even weirder way to hit a guy.

He glanced to the end of the hall.

Stoker asked, "How long is this going to take?"

Wells said, "As long as it takes, Detective."

"Look, lady," Stoker said, "this is all real cute, but we need our crime scene back."

"Detective," Wells said in a calm, even tone, "you don't have a crime scene. I do. When my team is done with my crime scene, I will hand it down to you. Until then, think of this as an opportunity to practice patience."

The look on Stoker's face demonstrated that he badly needed the practice.

The older man, Professor Sherwood, emerged from the crime scene looking ashen, but not displeased. "I got some good readings," he said, "in spite of the environmental obstacles."

"That's good," Albert said. "Now it's my turn." He reached behind his computer's screen, into the side of the case that held the jumble of simple shapes, and pulled out one of the objects. It was a sphere the size of a softball attached to four open-ended cylinders. It was like someone had glued a grapefruit to four juice glasses and painted the whole thing black.

The young man pressed a hidden button. As soon as the object started to emit a loud whirring noise, Albert lobbed it into the room, directly over the victim. It stopped at the top of its trajectory, stabilized with the four cylinders pointed downward, then bobbed in midair. Soon it was joined by three more drones, all identical to the first, all lobbed into the room by Albert. It would have seemed quite graceful if not for the earsplitting racket produced by the four of them. Rutherford winced at the noise.

"Yeah, I know," Albert shouted, seeing Rutherford's discomfort. "The ducted fans give more lift and cut way down on the air disturbance, but they don't help with the noise as much as I'd hoped. I tuned them so that they'd at least create a pleasant chord, but it was the best I could do."

Albert pressed a green button on his computer screen and the drones immediately scattered to the four corners of the room. Each emitted a red laser that scanned the contours of the space and every object in it. Rutherford looked at the computer screen, where a sketchy model of the crime scene was slowly taking form. After five seconds of shooting lasers around the room, each of the drones emitted a bright white flash. They dropped halfway down the walls, one of them moving forward to allow for the desk, then ran through the entire light show again. Finally they sank to almost floor height. Rutherford saw the lasers shooting across the room from under the bed frame, again exploring every crevice of the crime scene.

After emitting one final burst of white light, they returned to their starting position in the center of the room, then one by one flew back to Albert, who caught them and returned them to the storage cubby of his computer case.

"Done," Albert said. "Just let me pack up, and the place is all yours again."

"I thought she told you to be thorough," Rutherford said.

Albert smiled. "She did, and I set the scanners for *thorough*."

Rutherford looked at the screen and saw that what had been a low-resolution wire-frame model of the room was now a detailed, full-color re-creation, complete with the victim's body and a glimpse of Albert and Rutherford waiting outside the door. Albert must have noticed he was looking, because he spun the image around and zoomed in close enough for Rutherford to read his own name tag.

Rutherford said, "That's amazing."

Albert said, "Thanks, but it's not much really. The drones mostly just shoot lights and take pictures. All of the real processing's done by the computer."

That didn't make it any less amazing to Rutherford, but he chose not to say so.

Albert closed his computer, and he and Rutherford left the room to join Wells and the detectives. Professor Sherwood was still wandering around, waving his buzzing wand at various objects.

Wells said, "Detectives, Officer, thank you for your cooperation. The crime scene is yours again. We look forward to reading your report."

"I told you, lady, we don't report to you," Stoker snarled.

Wells's smile did not fade. "Call it what you like, Detective, but you will be writing a report, and we will receive a copy of it. Part of our understanding with the department is that we will receive all of the relevant paperwork generated by the investigations we take part in."

"Will we get a copy of that scan you just took?" Rutherford asked.

"Of course," Albert said, "It's evidence. But the Seattle PD doesn't currently have a computer that could run it."

Professor Sherwood approached the group, still looking down at his wand. As he neared the detectives, he seemed transfixed by what he saw on the wand's readout. He waved the wand toward Volz and the buzzing grew louder. Professor Sherwood squinted at the readout and smiled.

"What?" Volz demanded, sounding slightly alarmed. "What's it say?"

"Nothing, Detective," Professor Sherwood said, with a knowing grin. "Don't worry about it. I'm certainly not detecting anything that isn't legal in this state." He winked.

Wells handed Stoker her card and quickly explained that if—ahem, when—her organization had determined the identity of the culprit, their findings would be forwarded to the case's lead detective so that the Seattle PD could make the collar. She thanked them for their cooperation. Stoker, Volz, and Rutherford stood and watched as Capp's people left. Through the open door Rutherford caught a brief glimpse of the kid who'd found the body, still being interviewed by a uniformed officer while the older European man and the woman in the helmet watched.

Looking at her again, Rutherford was struck by the strange size of her helmet. It seemed only slightly larger than a normal-sized woman's head.

I doubt that thing's DOT approved, he thought, *unless her cranium is the size of a fist.*

The forensics team had been waiting for their crack at the crime scene. Technicians filed into the house, lugging their equipment and supplies.

Volz mumbled, "I still don't know what to make of the bruises."

"I know it," Stoker agreed. "A guy would be hard-pressed to kill someone by punching him in the head, even if he did take three or four swings, and that's making a fist the right way. Swatting like that, you'd have to be Superman."

Maybe the kid was hit with an object," Rutherford offered.

Stoker and Volz stared at him in silence until they were satisfied that he was uncomfortable enough for them to continue. Volz said, "An object?"

"Yes," Rutherford said. It was something that had occurred to him while he was in the room with Albert, only the lasers had distracted him from thinking it through.

"An object . . . with fingers and a thumb," Volz clarified.

"Yeah, well," Rutherford stammered. "I have a theory about that. I think it's . . ." Rutherford trailed off, having realized that he didn't want to finish the sentence out loud.

"You think it's what?" Stoker prompted him.

"A sex toy," Rutherford forced himself to say.

"A sex toy?" Volz repeated.

"Yes, I think it's a sex toy. They make them of . . . of this," Rutherford said, holding up his hand in an imitation of the pointed fist suggested by the bruise.

Volz laughed. "It's always the quiet ones."

"Wait, guys," Rutherford said, "I'm not into that kind of thing."

"And you're not that quiet," Stoker said.

"Guys, seriously," Rutherford almost whined. "I've never seen one in person, they aren't my thing, but I know for a fact that they make them."

"How would you know that?" Stoker asked.

"I saw one on TV."

Volz shook his head, fighting back a laugh. "You always watch videos of things that aren't your thing?"

"It wasn't a video," Rutherford said. "It was a show on TV."

Volz said, "I don't know what kinda crazy cable channels you've got."

"It was on the Discovery Channel," Rutherford said. "That show *MythBusters*."

"Sure," Volz said. "The myth of the sexy fake fist."

"No! They weren't using it as a sex fist."

"Then what were they doing with it?" Stoker asked.

"They were, uh," Rutherford stammered. "They were using it to punch a shark in the nose."

Stoker and Volz looked at Rutherford, then at each other. Finally Stoker shook his head and said, "Oh, what a tangled web we weave, when first we practice with a fist-shaped sex toy."

THREE

When Captain Weinart arrived, he was irritated to find that Capp's people had already left. Stoker and Volz tried to cheer him up by insisting that Rutherford explain his theory.

Rutherford's idea about the murder weapon, coupled with his explanation of how he knew about it, did quite a bit to lift the captain's spirits, leaving him in a playful enough mood to order Stoker and Volz to take Rutherford under their collective wing and help him investigate his theory.

They started by researching the object in question online. Rutherford was assigned a computer on a desk where his monitor was easily visible to passersby. His job was to compile the names and addresses of various manufacturers, as well as photos of the various models of fist-shaped novelties available on the intimate accessories market.

The constant jabs from his fellow officers had slowed his progress, but it didn't take long for Rutherford to find a solid lead that resolved the biggest problem with his theory. Stoker had been skeptical that any human would be strong enough to beat a man to death with a piece of soft, pliable latex, regardless of its shape, but Rutherford found a similar product cast in chrome-plated metal. Only one company made one that was human sized.

He called Stoker and Volz over to look at his findings.

"Wow," Volz said.

"Yeah," Stoker said. "I gotta admit, you could definitely beat a guy to death with one of those."

"And the finger positions do look like a match." Volz shook his head. "Kinda blurs the line between a toy and a tool."

"It seems like it would be . . . cold."

"And you probably wouldn't want to heat it up in the oven."

"Certainly couldn't put it in the microwave."

"No, that'd void the warranty."

"On the microwave or the fist?"

"Probably both," Rutherford cut in, "but that's not the point. I checked the victim's credit card statements, and he hasn't bought anything from any of the usual online sources for this kind of thing, which means he probably bought it at a store, in person. Or it belonged to the assailant. Either way, we should check it out."

Stoker and Volz admitted that it was a lead—and a potentially entertaining one, at that. They had Rutherford compile a list of the stores in King County that carried that particular bit of recreational equipment.

Rutherford found that there were four shops in the area that carried the Original Metal Mitt. He presented his list to Stoker and Volz, who explained that they would be driving from store to store. Rutherford would go in *undercover* as an interested buyer. They seemed to think it would be fun. Rutherford argued that it would be a waste of time, not to mention fairly embarrassing. This only seemed to reinforce Stoker and Volz's opinion that it would be fun.

Rutherford offered to run home and change into street clothes. They asked him what he had in mind. He described a casual ensemble (using the actual words "casual ensemble") consisting of khakis, a polo shirt, a cable-knit sweater, and a pair of plimsolls.

Volz asked, "What the hell are *plimsolls?*"

"They're a lightweight sneaker, with a canvas upper," Rutherford said.

Stoker said, "What, you mean like Keds?"

"Yes," Rutherford said. "Like Keds."

"Then just say Keds!" Stoker barked.

"But they aren't Keds."

"Then don't buy knockoffs," Volz said. "Spring for real Keds or don't bother."

They told Rutherford not to worry about it. They had already procured his disguise.

An hour later, the three of them were driving north on Aurora Avenue. Rutherford sat in the backseat, wearing ill-fitting sneakers, stained jeans, and a T-shirt he was sure had not been washed since Stoker's last visit to the gym, which appeared to be some time ago. The look was completed by an army-surplus jacket Volz had bought for five bucks off a guy in the holding cell.

Volz was not driving particularly well that afternoon, as he was splitting his attention between watching the road and glancing at Rutherford looking miserable in the back seat.

Stoker, riding shotgun, craned his neck around to coach Rutherford on the plan. "Remember, you can't let these guys know who you are. If they get the feeling you're law enforcement of any kind, they'll clam right up. Even if they're not doing anything illegal, they still won't want to talk to a cop. Understand?"

"Why couldn't we just get a court order?" Rutherford asked.

"Because we would have had to go talk to a judge about sex toys, which we don't want to do unless we know we're right. Understand?"

"Yeah," Rutherford said. "I get it."

Stoker smiled. He looked almost giddy. "Okay, so what are you going to do?"

Rutherford wasn't stupid. He knew that Stoker and Volz were messing with him. He also knew that this was an opportunity. He was being sent out undercover to investigate a lead he had come up with on his own. If it panned out, it could be a real feather in his cap. Playing along with these two grinning jackasses was a small price to pay.

"I'm going to go into the sex shop," Rutherford said, "where I'll express interest in the Metal Mitt. I'm going to ask if they've sold any recently, and if they did, I'll attempt to get any information I can about the customer."

Volz started shaking slightly. To Rutherford's alarm, he could see in the rearview mirror that the detective's eyes were squeezed shut. Stoker noticed too and hit Volz on the shoulder, saying "Hey! Eyes on the road."

Volz opened his eyes and said, "Sorry man," in a weak voice.

Stoker turned his attention back to Rutherford. "And where will we be?"

"Out here in the car, listening to me over the wire I'm wearing."

"That's right," Stoker said. "We'll hear everything, and we'll be recording it, so we can listen to it again later."

The first shop was a small establishment in a strip mall just a few minutes north of downtown. Rutherford saw the Metal Mitt immediately. It was on a high shelf behind the counter: a fist and eight inches of forearm, cast in chrome and packed into a brightly colored cardboard box with a clear plastic window on the front.

Rutherford pointed to it and asked the cashier if that was the Original Metal Mitt. She looked at him with dead eyes and said, "Yup. Accept no substitutions."

"I didn't expect it to come in a cardboard box," he said.

"We can dispose of the box so you can carry it home au naturel, if you'd prefer, sir."

"Oh, that's not necessary," Rutherford said. "Um, just out of curiosity, how many of that item do you carry at any given time?"

"What, sir?"

"I mean, is that the only one, or do you have more in the storeroom?"

"How many do you expect to need, sir?"

Rutherford was getting flustered. "I'm just curious to know how many of them you sell."

"Not many," the woman said. "They're crazy expensive, and it's the kind of thing people come in to point and laugh at before buying something less scary."

"So if someone did buy one, you'd remember what they looked like," Rutherford said.

"I suppose," the cashier said.

"And has anyone ever bought one here, that you know of?"

The cashier narrowed her eyes. "No. Why do you ask? Are you worried that I'll tell on you, or are you looking for a . . . *kindred spirit*?"

The second and third shops went little better. In each, one copy of the item in question sat on a shelf behind the counter, displayed in its box, seen by everyone, but bought by no one. It was the sex-shop equivalent of the one high-end sports car that a car dealership keeps in the showroom for customers to look at while they negotiate the price of their new hatchback.

Each shop visit went much the same—Rutherford asked the same humiliating questions, received similar humiliating answers, and returned to the car to listen to a new wave of humiliating laughter.

The final stop was less than a mile from the university. Of all of the shops visited, it was the closest by far to the scene of the crime.

"Why didn't we start here?" Rutherford asked before exiting the car.

Stoker said, "Because if we'd hit pay dirt here, you would have been robbed of this valuable undercover experience. We didn't want that."

Rutherford cursed silently to himself as he walked across the empty parking lot to the windowless building. This shop was different from the others in that it was attached to a low-rent strip club, like the pro shop in a bowling alley.

Upon entering the shop proper, Rutherford immediately realized this store was different in a second way. Their Metal Mitt was also displayed on a shelf behind the counter, but it was not in its box.

The cashier was a tall man with dim, lifeless eyes, an intimidating nose and Adam's apple, and muscular arms. He was wearing the kind of black, silky, skintight shirt that professional athletes often wear under a uniform and amateur athletes often wear as a uniform.

Rutherford strode purposefully through racks and aisles of esoteric merchandise. He looked the cashier in the eye, pointed to the Metal Mitt, and said, "I am interested in that." Later that night, Rutherford would look back and marvel at the change in his demeanor between the first shop and the last one. Despite outward appearances, he hadn't gained confidence. He'd simply become desensitized to this specific type of embarrassment. He wondered if that was all confidence was in the first place.

The cashier looked where Rutherford was pointing and seemed to pause for a half second.

"What about it?" the cashier asked.

"What's the deal with it?" Rutherford asked.

"If you don't already know, you're not going to like it."

"No, I mean, I've seen things like it before, in other shops," Rutherford said, trying to sound like a comparison shopper instead of a cop. "Is that a Metal Mitt, or is it another model?"

The cashier squinted at him. "Does it really matter?"

"All the other Metal Mitts I've seen have been in boxes. Why isn't this one?"

"What's it matter? You aren't buying the box."

"You wouldn't be trying to sell a used one, would you?"

"We don't take returns. Besides, what do you care? It's washable."

"Have you washed it?"

"It's never been used. You ask a lot of questions," the cashier said.

And you aren't answering any of them, Rutherford thought. He looked at the chrome fist. The cashier was certainly acting weird, and the fact that the fist was out of its box was suspicious. *Could it be the murder weapon?* He could see lots of smudges around the base of the arm. *The chrome really shows every fingerprint. Of course, the murderer probably would have wiped it down after the attack, but they might have missed something.*

Rutherford looked at the cashier, who was staring back at him with great intensity, as if willing him to just go away.

If he's the murderer, Rutherford thought, *he's going to get that thing out of here as soon as I leave. He might give it a more thorough cleaning, or if he's smart, he'll throw it into Lake Washington. The water is only a couple of miles from here. It could be gone forever five minutes after we leave. A distant memory by the time we came back with a warrant.*

"I'll take it," Rutherford said.

"What?" the cashier asked.

"I said I'll take it," Rutherford said. "I want to purchase that fist." He pointed at it for emphasis.

The cashier looked at him uneasily, then reached up to remove the fist from the shelf.

"Uh, wait," Rutherford said. "I'd rather you didn't touch it. I want to keep it as clean as possible. I'm sure you understand."

The cashier froze in his tracks. "I told you, it's washable," he said, looking confused and more than a little alarmed.

"How about this," Rutherford offered. "You tell me how much it costs. I'll pay for it. You give me a bag, and I'll come around and get it. That way it won't get contaminated."

The cashier repeated, "Contaminated?" and Rutherford knew he'd blown it.

They stared at each other for two seconds that felt like two hours, then the cashier grabbed the Metal Mitt by the forearm and swung it at Rutherford's head with all of his might.

Rutherford saw the blow coming. He shielded his head with both arms and lunged away from his attacker, which probably saved him from a particularly embarrassing concussion, although his left forearm bore the brunt of the blow and would likely have a nasty bruise tomorrow.

Rutherford was off-balance, but he caught himself with the counter before he fell over completely. The cashier had already vaulted the counter and was running toward the door, Metal Mitt in hand. He tried to slow Rutherford's inevitable pursuit by deliberately knocking down a rack of rubber garments and a shelf of DVDs that would probably never sell anyway.

The cashier burst out of the front door and ran down the street, the chrome fist gleaming in the sun. Rutherford wasn't far behind. The cruiser was still out front, and Stoker and Volz watched in slack-jawed shock as he emerged from the shop and continued his pursuit on foot. "Suspect assaulted me," Rutherford said, blurting out the words in staccato bursts between breaths. "Used fist as a club. Not injured. In pursuit."

Neither Volz nor Stoker liked Rutherford, but he was an officer of the Seattle Police Department. An attack on him was an attack on them. Rutherford didn't doubt for an instant that they would assist him if they could. He was not surprised to hear a roaring engine and squealing tires behind him as he chased the cashier out of the parking lot and down the street. He was sure they were also calling for backup, a call he could easily imagine but was grateful he could not hear.

The suspect struck Officer Rutherford with a metal sex fist, which he still has in his possession! He's going south on Twenty-Fourth Avenue, armed with said metal sex fist!

The suspect was in good shape, and the ease with which he moved implied he was accustomed to running. He turned left and cut diagonally through a bank parking lot.

Rutherford didn't look particularly athletic, but he was small and light, and had lettered in cross-country in high school. He was gaining on the suspect.

Stoker and Volz's car had only just drawn even with Rutherford when the suspect zagged in a direction the car couldn't easily follow, off the sidewalk and away from the road. Rutherford, of course, continued his pursuit. The car turned left at the next intersection, but it was a futile maneuver. The suspect ran back onto the sidewalk, then dodged traffic across Twenty-Fifth and darted into the bustling open-air mall across the street, heading southeast, toward the mall's westernmost Starbucks.

Rutherford heard honking horns and squealing brakes, and knew that the two detectives in the car were no longer a factor in the chase. For the time being at least, he was on his own. He poured on the speed as the sex-toy-wielding suspect disappeared into the crowd just beyond the Pottery Barn.

Rutherford was about twenty feet behind his assailant and closing the gap nicely until they hit the crowd. People saw the tall man with the chrome fist coming and got out of his way, but then they filled in behind him to watch him go, blocking Rutherford's path.

He saw the suspect run past Restoration Hardware. The window held a display of chrome-plated bookends. For a strange, giddy moment, Rutherford pictured the fist sitting there, looking at home among the other gleaming tchotchkes.

The suspect turned to the left, again fighting through traffic. Rutherford was able to cut the corner and gain back a little of the ground he had lost.

They ran through a dark alley between two rows of less successful shops that could only afford the mall's smaller stalls. They passed confused shoppers and an ill-advised playground area that seemed to be made solely out of Astroturf and brightly painted metal pipes.

The footpath widened and they again emerged into the sunlight. The suspect's path was less crowded than Rutherford's, but his good luck did not hold.

Between the Gap and a high-end cookware store there was a fountain. It was minimal, as far as fountains are concerned. It consisted of a small hole in the ground that would spurt water at semi-regular intervals. On hot days, parents would laugh and watch their children play in it. On cold days, children would laugh and watch their parents accidentally step in it. At this moment, a young mother was filming her daughter as she carefully approached the column of water when the suspect, neck craned around to see behind him, hit the wet patch on the pavement.

His feet went out from under him and he fell to the ground, yelping involuntarily as his tailbone hit the pavement. He lost his grip on the fist, which bounced on the concrete with the sound of a ringing gong. He scrambled up onto all fours and grabbed the fist with one hand, then glanced back the way he had come just in time to see Rutherford use his momentum to launch himself off a bench.

Rutherford landed on the suspect, knocking him back to the ground, but the suspect, being a larger, stronger man, easily threw him off. In an instant, they were both back on their feet in the center of a circle of shoppers. The suspect swung the fist at Rutherford, but missed. Rutherford punched the suspect in the face, which stunned him, but had little effect. The suspect swung the fist again, but the water had made the smooth chrome slippery. Instead of hitting Rutherford, he accidentally threw it through the window of the cookware shop, where, again, it looked oddly at home with the store's actual merchandise.

The suspect turned to flee again, but staggered to a stop when he saw Detective Stoker standing in his path. Stoker held him at gunpoint until Volz and two bicycle cops and a police cruiser arrived, and then the uniformed officers took the suspect into custody.

Once the excitement had died down and they were back in their cruiser, Stoker said, "Kid, I gotta hand it to you. You did good today, and we're going to make sure everybody hears all about it."

"All about it?" Rutherford asked.

"Every detail," Stoker said.

"Even the part where I got hit with a sex toy?"

Stoker turned and looked at him. "Are you kidding? *Especially* the part where you got hit with a sex toy, Officer Sinclair."

FOUR

The next morning at 0900 sharp, Rutherford was settling into his new assignment, which was to sit outside the captain's office and wait nervously. It was not a difficult assignment, and Rutherford had already mastered it. Especially the last part.

Rutherford had left for home the night before feeling unusually optimistic. He'd made a point of relishing the feeling, which was good, but the mood hadn't even lasted through his evening commute.

The arrest of the fist-wielding cashier had been Stoker and Volz's collar, so they were the ones in charge of interrogating him, crossing the t's, and dotting the i's. As such, they would be filling out reports about the undercover operation and the pursuit and apprehension of the suspect, just as Rutherford had done. During his drive home, it occurred to Rutherford that he was trusting two men who were openly hostile toward him to treat him fairly.

If everyone told the truth, there would be no problem, and Rutherford would come out looking pretty good. He was proud of his actions, for the most part, and as long as they were reported accurately, he was sure he'd be fine.

If either Stoker or Volz lied in his report to make himself look good at Rutherford's expense, the other detective's account would confirm Rutherford's, and the liar would be exposed, which suited Rutherford just fine.

Of course, if both Stoker and Volz falsified their reports in exactly the same way, then Rutherford would look like a self-aggrandizing liar, and the day's marvelous opportunity and his excellent work would become a career-crippling liability.

Rutherford realized that he was essentially engaged in a high-stakes game of Rock, Paper, Scissors against two opponents who were not only working together, but who knew in advance what tactic he would choose.

It was not an ideal situation, but what could he do? They were his superiors, and they were the arresting officers. He couldn't demand to be allowed to review and edit their reports. Besides, he didn't think they would lie. They were detectives, after all, and as much as he didn't respect them, he hated to think that someone who falsified reports and played politics could attain that title.

Which is to say, he definitely *did* think such a thing was possible, and he hated it.

Then he got home and turned on the TV. The first thing he saw was a news anchor talking in her serious voice and making her serious face while a graphic of a Metal Mitt superimposed over a Seattle PD badge floated to her right. This was not good.

Rutherford sat on the edge of his couch and listened.

"—exclusive, shocking footage obtained from a citizen reporter tells the story." The anchor and the badge-fist logo faded out. Smartphone footage showed a small child playing in the fountain at University Village. The game she was playing was the old childhood favorite: *I approach something cautiously while my parent forcefully encourages me to get closer in hopes that the very thing I fear will happen and make a cute picture to show my dates when I'm sixteen.*

The anchor's voice cut in. "When this local woman brought her daughter to the mall today, she never expected that her little girl's safety and innocence would be endangered by both human depravity and police incompetence."

The little girl in the video shrieked and ran as the suspect darted into the frame, slipped in the fountain, fell, and dropped the gleaming sex toy to the ground. Rutherford winced as he watched himself struggle with the man. He didn't look forward to explaining to his mother why he was on TV, dressed in filthy castoffs, fighting another grown man.

He especially didn't look forward to explaining what that other man was using as a weapon.

Sure, he was a cop. Dealing with this kind of thing was his job, but when talking to one's mother, "that's my job" does not end the conversation. Instead, it leads to a broader discussion of all the great jobs you could have instead, if you hadn't decided to waste your potential.

The anchor identified the Metal Mitt, and proceeded to describe in clinical terms how it was used.

Well, now I won't have to explain that to Mother, Rutherford thought. *That's a break.*

The anchor wrapped up the story, saying, "The Seattle Police Department declined to make any statement regarding the events depicted in this footage, but unofficial sources say that the fiasco is the result of an inexperienced officer who was overzealous in the apprehension of a suspect, and that these events should not reflect negatively on his supervisors."

But I will have to explain the situation to everyone, he thought. *Everyone except Stoker and Volz, whom I can safely start referring to as "the unofficial sources." At least now I don't have to wonder what their report will say.*

Rutherford's phone vibrated, making the entire end table resonate. He picked it up and saw that he had received a text from his older sister Vanessa. Clearly, she had been watching the local news as well, which was just his luck. The message was a question mark followed by an exclamation mark. He put his phone down, resolving to respond when he had both a little more energy and an idea of what to say.

Mercifully, the local news ended. The national news was the familiar nightly slog of some people complaining that the government was overreaching while others complained that it wasn't doing enough. Rutherford had almost managed to calm himself when the final segment of the night ran. Traditionally, this was the spot for some light, amusing story. This night it was footage of two men in a mall fighting over a sex toy, which was pixelated to protect young eyes from seeing what it was, and allow adult minds to assume it was something worse.

The national news anchor thanked the Seattle affiliate for supplying the story. Rutherford did not.

Later, he didn't thank the major Internet social networks when the story went viral, receiving an astronomical number of views, or when one quarter of his connections shared links to the video, introducing it to the other three quarters of his connections in the process.

In the middle of the long line of message notifications on his smartphone, there were three more texts from Vanessa. After her initial question mark and exclamation mark message, she had sent a single question mark, followed by two question marks, and then she'd jumped all the way to five question marks. She was too upset to talk to right now. He'd maybe respond tomorrow, when she had calmed back down to two question marks.

He woke the next morning to find a phone message from Captain Weinart, telling him to report directly to the captain's office at police headquarters, first thing, and not to bother wearing his uniform.

There was also a stream of new social media notifications and yet another text from his sister—this one consisting of a single exclamation mark. He chose to ignore all of it for the time being.

He shuffled around his apartment in a depressed fog. It was a modest one-bedroom decorated with tasteful thrift store finds, featuring a glorious view of the parking lot. He'd have preferred a view of the city, the water, or the mountains, but he'd told himself that his homes would get better with time. Now he looked at his modest dwelling and wondered if he'd be able to afford it in a month.

Rutherford usually enjoyed his morning commute, darting nimbly through traffic in his Mazda Miata. Today he didn't *dart* so much as *trudge,* and instead of seeming svelte and maneuverable, the little convertible felt tiny and vulnerable. He turned on the radio, hoping to get his mind off his work problems.

The morning zoo host was conducting a phone interview. A man on the other end of the line said in a thick New Jersey accent, "We're proud of our products, but I gotta make it clear that the Metal Mitt was never intended for use as a weapon."

"I'm sure it wasn't," the DJ said. "I think it's obvious that it is intended for two caring, consenting adults to use in the privacy of their homes, not a rookie cop and a murder suspect in a crowded mall."

"That's right," the interviewee said. "Although it don't gotta be two people. Any number is fine by us. We don't judge."

Rutherford turned off the radio.

Now he was waiting outside his captain's office like a naughty child waiting to be paddled by the principal. Since he'd been told to wear street clothes, and he'd wanted to feel as comfortable and confident as the situation would allow, he was wearing his favorite suit. It was a neat single-breasted in a tight herringbone, matched with his finest wingtips and a bright blue tie, fastened with a perfectly symmetrical half-Windsor knot.

He sat and brooded for ten minutes, both loathing the wait and dreading its end.

When the door finally opened, he resisted the urge to cringe, instead springing to his feet.

Captain Weinart stepped out and looked disapprovingly at Rutherford, then nodded and said, "Officer Sinclair."

"Good morning, Captain," Rutherford said. "I'm sorry, but my last name is Rutherford."

"Detective Volz told me you preferred to be called *Sinclair*. Are you calling Detective Volz a liar, Sinclair?"

"Sir, I'm just saying that—"

"Because I trust Detective Volz. I've known him for a long time, Sinclair."

"I'm aware of—"

"And I barely know you at all."

"Yes, Captain. That's true."

"You like to play a lot of games, don't you, Sinclair?"

"No, sir."

"So now *I'm* lying, Sinclair?"

Weinart stared at Rutherford in silence until he was certain that the younger man had squirmed enough, then said, "I called you here this morning because of that stunt you pulled yesterday."

"Yes, and I'm glad you did," Rutherford lied. "I'm anxious to explain what happened."

"Well that's a shame, 'cause you're not going to get the chance," Weinart said. "You're to report to the main entrance. There's a car waiting for you."

"Where's it going to take me?" Rutherford asked.

"Away," Weinart said. "And that's enough for me."

With that, the captain stepped back into his office and slammed the door behind him.

Rutherford left HQ and looked for the mysterious car that was supposed to be waiting for him. He expected a black town car, or if he was unlucky, a taxi. He found neither. He suspected that was because the load/unload zone in front of the station was taken up by a huge UPS van. The two front doors were slid open, as usual. The driver, in his distinctive brown shirt and shorts, was sitting in the driver's seat and looking at his chunky delivery tablet.

The driver glanced toward the police station's entrance and noticed Rutherford. He immediately stood and came out the passenger-side door.

"Officer Sinclair?" the driver said.

"Uh, I . . . I suppose," Rutherford stammered.

The driver looked healthy, but he was bony and there was something old-fashioned about his features. His face would have looked more at home in a black-and-white photo of victims of the dust bowl than on a modern UPS driver. His eyes seemed friendly, but he didn't smile as he stepped to the side, motioned toward the passenger door of the UPS truck, and said, "Right this way, officer."

Rutherford didn't understand what was happening, but decided to ride it out. He stepped up onto the shiny metal steps of the UPS van. As he reached the second tread, the bulkhead behind the driver's seat slid open, revealing what seemed to be a well-appointed conference room in the truck's cargo area.

The ceiling was some sort of frosted glass material, which allowed natural light to pour into the space. The interior was a bland, tasteful beige with large flat-screen monitors on the side and rear walls of the room. They were showing feeds from cameras Rutherford figured were hidden on the exterior of the truck, giving the impression of windows. In the middle of the room there was a conference table made of a dark, rich wood with a padded bumper around its edge. Its surface was empty, save for a tablet computer. There were several swivel chairs. At the opposite end of the truck, standing at the head of the table, Rutherford instantly recognized the software billionaire, Vince Capp.

Capp stood and spread his arms in welcome. "Sinclair Rutherford, it's good to meet you."

Capp walked around the table toward Rutherford. Rutherford stepped forward to meet him, then stopped after one step, startled by the sound of the door sliding shut behind him with a definitive *click*. Capp took Rutherford's right hand in his while grabbing Rutherford's right elbow with his left hand and looking him square in the eyes. Not in the eye, which was what most people did, but in the eyes. It was as if Capp's left and right eyes were working independently to make specific contact with both Rutherford's left and right eyes. All of these actions worked together to create an effect Rutherford would later describe *as terrifyingly reassuring.*

Capp was a stocky man in his late fifties. He had hair that was expertly cut and hastily styled, and a suit that was impeccably tailored and noticeably rumpled. He wore no tie, and his shirt was unbuttoned just far enough to make him comfortable without making anybody else uncomfortable.

Capp introduced himself briefly, then quickly changed the subject. "I'm told they call you Officer Sinclair. Why do they use your first name?"

"To bother me," Rutherford said. It hadn't even occurred to him to lie. He added, "You know, guys."

Capp smiled and nodded. Clearly, that was the only explanation required.

"So, you'd prefer to go by your last name, professionally?"

Rutherford said, "Yes. You know, until I get to know people."

Capp gave a big, toothy grin. "Understandable," he said. "Rutherford is a cooler sounding name anyway. Please have a seat. Why the suit?"

Once seated, Rutherford surveyed his suit, trying to figure out how to answer. Finally, he settled on the truth and said, "I was told to wear street clothes for a meeting with my captain."

Capp nodded again. "Ah, I see. And the suit's an attempt to put your best foot forward."

"Yes."

"Well, that's good, Rutherford, but you don't have to do that with me. Feel free to dress more casually in the future, okay? No suits required."

Rutherford couldn't imagine why he'd be meeting with Capp in the future, but he didn't know why he was meeting with him now. While his brain struggled with that issue, Rutherford's mouth blurted, "But I like wearing suits."

Capp waved his hand dismissively. His expression said, *Thanks, but don't bother.*

The truck pulled into traffic. The flat panels that hung on three of the walls now showed buildings sliding past and the cars following behind them. Rutherford noticed a lack of engine noise, but chalked it up to sound insulation.

Capp spent a moment watching Rutherford look around before saying, "I'm sure you have questions."

"Yes," Rutherford said. "Where are we going, and why are we in a UPS truck?"

Capp chuckled amiably. "We're going to Boeing Field, where my jet's waiting to take me back to the Bay Area. I wanted to devote some time to meeting you one-on-one, and this was the only slot I had available. We're in this UPS truck because it's a prototype my automotive concern, Stephenson Motors, is working on."

"For delivery trucks?"

"No, for what you see. High-end corporate transport."

Rutherford furrowed his brow and looked around the truck's interior again. He knocked on the table, noting again the padded, segmented bumper that ringed its outer edge. He looked up at Capp and said, "Air bags?"

Capp smiled. "Yes, they're all the way around the table, and the walls and ceiling are lined with them too. Which ones go off depends on where the impact comes from."

Rutherford nodded. "I see. Yeah, that makes sense. I assume you'd paint the final model black."

"Nope," Capp said. "This one has the final paint scheme."

"It's not very glamourous."

Capp shook his head. "That's a common misconception. For the most part, high-end executive travel isn't about glamour. It's about efficiency. Limousines were designed so that three or more important people could travel together and conduct business while stuck in traffic. Only people whose time was extremely valuable could justify the expense. Because those people were both wealthy and powerful, limos became status symbols. Then they became clichés. Then people started renting them out for parties. Limo makers followed the money and started making them look like martini bars inside, and they stopped being places where anyone who wanted to be taken seriously would try to do business."

"Okay, that all makes sense," Rutherford said, "but why paint it like a UPS truck?"

"Again, efficiency. We can park in commercial loading zones and nobody will bat an eye. We can pull up to loading docks in the backs of hotels and conference centers and nobody gets suspicious. Also, people tend to cut UPS trucks a little more slack than they do limos. They figure it's some average person driving, trying to make a living, not some rich guy out to make more millions or teenagers en route to the prom."

"But won't UPS mind you using their name?"

"Mind? They'll probably try to buy the idea from me. If they don't, FedEx will. If they can make a profit transporting merchandise for companies, imagine what they can make transporting executives."

Capp paused, chuckled, and leaned forward in his chair. "But we aren't here to talk about the truck, Mr. Rutherford, we're here to talk about you."

"What about me?"

"All about you. Your record as a policeman is short and unremarkable, which makes what you did yesterday all the more surprising."

Rutherford winced. He had spent the entire night and morning hearing how everyone but him viewed his actions, and it had started to color his own memories. "Well, I'm not entirely proud of what happened yesterday."

"You should be. You scooped my team. You got to the killer before they did, and you drew a lot of attention to yourself while you did it."

Rutherford said, "He's a suspect, but there are still a lot of unanswered questions."

"No there aren't. He spilled his guts last night after you went home. The victim went to the sex shop with a friend who was a regular. While the owner, the guy you met yesterday, was distracted, the victim stole the fist. He intended to give it to another friend as a gag gift, a trophy for having won a bar fight. Anyway, the shop owner tracked the victim down through his friend, the regular. Things got out of hand and it ended with a murder."

Rutherford considered the story. "Yeah, that all makes sense. Your team would have gotten there eventually."

"Yes," Capp agreed. "But you didn't get there eventually. You figured it out immediately—and in spectacular fashion. You probably know where I'm going with this."

"I really don't," Rutherford admitted.

Capp said, "Don't be coy. It doesn't suit men like us. Rutherford, I come from the technology sector. In the rest of the world, when someone beats you, you destroy them. In my world, when someone beats you, you try to buy them out or merge with them. If that doesn't work, *then* you destroy them."

"You want me to be one of your people?"

Capp grimaced. "Ugh, is that what the cops call them? *My people?* Makes me sound like a cult leader. See, that's one of the challenges we face. Branding. Internally, the team's called *the Authorities.* I think it has a good feel. *Call in the Authorities. The Authorities caught up with the suspect.* That kind of thing. We haven't really gone public with it yet. We want to build some buzz first, and we haven't settled on a logo we like."

"Why would a team of investigators need a logo?" Rutherford asked.

Capp answered the question with a question of his own. "What do you think a badge is? The Authorities need proper marketing, just like any other commercial proposition."

Rutherford let the badge comment pass until he had more time to think about it. "How can it be commercial?" he asked. "Where's the money in solving crimes the police are already investigating? The cops aren't going to pay you for help. We barely get paid ourselves. Is the plan to rent your team out as private investigators?"

"That's one possible revenue stream, but I'm thinking bigger. That's why I'm only assigning them to really interesting, high-profile cases."

"But, yesterday's case wasn't very high profile."

"It wasn't before you came along, I admit. You made it high profile, which is why we're talking. I sent the Authorities in because it sounded interesting. A body found in a room with no weapon. I thought it might turn into a cool *locked room mystery* kinda thing. Didn't pan out that way, though."

Rutherford nodded. "The door didn't even have a doorknob."

"Yeah, turns out. Anyway, once the Authorities get some successes under their belt and make a name for themselves, there will be lots of possible ways to generate income. Patents and sales of proprietary tech and equipment. Licensed self-defense training centers. Books, movies, or TV shows detailing the higher-profile cases. Classes, seminars, and media teaching their methods and management techniques."

"Really?" Rutherford asked. "Management techniques?"

"Oh, yeah. Upper-level managers eat that stuff up. The company gets a tax write-off. The attendees get a weekend away and a three-hour talk where they learn about my system."

"And what is your system?"

Capp glanced around, as if verifying that they were still alone in the back of the moving truck. "I identify a market segment that is stagnant or underutilized. After hiring the best people available, I set the team a definable goal, assign a competent manager to coordinate their efforts, and do my best to set them up for success. Then I stay out of their way and let them do what they do best."

"That's going to be a short seminar," Rutherford said.

"Nah, once we break it down into a slide show it'll fill three hours easy. The main purpose of PowerPoint is to slow communication down so the ideas are easier to catch. Anyway, seminars are just one possibility. Right now our main objective is to get out there and see what works. We'll figure out how to make money from it later."

Rutherford was confused and overwhelmed, and Capp seemed to realize it. He leaned forward a bit, smiled reassuringly, and said, "Look, Rutherford, I have a good team, but they've been toiling away for the last six months, and it's become clear that something's missing. We have a great detective, a top-notch tech expert, and our head of personal security is a monster."

Rutherford said, "Really?" He'd been curious about the badass woman with the helmet and the weaponized cane. It was interesting to hear that, at least according to her employer, her skills lived up to her look.

"Oh, yeah," Capp said. "Your first warning that you're being attacked is when you wake up in the hospital. Beyond the core team, the management is great, and we have a long line of experts who want to work with us to test innovative crime-fighting techniques."

"It sounds like you're all set," Rutherford said.

"I know it does, but there's still something missing. You."

"*Me?*"

"Yes, you. You don't have a lot of experience, but you'll get that with us. What you do have is a set of talents we can use."

"But you said you already have a detective."

"That's true," Capp said. "But no one's good at everything. Every person on Earth has weaknesses, and since my team is made up of people, my team has weaknesses too. I think you'll fill in some of those gaps nicely."

Rutherford took a deep breath and spent a long time letting it out. "I'm sorry, Mr. Capp. I'm having trouble getting my head around this. You're offering me a job?"

"I'd prefer to say that I'm offering you an amazing opportunity to come work for me. Your official title will be *Detective*. You've graduated from the state-run police academy, so the governor has agreed to issue you a special commission for the duration of the time you work with my group. You'll be a fully authorized law enforcement officer, the only one on the team. It'll be handy to have someone who can actually detain and arrest suspects. I'll start you at twice your current salary with full benefits, and you'll get to wear real clothes. No more stuffy uniform. The team is based out of Seattle, but when we get out of the beta phase you may be traveling a great deal, and if we set up regional teams, you might have the opportunity to relocate."

Rutherford said, "Wow." He thought for a moment, grasping for something more articulate to say, and finally repeated, "Wow."

"I know," Capp said. "It's not the kind of offer you get every day."

"No," Rutherford said. "It isn't. What if I say no?"

Capp laughed. "Rutherford, it's a job offer, not an ultimatum. I'm not going to punish you if you turn me down."

Rutherford blushed. "I'm sorry. You're right. Of course not."

"Life will punish you on its own," Capp said. "If you say no, we'll drive you home. You'll have the rest of the day off, then tomorrow you'll put your uniform on and go back to your current job, where if they don't fire you over all the press coverage of yesterday's incident, you might manage to make plain clothes in six or seven years. Even if you get lucky and they eventually start treating you with some portion of the respect you deserve, you'll remember the offer I just made you every. Single. Day. And you'll always regret that you said no."

"What if it doesn't work out?"

Capp sighed. "If you want to quit, you can quit. I'm hiring you, not buying you. If nothing else, you'll have a heck of an interesting bullet point on your resume. If you're fired, the police will probably take you back, and even if they don't, you'll still have that really interesting bullet point on your resume. I'm not universally beloved. There are people who have gotten some pretty choice jobs off the fact that they were fired by me. It's not going to happen, though. If I thought it was likely that I'd end up firing you, I wouldn't be hiring you. It would be counterproductive."

Rutherford studied Capp's face, trying to decide whether or not to trust him.

Capp looked back. He was still smiling, but the effort he'd expended in his attempt to hire Rutherford seemed to have noticeably dulled his enthusiasm. What Rutherford didn't know was that the diminished enthusiasm was, in fact, part of the effort.

Rutherford said, "It's definitely a tempting offer."

"Yes," Capp agreed. "And you need to make a decision. We're pulling into the airfield now. When I step out of this van, the offer's rescinded."

"Seriously?" Rutherford asked.

Capp said, "Yes." He was no longer smiling, and Rutherford couldn't picture what a smile from Vince Capp would even look like, even though he'd been looking at one for the last ten minutes.

On the rear flat screen Rutherford saw the chain-link entrance gate to the airfield receding in the distance. He felt the truck slowing and turning as if pulling up to park beside a plane. He returned his gaze to Capp, who tilted his head and raised his eyebrows, as if asking Rutherford if he really wanted to push his luck this far.

As the truck came to a stop, Rutherford blurted, "Of course I'll do it! I'll take the job! Are you kidding? I'd be a fool not to."

Capp was smiling again in an instant. "Excellent," he said. He stood, turned on the tablet that had been sitting on the table, turned it around, and slid it along as he walked over to where Rutherford was sitting. The document on the screen was a block of text so fine and tightly packed that from a distance it read as a dark gray box. There were two sets of two lines at the bottom. The lines on the left already bore Capp's signature and the date.

Rutherford looked up at Capp and asked, "Can I read this over before I sign it?"

"Sorry," Capp said. "No time. I have a plane to catch, and I need to have this nailed down before I leave. The agreement just formalizes what I've already told you."

Rutherford looked at the tablet again.

"I know," Capp said. "I feel bad about how this has worked out. I wish there were more time. Look at it this way. You already said you want the job. As for the contract, I'm either trustworthy or I'm not. If I'm not, I'll find a way to screw you no matter what the contract says. If I am, then I'll take care of you no matter what the contract says. So, really, the question isn't, *Do you want to sign the contract?* It's, *Do you want to trust me?*"

Rutherford glanced at the contract one last time, then looked back at Capp, who was smiling and holding out a stylus.

Later, when he had time to think, Rutherford would notice bitterly that Capp had phrased his last statement very carefully. He hadn't posed the question of whether he should be trusted. He'd asked if Rutherford wanted to trust him, and of course the answer to that was *yes.*

Rutherford signed and dated the contract. In the space of ten seconds, Capp shook Rutherford's hand, patted him on the back, congratulated him, welcomed him aboard, thanked him for making the right decision, took back his tablet and stylus, and stepped out of the truck onto the tarmac. Not knowing what else to do, Rutherford followed.

A private jet that resembled a silver shark with wings sat out in the open, radiating cool vibes and hot sunlight. The pilot and a flight attendant stood by, looking professional in dark uniforms and dark glasses, worn to cut the blinding glare from the aircraft. A black sedan waited to one side. Standing beside the sedan, Rutherford recognized Terri Wells from the crime scene the day before. She approached, shielding her eyes with a leather portfolio.

Capp turned to Rutherford, who was surprised to see that the technology mogul was now wearing sunglasses. He hadn't seen him put them on.

"Sinclair Rutherford, I believe you've met your new supervisor, Terri Wells. Terri, Mr. Rutherford has decided to join us."

Terri shook Rutherford's hand and gave him a smile that felt like three hugs. "That's great news. May I call you Sinclair?"

Rutherford started to say *of course*, but was cut off by Capp saying, "I think it'd be better if you called him Detective Rutherford, or just Rutherford. Yeah, stick with *Rutherford*. Do you mind if she just calls you *Rutherford?*"

"No," Rutherford said. "That's fine."

"Great, Rutherford it is. This is going to work out just fine." Capp started walking backward toward the jet, but continued talking. "Terri here will help you through the paperwork, introduce you to the rest of the team, and get you all squared away."

Capp bounded up the stairs. Just before he disappeared into the plane's interior he turned, waved, and shouted, "I'm really excited to have you on the team."

The pilot and the flight attendant followed Capp into the plane, pulling up the stairs and closing the door behind them.

Rutherford turned to Wells and said, "He's really something."

"Yes," Wells agreed. "He is something." She cast a quick downward glance, quickly taking in Rutherford from head to toe. He was once again grateful that he'd put so much effort into his clothes today.

For an instant her smile faded, but only for an instant. "Well, Rutherford," she said, "if you'll come this way, I'll drive you to the office."

Wells walked toward the car. Rutherford took a few large, fast steps to catch up. When he was beside her, he said, "That sounds great, Mrs. Wells."

"Please, call me Terri."

"Thank you, Terri. You can call me Sinclair if you'd like."

She shook her head. "No I can't, Rutherford. You heard him."

FIVE

It was much easier for Rutherford to keep track of his location now that he was riding in the shotgun seat of a car. Sure, there were those monitors built into the walls of the UPS truck, but he hadn't really paid much attention to them after Capp had started talking.

Terri was driving, sticking mostly to the confusing tangle of surface streets and railroad tracks that most people avoid by taking Interstate 5 or Highway 99 into the city. Traffic wasn't great, and Terri needed to concentrate, so conversation had dropped off drastically. At the first stoplight, she handed Rutherford the leather portfolio she'd been holding at the airport.

"I assume Mr. Capp already had you sign the contract, yes?"

"Yes."

"Okay, well, you'll find the rest of the paperwork in there. If you want to look it over and sign what you can while we're driving, that'd save us some time." It was said with a brittle cheeriness. She sounded like someone who was trying to sound happy.

Rutherford said, "Sure, I'll take a look, but riding in the back of that van didn't sit very well with my stomach, and reading in the car . . ."

Rutherford trailed off as he slowly registered the decidedly negative emotion behind the look Terri was giving him.

"I'll get through as much of it as I can," Rutherford said.

"Thank you," Terri said, a little too gratefully. "I appreciate it."

The paperwork all seemed pretty straightforward. He'd have to fill out some of it later, like the authorization for direct deposit and the enrollment in the health and dental plans. He read every word of the nondisclosure agreement. It allowed him to testify in court and share evidence with law enforcement agencies, but it was rather draconian in all other matters. He was uncomfortable with it, but he figured he was already committed. He reached into his jacket's inner pocket and pulled out his favorite pen.

Terri glanced over and saw him signing. "Is that a fountain pen?" she asked.

"Yeah," he said. "It's not real, though."

She looked confused.

"I mean, it's a real fountain pen," he explained. "But it's a knockoff of a much better pen." He glanced forward, trying to say *please look at the road* without actually having to say it.

Terri returned her attention to the road and said nothing.

"See," Rutherford explained, "I've always wanted a Parker 51. Many collectors consider it the best fountain pen ever made. I can't justify spending that kind of money on a pen, so I got this Hero 329. It's made in China. It's not as good as a real Parker, but it's closer than you'd think. Really, the biggest difference is the nib. A real Parker has a gold nib. The Hero doesn't."

Terri kept driving and said nothing.

"Terri," Rutherford said, "please open your eyes."

She opened her eyes and immediately applied the brakes, then muttered an embarrassed apology.

Rutherford decided to change the subject.

"I should probably call my captain to tell him what's happened."

"No need," Terri said. "You're on a leave of absence until your employment paperwork goes through, then you'll officially leave the force with all need for advance notice waived. Mr. Capp had that arranged before you got into his truck."

"That's presumptuous," Rutherford said.

Terri chuckled to herself. "He'd call it *confident*. Knowing what he intended to offer you, do you really think there was a chance you would turn him down?"

Rutherford thought for a moment. "I guess not."

"Yeah, well, he didn't have to guess."

They rode in silence for a while before Rutherford thought of a good enough question to justify breaking the silence.

"What did you do before you came to work with the Authorities?"

"I was in upper management at one of Mr. Capp's other companies."

"A security company?"

"No. Software."

"Security software?"

"Back-end software for retail point-of-sale systems."

"Really?" Rutherford said, not attempting to keep the surprise out of his voice.

Terri glanced at him, and for a moment her amazing smile reappeared. "Yeah," she said. "I know it seems weird, but my job's pretty much the same here as it was there. I give my team the things they need, including direction, to achieve whatever impossible task our employer is demanding of us that week."

"Well, I'm happy to be on your team," he said.

"Glad to hear it," Terri said. "Because, no offense, but right now the impossible thing he's demanding is for me to get you settled gracefully into your new job."

"But no offense," Rutherford sniffed.

"I, look, Rutherford . . . Sinclair . . ." Terri stammered. "I'm sorry, but I didn't mean it as an insult. I'm betting Mr. Capp didn't really tell you much about your role in the team, did he?"

Rutherford thought about it.

"He said that the team has some gaps I can fill, and that I'll be able to detain and apprehend suspects because I'm the only sworn law officer. Is there more to it than that?"

"Yes."

"Okay, so, what else will I be doing?"

"I could tell you, but it'll be easier for me to show you. All of your questions will be answered in the next half hour," Terri said. "We're here."

They had returned downtown, and were driving along a narrow road one block inland from the waterfront. Rutherford could smell salt in the air. As they rolled through an intersection, he caught occasional glimpses of the gaps between the buildings. Tourists were exploring a garish gift shop that took up an entire pier, totally blocking any view of Puget Sound or the Olympic Mountains beyond.

Terri steered the car into a multistory parking garage that had been retrofitted into an old brick building. A valet rushed forward to open her door, but instead of exiting, she held a plastic tag about the size of a credit card up to the window. The valet immediately backed off and Terri drove the car up the ramp into the guts of the garage.

THE AUTHORITIES 61

Despite the sunny weather, there was very little light inside the parking structure, just enough that a driver would have to think about whether or not she needed headlights. The ceilings were lower and the lanes tighter than Rutherford would have thought sensible. Judging from the look of concentration on her face and the death grip she had on the wheel, Terri seemed to agree.

They worked their way to the top floor and pulled into an empty space that under normal circumstances could have held three cars. The valets probably could have squeezed in four. The ancient brick wall was interrupted by a dull patch of gray concrete. Terri pressed a button on her key fob. A rectangular chunk of the concrete patch receded and slid off to the side, opening a hole more than large enough for the car.

Terri drove through the opening, into a room with polished concrete floors, white painted concrete walls, and space for at least three large SUVs.

Theirs was the only car present, but Terri parked to the side, leaving room for later arrivals. As they got out of the car, Rutherford saw the hidden door slide shut behind them. He spun around, taking in the room. He stopped when his gaze fell on Terri, who was standing next to a frosted glass door, waiting.

Terri held the door open as Rutherford walked through.

"Welcome to the Authorities HQ," she said.

Rutherford emerged into a large office space, at least six thousand square feet. It was surprisingly empty. Cubicles with low, built-in partitions were amply stocked with computers and electronic equipment, and a conference table and chairs sat in the middle of the room, with rolling whiteboards at one end of the table and a large flat screen slung from the ceiling at the other. Everything you'd expect in a modern office space. There just wasn't nearly as much of it as you'd expect.

The wall behind him was made of brick, which had been carefully selected to match the look and character of the bricks the building had been made from over a hundred years before. A second wall was obscured by a bank of sealed offices with frosted glass façades and names printed on the doors. In the middle of the open space, there was the predictable elevator and stairwell that defined the building's spine. The other two outer walls were mostly glass, and provided a panoramic view of Puget Sound, West Seattle, the waterfront, the ferry terminal, and the equally antique building across the street.

"This is all yours?" Rutherford asked.

"It's ours. You're one of us now," Terri said.

"How many people work here?"

"Including you? Six."

"All this, for six people?"

Terri pointed at the ceiling. "We also own the roof deck."

"Why do we need all this space?"

"We don't. But we have it. Mr. Capp owned it already. Got it when he bought one of the Internet video companies that was competing to be the last company put out of business by YouTube."

"Hmm. Tough luck," Rutherford said.

"Not really. I think he just bought it to get this office. They had this crazy long-term lease in return for pre-IPO stock, which turned out to be worthless for the building's owner, but Capp gets to keep the top floor as long as the company name remains incorporated. He was going to make an apartment for himself out of it. The garage was part of that plan."

"But he didn't make an apartment."

"No," Terri said.

"Why not?"

Terri shrugged. "He changed his mind."

One of the frosted glass office doors opened, and a man poked his head out. Despite the fact that the guy now had a magnifying visor clamped to his head, Rutherford immediately recognized him as the operator of the drones.

"Ah, I thought I heard voices," he said as he emerged from his office. He rotated the visor upward. A pair of large black headphones was resting around his neck. He was wearing the pants and vest of another three-piece suit. His tie was loosened, his top button was undone, and his sleeves were rolled up.

Terri said, "Rutherford, I know you already met Albert Mok yesterday. Albert builds, procures, and maintains most of our equipment."

Albert stepped forward to shake Rutherford's hand. "Good to see you again, Officer Rutherford. Or is it Detective Rutherford now?"

Before Rutherford could answer, Terri said, "It's just Rutherford. That comes straight from Mr. Capp."

"Ah," Albert said. "Figures. Well, welcome aboard, Rutherford. Terri, Mr. Ivanov arrived about fifteen minutes ago. I gave him some tea and stuck him in your office. The others are all out, running some tests with Sherwood's apparatus."

"Great," Terri said. "When Peter and I are done with Rutherford, I'll hand him over to you so you can get him set up."

"Works for me. Also, I got an e-mail. The van will be here tomorrow morning."

Rutherford heard the entire exchange, but while he knew what all of the words meant, without context, little of it made any sense to him.

Terri said, "When things happen, they happen all at once."

Rutherford understood that statement, and agreed with it wholeheartedly.

"Always," Albert agreed. "Now if you'll excuse me, my soldering iron is calling to me."

Albert went back into his office and Terri ushered Rutherford into the corner office. A portly man in his late fifties was waiting there, looking out of the large windows at the intersection four floors below.

"Peter!" Terri said. "Thanks so much for coming. I'm sorry you had to wait."

The man stood. He was wearing low-top hiking shoes, jeans, a paisley shirt, and a red velvet jacket. He had long, wavy hair that he probably thought was silver, but was closer to the color of tin. He grasped Terri by the shoulders and mimed kissing her on both cheeks.

"Terri, my pet, it's always a pleasure to see your smiling face!" The man's voice didn't have any particular accent, but dripped with affected smarm, as if he was trying to give the impression of being a smooth-talking scoundrel, but wasn't quite a good enough actor to pull it off. He turned to Rutherford.

"And you must be the new hire! I would love to say that you are exactly as I pictured you, but I cannot."

Terri smirked. "Rutherford, this is Peter Ivanov. He's the head of the costume department at the Pacific Northwest Opera. Mr. Capp is a patron, so they occasionally loan us Peter."

Rutherford shook his hand and said, "Good to meet you."

Peter said, "Yes. Now please take off your jacket."

Rutherford raised his eyebrows at Terri, who nodded once. Not wanting to be labeled uncooperative on his first day, he took off his jacket and handed it to Peter, who felt the fabric, smiled at Rutherford as if slightly impressed, and placed the jacket gently on a chair. He produced a tailor's tape measure and started moving Rutherford's limbs around like a giant action figure, measuring his various dimensions.

"Tell me, Mr. Rutherford, where did you procure this suit?"

"Oh, at a thrift store. I can't afford to buy anything really good new, but you can find some great stuff used if you're patient, and you're not afraid to have things dry-cleaned and tailored."

Yes," Peter said, "And if you don't mind the melancholy of knowing that you're wearing a dead man's clothes."

Rutherford spent a moment trying to decide if he'd just been insulted, then turned to Terri and asked, "What's this for?"

"Your uniform."

"Please," Peter said. "It's a costume."

Rutherford said, "I was told I wouldn't be wearing a uniform."

"You won't," Peter said. "You'll be wearing a costume."

"Mr. Capp told me I'd be in plain clothes," Rutherford insisted.

"*Plain clothes,*" Peter muttered. "My clothes are never plain."

"Yes, I'm sure he did," Terri said, "but did he ever tell you that you'd get to pick those clothes yourself?"

"Well, no, but I naturally assumed I would."

"Yes. Of course you did," Terri said, "and Mr. Capp knew you would."

Rutherford spent several seconds feeling foolish. There was no point in getting mad at Terri. He could tell from the look on her face that she wasn't thrilled about the situation. She was neither the one who had misled him nor the one who had been misled. She was just the person who got to break the news. Besides, she was now his immediate supervisor. Getting angry with her would be a terrible way to start their relationship.

After a long silence Rutherford said, "Well, it's not so bad. The *costume* will look like plain clothes, and it'll be bespoke, which is amazing."

"All true," Peter said, still measuring Rutherford's various parts. "The custom garments won't be ready for a week or so, but I have a full off-the-rack ensemble for you to wear until then. It's waiting in the dressing room."

"In his case, wouldn't off-the-rack be better anyway?" Terri asked.

"Please," Peter said, rolling his eyes at Rutherford. "Off-the-rack is never better."

"Look," Rutherford said. "If I'm going to be wearing suits, I have a few that are tailored to fit me already. I could wear them until the new ones are ready."

Terri and Peter exchanged an uncomfortable look, and the designer stood up and started rolling up his measuring tape.

"What?" Rutherford asked. "I won't be wearing suits?"

He remembered how Capp had reacted to his attire earlier. *Feel free to dress more casually in the future, okay? No suits required.*

Rutherford said, "Look, I know that business casual is pretty much the norm these days, but a detective shouldn't show up at a crime scene in Dockers and a button-down."

Peter snorted. "The *victim* shouldn't show up at a crime scene in Dockers and a button-down."

Rutherford said, "I know, right? A good detective should look like a professional."

Peter said, "On the police force, perhaps, but—"

"I think," Terri cut him off, "it might be best if we just show him and give him a moment to think it through himself."

Peter looked dubious, but said, "Of course."

They guided Rutherford to the corner of the office space, where a windowless hallway led to the restrooms. Terri pointed him toward the men's room. "There's a full shower and changing room in there."

Peter said, "Your costume is hanging in a bag marked *Pacific Northwest Opera.* The shoes are in the box beneath it."

Rutherford went into the men's room. He was in there for less than thirty seconds before he emerged, still dressed in his own clothes.

"I'm sorry. I think there's been a mistake. I found the bag, but it's full of—"

"There's no mistake, Rutherford," Terri said, wearily. "Please just put it on. That way we can tell the very busy Mr.

Ivanov if the costume fits or not, and once he's gone on his way, we can discuss it further."

Rutherford returned to the men's room, and this time he emerged in full costume. Without saying a word, he lifted his arms and spun around once.

"Good," Peter said, approaching to check the fit by tugging at various corners of the garments. "Let's take a closer look."

"The jeans are a touch loose," Terri said.

"That's by design. A character choice, if you will. We didn't want a skinny-jean look. We wanted to give the impression that he buys his clothes carelessly and infrequently."

"That's why the knee is blown out," Terri said.

"Exactly. One of my seamstresses spent quite a bit of time distressing the jeans with a belt sander. How do the sneakers fit?" Peter asked Rutherford.

"Fine," Rutherford said.

"We got your size from your uniform vendor, Blumenthal's, but you know how it is. These things are never exact."

"Where did you find a vintage ZZ Top tour shirt?" Terri asked.

"One of our set carpenters was wearing it. It has a patina that you just can't fake, and the carpenter got an extra fifty bucks for a shirt he was wearing to paint in anyway."

"I bet this is one of the least expensive costumes your shop has ever produced," Terri said.

"True, for the most part. The leather jacket is a designer piece, though. I thought the car-coat length would add some visual interest. We got one that's a bit large so that it will accommodate the shoulder holster. Also, it will flap nicely when he runs. Everything else was fairly inexpensive. How do the fingerless driving gloves feel?"

"Like I'm a break dancer," Rutherford said.

"Great," Peter said. "We were hoping for an urban vibe. So tell me, what do you think?"

Rutherford came very close to answering in no small detail, but Terri cut in before he could speak. "Rutherford, Peter here is an important man, whose work has won numerous awards. He has Mr. Capp's full confidence, so please, tell him how everything fits, if your range of motion is limited, that kind of thing."

Rutherford swung his arms around, touched his toes, ran a quick lap of the room, and told Peter that the clothes fit fine. Peter said his good-byes. As soon as the elevator doors closed, Rutherford turned to Terri, ready to bombard her with a mix of questions and recriminations, but she was already holding up a hand to stop him. Her eyes were sympathetic as she said, "We definitely need to have a talk, but it'll be better for both of us if we do it calmly. If you'll go have a seat in my office, I'll get us each a cup of coffee and we can discuss the situation like adults."

SIX

Five minutes later, Terri came into her office with two steaming mugs. She handed one to Rutherford, who was sitting in her spare office chair. She leaned on her desk instead of sitting behind it.

"Okay, I can tell your uniform was a bit of a shock. I think you handled it pretty well, all things considered. Thanks for not causing a scene in front of Peter. None of this is his fault."

Rutherford sipped his coffee and shrugged.

Terri said. "Mr. Capp told you that you could fill certain gaps in the team's skill set, and that your title would be detective. Did he tell you how you got his attention?"

"Yeah, my work bringing down the murder suspect yesterday."

"Which he saw all over television and the Internet."

"Yeah," Rutherford said. "I guess."

"Last question, then I'll start answering yours: Did he tell you what we do here, and why we're doing it?"

"Of course. He said that you investigate high-profile crimes and test experimental crime-fighting techniques. In the long run, he hopes to make money off your success and notoriety."

Terri nodded emphatically, "And that's the problem. We've consulted on eight cases in Seattle and Tacoma in the last six months, and we've solved seven of them. All without getting any attention. You solved the eighth and made national news. We've had plenty of success, and we've hoped that word of mouth and acting mysterious would take care of the notoriety. Mr. Capp likes to say that the best way to call attention to something is to try to hide it."

"But it hasn't worked."

"No, so now we're going to try the second-best way to call attention to something."

Rutherford frowned. "What, you're going to yell, 'Hey, look at this'?"

"No, Mr. Capp thinks that's the third-best way. The second is to act like you're hiding something while *accidentally* drawing attention to yourself. Yesterday, you did two things. One of them was catch a murder suspect. Do I need to tell you what the other was?"

"So I'm here because my sex-toy video went viral?"

"That's the worse sentence anyone's ever said in my office, but yes," Terri said. "You got more publicity with one bust yesterday than we've gotten the entire time we've worked together as a unit. Mr. Capp thinks we've been too quiet and we've made our work look too easy. You're here to be loud and make things look difficult."

"But yesterday was a fluke!"

"Yes, it happened by accident. But now you'll have a whole team behind you, not to mention Mr. Capp's considerable resources, to help you do the same thing deliberately. Yesterday you presented the public with a familiar, relatable image: *the rebel cop who plays by his own rules.* Mr. Capp's marketing team feels strongly that—"

"He spoke to a marketing team about me?!"

Terri paused, tolerating the interruption. "The marketing team feels strongly that your actions established a brand, and that those actions can be repeated to strengthen that brand into something we can capitalize on."

Rutherford sagged into his chair. "So my job is to embarrass myself on YouTube to draw attention to the rest of the team."

Terri circled behind her desk and sat in her chair. "Nobody's saying you have to be embarrassed. It's all a matter of perspective. Listen, I'm an administrator. We have a detective, a security expert, and a techie. You're here to look dangerous, chase suspects on foot, get into fistfights, drive cars through fruit stands, and handcuff perps. The exciting stuff that looks good on TV. Lots of guys would see it as a dream job."

"Yeah," Rutherford said, "but I'm not one of them."

"I know, Sinclair, and that's why I said that it was going to be impossible to get you integrated into your new job. I didn't mean it as an insult. You present yourself as a decent, dapper, smart young professional."

"Thanks. I try."

"You do it well, and it's now my job to order you to cut it out."

"I don't know if I can."

"It's your job to try. We all have to do things we don't enjoy as part of our jobs. That's why they have to pay us. Do you think I'd be wearing this business suit if I didn't have to look professional?"

Rutherford said, "Well, it is a nice business suit, and you do wear it well."

Terri smiled. "Thank you, Rutherford. Coming from you that's quite a compliment."

"I don't know," Rutherford said. "It might be better for everyone if I just tap out now and go back to the force."

"That'll only be better for Mr. Capp's lawyers. They'd enjoy a nice cut-and-dried breach of contract suit to sink their fangs into." There was no joy in Terri's voice as she said it. She wasn't threatening or gloating, just explaining.

"Would he really sue me?"

"Sinclair, he didn't get where he is by letting people off the hook. The only people he talks to more than his marketing team is his legal team."

"So I'm stuck."

"Yes, you're stuck, but not in mud. You're stuck in liquid gold."

She saw the confusion on Rutherford's face and spoke up again before he could ask any questions. "That was a bad metaphor. The point is that this is still a great opportunity. You're going to be the public face of a group of the best experts available, working on high profile cases. This could be a great learning experience for you, and a huge boost to your career."

He thought for a long moment, then said, "Well, I'm in it now. The only logical thing is to try to make the best of it."

Terri smiled. "Good man. Now, look, I'm here to help in any way I can, but I'm also here to make sure you do your job. If that means I have to push you, I will."

"I don't doubt it," Rutherford said.

"Good. Right now I'm going to push you out of my office. Let's go see Albert and get you your equipment."

They found Albert precisely where they'd left him—in his office workshop, soldering a small object Rutherford couldn't see clearly to a larger object he couldn't identify, which was inside the chassis of one of the scanner drones, which was itself a mechanism Rutherford didn't understand.

Terri excused herself, stating that she'd be in her office tending to business.

"All right," Albert said, rubbing his hands together in anticipation. "Now that costuming is behind you, we can get on to the fun part."

"I guess costuming is sort of a jolt for everyone."

"No," Albert said. "None of the rest of us got costumed. You're the only one whose image is being engineered. The rest of us were cast to type, so to speak."

"So the ninja dresses that way on her own?" Rutherford asked, stunned.

Albert looked puzzled. "The ninja? Oh, you mean Sloan. You call Sloan the *ninja*?"

"Yeah, that's what the cops who've met your team call her. You call the ninja *Sloan*?"

"Yeah, that's what her parents called her, Megan Sloan, and they met her first. I guess I see why you guys might think she looks like a ninja. I always think of her as looking more like a Power Ranger. Anyway, you'll meet the rest of the team soon enough. Right now, let's talk about toys."

Albert opened a cabinet and pulled out a rectangular slab of glass and metal. "Your new phone," he announced, handing it to Rutherford.

Rutherford turned it over in his hand. It looked like a sheet of glass glued to the top of a thin bar of stainless steel. There were no physical buttons, but markings etched into the sides indicated the power and volume controls. Two large glass lenses spaced about two inches apart were recessed into the back of the phone. He touched the power symbol and the entire front of the phone came alive with an image that stretched all the way to the edges of the glass.

"The specs are a little better than a high-end phone right now," Albert said. "It'll be hopelessly outdated a year from now, but by then we'll have upgraded. It's got a huge battery, so a day of constant use won't be a problem. It has radios for every type of cellular protocol used in North America. If you can talk on it, you can use this phone on it. The phone runs vanilla Android with some proprietary apps. You'll also get a tablet that has most of the same functionality, but with more memory and a much larger screen."

Rutherford said, "Cool. Do I stick the SIM card from my current phone in it, or what?"

"No, we wouldn't make you pay for your own cell service. Besides, you could never afford it. Part of why the phone needs such a big battery is that it's always in contact with our computing cluster. We can watch your camera feed and use your screen to direct you to anything we think needs your attention, and you'll be in constant voice contact with the rest of the team over an earpiece."

Albert turned his head and tapped his ear with a finger. Rutherford leaned forward and saw that deep inside the curves of Albert's ear there was a small piece of flesh-toned plastic, perforated with tiny holes.

"It's got a built-in microphone. We can use it to directly call any other member of the team, or broadcast to several people at once, like a big Google Hangout."

"Cool," Rutherford said.

"I'm glad you think so," Albert said, "because I'll have to scan your ear canal before I can make yours. Used to be I'd have had to clamp your head into a vise to hold it still, but we've made some improvements."

"Glad to hear it," Rutherford deadpanned.

"Now, you'll just have to wear this for five minutes." Albert held up an old open-face motorcycle helmet with a large metal box bolted to its right side.

Rutherford put on the helmet, and Albert plugged the cord dangling from it into the same oversized portable computer he'd had at the crime scene the day before. Then Rutherford watched as a detailed map of his inner ear slowly filled in on the computer screen. It had been an eventful morning. This was the first time he'd had a moment to actually think about anything.

He checked his phone. His social media was still being blitzed, but there was only one new text from his sister Vanessa. This one consisted of five exclamation marks, then, in parentheses, *Don't make me use words.*

Rutherford texted back, *You just did. Don't worry. I'm embarrassed but fine. Will call tonight.* He put his phone away, sat quietly for a long moment, then said, "Albert, can I ask you a question?"

"As long as you try not to move the right side of your face as you do it."

"How did you get into this?" Between trying not to move half of his mouth and the way the helmet was constraining his jaw, Rutherford slurred the words in a way he realized was barely intelligible.

"It depends on what you mean," Albert said. "If you mean, *How did I end up as the gadget-master for the Authorities*, I was already working on this kind of thing for fun. I wrote a few proof-of-concept apps and drew up some designs, just stuff I was excited about. My scanner drones were part of it. I showed them to my supervisor, who worked for a guy who worked for a guy who answered to Capp. Word filtered up. Capp wanted to see what else I was working on. After I showed him, he offered me this job. I'd been thinking up spy-type gadgets ever since I saw my first James Bond movie as a kid. This isn't quite the same thing, but it's close enough that I jumped at the opportunity. Scan's done."

Rutherford unstrapped the helmet and squeezed his head free. Albert unplugged the cord and tapped a few keys.

"I was ten," Albert said absentmindedly, "and *Goldfinger* was on cable. I took one look at that Aston Martin and I knew I wanted to grow up to be just like Q."

"Q," Rutherford said. "Not Bond, or Goldfinger, or even Odd Job? Q?"

"Yeah. Have you seen many of the Bond movies?"

"All of them, most more than once."

"Nice! Well, if you think about it, the only people who get to give Bond crap without getting killed for it are M, Moneypenny, and Q. Bond comes into the office, gets talked down to and bossed around, then he goes out into the field to get shot at. M sits in an office, looking miserable, and Moneypenny spends her day being used as a target dummy for flirt practice. Q has a lab, underlings, and gets to play with all the toys. He's got the best job of anyone."

"I see your point."

"I thought you might. Now, let's get you your sidearm."

"What would that be, a Walther PPK?"

"Well done, but no. We've got something much cooler for you. Our employer has a diverse portfolio of investments. One of his interests is a gun manufacturer. He and I looked over what they had in their new product pipeline to see if we could find a distinctive weapon to fit your image. He'd like to get some cross-promotion going. You know how NASA capsules used to land in the ocean back in the day?"

"Yeah," Rutherford said, confused by the sudden change in topic.

"To help the astronauts survive until the helicopters got to them, NASA gave them rafts, right?"

"Of course."

"Russian capsules didn't land in the ocean. They landed in the Siberian wilderness. They didn't have to worry about drowning, just bears and wolves. So, instead of rafts, they were equipped with these."

Albert reached into a cabinet and produced a chunk of black steel and polished walnut roughly the length of a grown man's forearm. He pointed the monstrous pistol's muzzle at the floor and turned the handle toward Rutherford. "It isn't loaded."

Rutherford took the firearm. At first he held it gingerly, as if it were radioactive waste, then he grasped it firmly with both hands, as if it were very heavy radioactive waste.

"The TP-82. The cosmonaut gun," Albert said, as if beginning an oral book report. "The original could fire bullets, shotgun shells, and signal flares, but only had a three-shot capacity. One round for each barrel."

Rutherford turned the gun around so he could look at its business end without pointing it directly at his head. Two shotgun barrels ran along its top and a third smaller rifle barrel was nestled below and between them.

"This model is designed to be a more functional, modern weapon while evoking the feeling of the original. It takes standard twelve-gauge shotgun ammo, loaded through the breech. The lower barrel is now a nine-millimeter semiautomatic, fed by a magazine in the handle. You can switch between the various barrels with a thumb switch near the safety. It really is a masterful piece of design work. I wish I'd done it. They added all of this functionality, but they still managed to make it three pounds lighter than the original."

Rutherford tilted the gun back and forth in his hands, feeling its heft. "*This* is lighter?"

"Yeah, the cosmonaut model weighed eight pounds."

"Am I really going to need this much gun?"

"Better safe than sorry."

Rutherford thrust the gun forward, still cradling it sideways in both hands. "And this is what safety looks like?"

Albert smiled. "For the person holding it, yes. Look, only the nine-millimeter barrel has to be lethal. We can load up the shotgun barrels with rock salt or beanbag rounds, and we've developed a twelve-gauge GPS tracking dart, because we didn't think you'd need a flare."

"Oh," Rutherford said. "That's cool."

Albert said, "Yeah, just don't ever fire the dart at a person, okay? It's strictly for use on vehicles. Preferably ones that have a metal body, because the dart will punch right through most automotive-grade plastics."

"Thanks for the warning. Anything else?"

"Yes," Albert said. "I recommend holding it with both hands when you fire it, both because of the weight and the kick."

"How hard does it kick?"

Albert executed one of the rarest of human sounds, the grim laugh, then said, "Noticeably. When you fire the shotgun barrels, you'll want to use the attachable stock or—at the very least—fire it from the hip and keep a death grip on the forestock."

"I won't hit much that way."

"Maybe not, but the gun also won't fly back and break your nose."

Rutherford looked down at the small cannon in his hands, held out in front of his body, then asked, "So, do I just carry it around like this?"

"Oh, no," Albert said with a start. "We have a custom holster."

He reached back into his cabinet and pulled out the largest, most cumbersome-looking shoulder holster Rutherford had ever seen.

Albert explained, "It's got loops for eight shotgun shells, pouches for two extra magazines, and the holster itself is on a swivel. That way the gun will lie parallel with your body, but you can easily pull it out through the front of your jacket. It's going to scare the hell out of anyone who messes with you."

Rutherford thought that he could probably scare an attacker just by showing them the holster and threatening to make them wear it.

"What's that?" Rutherford asked, pointing at a flat leather panel with a silver snap and what appeared to be a plastic grip positioned on the holster between the gun and the wearer's ribcage.

"That's where the removable stock goes. It attaches to the base of the pistol grip."

Glad I asked, Rutherford thought. *I'll be wanting to use that.*

Albert unsnapped the flap and pulled the stock from its sheath. The black plastic handle and a matching plastic butt plate were affixed to opposite ends of a shining metal triangle.

"It also works as a machete," Albert said, giddily.

Or not, Rutherford thought.

Rutherford removed his leather jacket. With Albert's help, he strapped on the holster, put the gun in the holster, and put the jacket on over that. Rutherford retuned to the restroom to look in the mirror. He had to admit that the extra bulk was not as obvious as he'd feared, possibly because of his slight frame. He was painfully aware of the extra weight though, also probably because of his slight frame.

When he emerged, Albert showed him where all of the gun's switches and levers were. He practiced removing the weapon from its holster as smoothly as possible while Albert made suggestions. Albert was explaining how the deadly looking stock attached to the gun when he got a faraway look in his eyes and stopped talking. He stood motionless for a moment, then said, "Yes, I'm here."

Rutherford had worked with enough people wearing radio earpieces to know when a person in the room with him was being talked to by a person who wasn't in the room with him.

"What is it?" Rutherford asked.

Albert held up a finger, asking for a moment, then said, "Okay. Rutherford, grab your phone."

He remembered leaving his new company-issued smartphone on one of Albert's workbenches. He darted into Albert's office and saw that the phone's screen was pulsating and the phone itself was vibrating audibly. He picked it up and glanced back to Albert, who already had his own phone out. Albert nodded, signaling him to answer the call.

Rutherford swiped the screen, and he saw a large image of Vince Capp sitting in a plush-looking chair, inside an equally plush-looking private jet. Along the bottom of the screen there were little moving images of Terri and Albert, along with the bearded European man, the older black gentleman with the buzzing wand, and the helmet of the woman he thought of as the ninja, but whom he now knew was called Sloan. It seemed everyone on the team was in on the call.

"Hello, everyone," Capp said. "I'm calling for a couple of reasons. First, I want to welcome the newest member of our team. I know you all met him briefly yesterday, but please say hello to Rutherford."

Almost all of the heads in the thumbnail images smiled, nodded, and made overtly welcoming noises. Sloan's helmet remained silent and motionless.

Capp continued. "I see that they have your clothes sorted out. That's good. Has Albert shown you the gun yet?"

Rutherford said, "Yeah, about that, I think I have to tell you—"

Terri's face disappeared from her thumbnail, then he heard her office door swing open with a powerful *whoosh*. He looked up, saw the expression on her face, and thought better about what he'd been intending to say.

"It's cool," Rutherford said, uncertainly. "The clothes fit well, and the gun, it's really something."

Terri's smiling face came back into frame.

"About the gun," Capp said. "One of the marketing stooges came up with a backstory about how you got it. I'll e-mail you the details, but if anyone asks, the gist is that a wealthy Russian arms merchant's daughter was kidnapped, and you saved her. The arms dealer was grateful, and gave you the gun as a gift. You named the gun *Tatiana*."

"After the daughter," Rutherford said.

"No," Capp said, raising his eyebrows, "the arms dealer. Nice, eh? Hey, Albert."

"Yes, sir?"

"How quickly can you get *Tatiana* engraved on the gun somewhere?"

"I can have a new forestock made. Should be able to turn that around in a week or so."

"Top man. On to business. I have good news. There's been a nice, juicy murder. The data mine pinged me just a minute before I called. Sounds like Dr. Dan Arledge has been killed. You probably don't know about him, but I do. You might have heard of some of his clients, and you've definitely heard of the companies they work for. He's a psychologist, very well-known in the tech industry. He was the go-to guy for upper-level tech execs who suffered from neuroses, success guilt, or excessive stress, which, between those three things, is most of them."

Rutherford heard the sound of a keyboard clacking as soon as Capp said the victim's name. He saw that Terri had her head down. She said, "Okay, I have his information here. He ran a place called *The Arledge Behavioral Health Clinic*, which figures. Where was he found?"

"His office, twenty minutes ago," Capp said. The police are there now. Get over there and do your jobs. Oh, and Rutherford?"

"Yes?"

"Do you smoke?"

"No."

"Wanna? I think it'd help sell the image. We could get you a per diem to pay for cigarettes, or better yet, cigars."

Rutherford swallowed hard and said the thing he needed to say. "Sir, I just don't know if I can pull off this bad-boy mystique you've set up for me."

Terri closed her eyes. Albert visibly clenched. Capp smiled. "We didn't set it up for you, Rutherford. We set it up, then hired you for it. And I believe you'll find a way to make it work. You're a smart young man. Smart enough to know that if you don't, I'll be forced to fire you, and that'll be the end of your career in law enforcement. And never say *mystique* again. It's out of character."

"I am who I am, sir."

"Yeah, well, work on that. Anything else?"

The bearded European gentleman spoke up. "I must ask a question. Forgive me, but you are an executive in the technology sector, and you are familiar with the victim. Have you ever been his patient?" He spoke with the careful diction and precise word choices of a man who would claim to not speak English well when in fact he just didn't know the language well enough to feel comfortable abusing it.

Capp said, "Thanks for asking, Max. No, I've never seen Dr. Arledge or any mental health professional. If I have any mental problem at all, it's that I'm too sane. If I saw a psychologist, I'd probably end up helping them."

SEVEN

The team arranged to converge on the crime scene, and within minutes Rutherford, Terri, and Albert were in the car, pulling out of the parking garage.

Rutherford was driving, because that was going to be a major portion of his job. Terri was sitting in the front passenger seat, chiding him, which was going to be a major portion of her job. Albert sat in the back seat, researching the victim and acting as if Terri and Rutherford weren't there.

Terri concluded a long, impromptu speech, summing it up by saying, "Don't you ever pull a stunt like that again."

Rutherford, for his part, had listened closely and understood every word she'd said, but still couldn't quite comprehend the situation. "What stunt?" he asked. "All I did was voice a concern to my boss."

"No, you voiced a concern to *my* boss, Mr. Vincent Capp, who hired me to be your boss. I try to please him by doing my job, which is making sure that you do your job. By doing your job, you will please me, which will please Mr. Capp, and that's how we all end up happy. By going directly to him with a problem, you told him both that you couldn't do your job and that I wasn't doing mine. That's how we all end up unhappy."

Rutherford considered this for a moment. When he finally replied, it was in a quieter tone. "Terri, I'm sorry. I didn't mean to go over your head."

"You complained to the person who pays my salary. I don't see how you could have thought you were doing anything else. But I understand. It's your first day. It's been eight kinds of crazy. Just know that it can never happen again."

"Are you saying that I should never voice any concerns to Mr. Capp?"

"Yes. That's exactly what I'm saying. For you to complain to him would be counterproductive, because all he'll do is tell me to fix it. You're a cop. Think of it this way. I'm your captain. He's the chief of police. He tells me if he has a problem with you. You tell me if you have a problem with him."

"And then what do you do?"

"Usually, try to hide that information from both of you."

Eventually, mercifully, they made their way across Lake Washington to Bellevue, a bedroom community that had profited greatly from the dot-com boom, and as a result had a downtown core of tall buildings larger than that of many freestanding cities.

The trip across the lake had taken, as usual, much longer than was reasonable. By the time they arrived, just shy of eleven fifteen, the police had a surprising amount of the street cordoned off. Parking was already hard to come by in this area, and the police disruption didn't help matters. Rutherford ended up parking two blocks away from where the police tape began.

They continued on foot, Albert lugging his oversized portable computer, Rutherford listing noticeably to the left, pulled down by the weight of his barely concealed handheld howitzer.

There was another black sedan, identical to the one Rutherford had been driving, parked much closer to the crime scene than he'd managed. The doors of the car opened and the other three members of the team emerged. Sloan wore a similar black pants suit and the same black helmet, and used the same cane she'd had the day before. Her presence had a noticeable effect on the surroundings. Conversations quieted. People passing, on foot or in cars, slowed down. It seemed to Rutherford that the only people who weren't made uncomfortable by her were herself and the people with her.

I guess I am one of the people with her, Rutherford thought. *Eventually she won't make me uncomfortable either. I can't imagine it happening, but it can't happen soon enough.*

Terri said a quick hello when they reached the others, announced that she was going to go make contact with whoever was in charge, told everyone to wait where they were, and asked Albert to handle the formal introductions. She did all of this without once breaking her stride. She reached the caution tape, spoke very briefly to the officer maintaining the barrier, and walked through.

Beyond the tape, two doors down, Rutherford saw a brick building that was obviously the crime scene, marked as such by the steady stream of cops coming in and out. Most of the parking spaces in front of the building and its two neighbors held dirty, beat-down pickups, all of which were cordoned off with caution tape. A few of the trucks were also being searched.

Albert clapped Rutherford on the back. "Everyone, I'd like you to meet Rutherford. I know we all saw him yesterday, but I was the only one who really got to talk to him. Anyway, he's the newest member of the team, and I should warn you, he's at a bit of a disadvantage. His earpiece is still printing back at the office, so he can't hear anything said on the party line. So, Rutherford, this is Max."

Albert gestured toward the older, bearded man, who shook Rutherford's hand. Max's clothes were mostly brown, but they were a kaleidoscope of textures, including tweed, flannel, suede, and corduroy.

Max said, "Welcome to our merry band, young man." His accent was still unidentifiable to Rutherford. "I must say," Max continued, "you impressed us all a great deal yesterday. That was good work with the sex toy."

"Uh, thanks," Rutherford said.

Albert said, "And this is Sloan."

Sloan silently nodded her helmet.

Rutherford said, "It's good to meet you."

Sloan stood motionless for a moment, then nodded again. After another long, silent moment passed, Sloan's helmet tilted slightly, as if she was puzzled. Everyone except Rutherford and Sloan let out a restrained laugh.

The tall, older African American man in the blue windbreaker stepped forward and shook Rutherford's hand.

"Hello, Mr. Rutherford. I'm Professor Duane Sherwood. It's good to have you aboard. It'll be nice to not be the new guy anymore."

"How long have you been with the group?" Rutherford asked.

"Just a couple weeks."

Albert cut in, "Professor Sherwood is with us temporarily. He's here to do research."

"Really?" Rutherford asked. "What are you studying?"

"The use of live bees in law enforcement applications."

Rutherford started to ask him to repeat himself, but Professor Sherwood held up a hand and got a faraway look in his eye. Albert and Max had that same look. Sloan remained impassive.

Albert said, "All right. Rutherford, we've got the go-ahead from Terri to come in."

Rutherford said, "That didn't take long."

Max smiled at him. "It never does."

They entered the building that housed the Arledge Behavioral Health Clinic and found it to be a construction site. The floor was bare concrete with a gap below the moldings that betrayed the former presence of thick carpeting. The air reeked of paint, paint thinner, adhesives, and solvents.

Judging by the bricks, and the shape of the structure they were piled into, Rutherford figured he was standing in the archetypical Seattle building. It had probably been built in the fifties or sixties during the Boeing boom, as something lowbrow like a neighborhood drugstore to cater to factory workers who couldn't afford to live closer to work. Then, in the nineties, when a new downtown had sprouted up around it, the building would have been purchased, gutted, and renovated to serve the highbrow needs of Microsofties and Amazonians. Now it was being renovated again to reflect the modern ideal of what an upscale twenty-first-century business should look like, which meant it would likely be furnished and decorated with a nod toward the fifties and sixties.

Of course, the midcentury modern facelift was only half finished. This point was driven home by the unfinished floor, the smatterings of raw wood and drywall, and the partially completed broken tile mosaic mural that was being assembled on the wall behind the reception desk.

A gaggle of construction workers lounged around the waiting room, most of them sitting on the floor, patiently waiting while the police searched their work site and trucks. If the police had any questions for the workers, they'd been asked before the Authorities arrived. The workers seemed bored but happy, likely because they were still on the clock despite being legally prevented from exerting themselves in any way. A single police officer was completing a lap of the room, collecting Terri's nondisclosure agreements, many of which had been signed only semi-legibly with squared-off carpenter pencils.

Everyone who was paying attention to their surroundings grew quiet the moment Sloan entered the room. One member of the construction crew was slumped, eyes downcast, on the verge of a nap. It was clear that all he saw of Sloan was the lower reaches of a slim feminine form and a cane. He started to compliment her on the quality of her said feminine form but stopped mid-syllable when he saw her helmet gazing down at him.

It struck Rutherford that when people couldn't see your face, they tended to assume you weren't smiling.

Toward the back of the lobby, Terri was using her smile to blind and disorient the senior officer on the case. She saw that the team had arrived, and excused herself, then came over to brief the group.

"Okay. Like Mr. Capp said, the victim is Dr. Daniel Arledge. He was a psychologist, and a successful one at that. He shared his practice with another psychologist, his junior partner, Dr. Tyler Shaw. Shaw's in his office being interviewed by a detective right now. The receptionist found the victim in his office." Terri motioned to a harried-looking young woman in professional attire, sitting quietly behind the reception desk, all of her attention focused on the steaming cup in front of her.

Terri continued. "The victim's car was here when she arrived, which is normal. He hadn't come out of his office all morning, which is less normal, but not unheard of. She finally had to knock to discuss a scheduling issue a few minutes before ten. When he didn't answer, she peeked in."

Max asked, "Is there any apparent cause of death?"

"It looks like blunt force trauma and a massive skull fracture, but that's not official until the autopsy, of course. I haven't seen the body myself, and I don't plan to look. Rough time of death is last night around nine. They say there were repeated blows to the back of the head. No sign of a murder weapon."

"Which would explain why they're searching these men's trucks," Max said.

The team seemed to consider this in silence for a moment, then Max and Albert both stifled a laugh, though Rutherford had no clue what was funny.

"All right," Terri said. "You know the drill. Sloan, Max, question the witnesses and have a look around. Albert, let's get a scan of the crime scene, the partner's office, and the lobby too while we're here. Oh, and try to get the storeroom. The builders have been locking their heavier tools and materials there overnight. The cops have already gone through it, but you never know what we'll need. Professor Sherwood, go ahead and let your bees have a sniff around. If we're lucky, they'll find something."

Professor Sherwood raised his buzzing metal wand. "Will do."

Rutherford looked at the device, which still seemed like nothing more than a handheld metal detector. "Do you really have a live bee in that thing?" Rutherford asked.

Sherwood's eyes lit up. "No, young man, I have thirty live bees in this thing. Each one trained to smell a specific compound. They have amazing little noses. Not noses, really. They have olfactory antennae, but the point is that their sense of smell is much more sensitive than a dog's. The bottom surface is perforated with holes. A small fan draws the air into the device. Each bee is fastened to a little mount, and if they smell what they're trained to smell, they trigger—"

"I'm sorry to interrupt," Terri said, "but you can explain that later. Right now we have a murderer to catch, a bunch of cops who want us out of the way, and a contractor paying a construction crew union wages to read copies of *Mental Health Monthly*."

Professor Sherwood said, "Of course," nodded to Rutherford, and headed to the office doors at the back of the lobby, where Albert was already unpacking his drones.

"What should I do?" Rutherford asked.

"You," Terri said quietly, glancing around the room to see if anyone was listening. "Until we're ready to make an arrest, your main job is to be seen looking like a badass."

"How do I do that?"

"I don't know. The outfit'll get you most of the way there on its own. Try to look unhappy. That seems to go with the attitude. Oh," she stopped talking and rummaged through her bag. "Here, put this in your mouth." She brought her hand out of the deepest corner of the bag and produced a single wooden toothpick.

"Agh," Rutherford moaned. "Has that been rolling around loose in there?"

"Yes, but that's good. Thinking about it will help with the *looking unhappy* thing. Put it in your mouth."

Rutherford did as he was told.

Terri nodded. "Yeah, now you look angry at the world. The squint's a nice touch."

"I'm not squinting. I'm cringing."

"Well keep it up." Then, in a much louder voice, Terri said, "No, Rutherford, I don't care that the guy confessed, he had rights, and you're on probation until you learn to follow the rules! Now you just stay out here and don't hurt anybody while the trustworthy professionals do some real detective work."

Rutherford's *squint* intensified. Terri looked pleased. She turned and went back to the officer she'd been schmoozing before.

Rutherford looked around the room and everyone made a show of not looking back. All of the seats were taken, so he would have to lean against a wall. That allowed him to pick any

THE AUTHORITIES

part of the wall he wanted. He chose one within earshot of where Max was questioning the receptionist. If he couldn't do any real detective work, he could at least watch it being done.

Sloan stood motionless next to Max, watching the receptionist intently. In case she decided to attack, Rutherford supposed.

"So you believe that the doctor was here all night?" Max asked.

The receptionist said, "I can't be sure, but he was here when I left yesterday, and his car was here when I got in this morning."

"So it's a good bet, yes?"

"I think so."

There was a sudden high-pitched whine from the back of the lobby. The receptionist, cops, and construction workers all craned their necks to see what was happening. Rutherford, Max, and Sloan knew it was Albert deploying his drones. Rutherford still looked. Max simply spoke louder. Sloan didn't react at all.

"Is it unusual for him to spend the night in his office?" Max asked.

"The whole night, yeah, that's not normal, but Dan . . . Dr. Arledge gets caught up in his work and stays late all the time. He sits at his desk, looking over case files until he gets sleepy, then he *rests his eyes* and lays on a couch he has in there."

"Ah," Max said, smiling first at the receptionist, then over his shoulder at Sloan. "Of course, the psychologist would have a couch."

The conversation paused while the receptionist and everyone except for Sloan reacted to the sudden lines of bright red laser light stabbing out of the door to the crime scene, followed by flashes of bright white light, both of which accompanied the unsettling dentist-drill whine of the motors.

"Actually," the receptionist continued, still watching the lights, "it's not that kind of couch. It's a normal sofa. Very few psychologists use the kind of couch you're thinking of anymore. They don't want to look like a *New Yorker* cartoon. The only thing worse for a psychologist would be to have a beard and a German accent." She looked at Max, then froze up completely. Max said nothing for a moment. For the first time since Rutherford had started watching, Sloan looked away from the receptionist and tilted her helmet toward Max.

Max laughed. "I am Dutch, not German, young lady, but no offense taken."

She looked relieved. Max watched her silently for a moment, then asked, "So it wasn't unusual for him to fall asleep here. Did he usually just go ahead and stay the night in his office?"

"Only rarely. He'd usually wake up and go home to finish the night's sleep or at least freshen up. I should have knocked earlier to check on him. I don't know why I didn't."

"You didn't, because why would you?" Max said. "You had no reason to suspect he'd been murdered. I understand why you didn't want to disturb you employer." Max paused. After a moment's thought, he said, "But I am curious why you didn't need to check on him earlier. Did he not have any appointments this morning? No clients coming in to see him?"

"No. He's changed his practice a bit in the last few years. He doesn't see as many clients any more, and almost never meets with them one-on-one. He mainly does group therapy."

Max thought a moment, then nodded. "I see. Yes. Thank you for putting up with all these questions. You're doing well. We're almost done. Please, tell me, did the doctor have any enemies that you know of?"

"No," the receptionist said. "He was a good man. There were people who were unhappy with him, but nobody you'd call an enemy."

"Who was unhappy with him?"

The receptionist shook her head, dismissively. "There was a patient who stormed out of his group therapy session a couple of days ago, but that's par for the course."

"Patients often get upset and leave the group therapy?" Max asked.

"That particular patient does. It's a big part of why he needs therapy."

Max said, "I see," and then all conversation in the lobby became impossible as Albert left the victim's office lugging his briefcase computer, the drones flying in an orderly line over his head. He put his computer on the floor and opened the next door over, the junior partner's office. The quadcopters entered the room in a calm, orderly fashion. All of the people who had been in that room left it in a rushed, disorganized fashion, chased out by pulses of laser light.

Among the refugees from the second office was a man in his late thirties wearing what Rutherford recognized to be a very nice inexpensive suit. The kind of suit one might get if he walked into a JCPenney and said, "Shoot the works, my good man, for I am a big shot."

Sloan leaned on her cane, silently watching the people spill out into the waiting room. Max turned, looked at the group, then pointed toward the man in the expensive cheap suit and asked the receptionist, "Please tell me, would that be Dr. Shaw?"

"Yes."

"Ah," Max said. "We should talk to him. Thank you for your time, young lady. You have been very helpful."

Max and Sloan crossed the room to ask Dr. Shaw a few questions. Rutherford considered following so that he could eavesdrop on that conversation as well, but then he realized Terri was looking directly at him. He remembered that his instructions had been to stand around looking tough, and while he could do that while listening in, crossing the room to do so would be a bit obvious. He resigned himself to staying put.

Terri smirked slightly, then went back to her conversation.

Rutherford frowned and went back to his work, which at the moment was frowning. He glared at the construction workers. He scowled at the floor.

He stretched, and flexed his shoulders. He wasn't accustomed to the shoulder holster, and the off-balance weight of the over-powered gun it held was wreaking havoc on his posture.

Hopefully, people think it's a gangsta lean, he thought. *But really, it's more likely they'll think I have scoliosis.*

He was just getting ready to start glowering out the window when he felt a light tap on his shoulder. When he turned around, he found himself looking at a woman in her late forties. She was dressed professionally but stylishly, with a briefcase in her hands and a nervous look on her face.

"Pardon me," she said. "Are you one of the subcontractors, or are you here with the investigation?"

"The investigation. I'm, uh, I'm a detective." Rutherford stumbled over using the word *detective* to describe himself, which he realized robbed him of most of the authority the title gave him.

"Oh," the woman said. "You wouldn't happen to know where I could find the general contractor, would you?"

"I'm sorry, no idea." Rutherford motioned toward the workers who were sitting around reading magazines. "Any of them might be able to tell you."

"I'll ask," the woman said. "Can you tell me how long you all will be here investigating?"

Rutherford said, "I'm afraid it'll take as long as it takes, Miss . . ."

The woman took the hint and extended a hand. "I'm Claire Sullivan," she said. "I'm the interior designer."

"Ah," Rutherford said brightly. "Nice to meet you." He cast his eyes around the room, then asked, "Do a lot of midcentury modern?"

"Yes. It's my specialty, and it's popular right now. When people get successful enough to hire a designer, they're usually old enough that their tastes sort of mimic those of the rich, successful people they saw on TV when they were kids. Besides, midcentury is an appropriate style for this application."

"Makes sense," Rutherford said. "I doubt many doctors want their waiting rooms done in French farmhouse."

"No," she said, smiling. "That would be a challenge. I could probably make the individual offices work, but you need something more formal for the waiting room."

Rutherford said, "Agreed. Most doctors' waiting rooms don't have nearly this much natural light, though. You got lucky there."

"Yes, well, this building was originally a mom and pop grocery store. When they converted it, they kept the windows in the front wall," Ms. Sullivan said. "It's really the only nod they've made to the building's former life. It's a shame. I would have held on to the shelves along the wall, or made the receptionist's desk out of one of the old check stands, but then, they made a lot of questionable decisions."

"Really? How was the place decorated before you came in?" Rutherford asked.

"Well, it was converted in ninety-five, and it showed. Exposed brick, quirky decorations, oversized mismatched furniture."

Rutherford nodded. "The set of *Friends.*"

"Bingo. If you want a sample, the doctors' offices are still intact. The plan is to move on to them after the waiting room's done."

Rutherford nodded and looked around briefly. "Well, I know this room is far from done, but I really like the finishes you've chosen. So tell me, are you going to go with wood, linoleum, or a very low pile for the floors?"

"I talked them into springing for terrazzo!" she said.

"Really? Good for you! If they hadn't agreed to that, would you have considered a polished concrete?"

"I thought about it," she said, "but I don't know that it would have been luxe enough to go with the mosaic mural."

"I see what you mean," Rutherford said. "Did you design the mural too?"

"Guilty," she said.

"*Guilty* isn't the word I'd use. It's hard to say until it's done, but I like what I see so far. Isn't it a bit festive for a doctor's office, though?"

"They're psychologists. They're all about new beginnings and a brighter future."

Rutherford said, "Good point. I especially like how instead of broken tile, you're using shards of gray-and-white pottery for the clouds to give them a bumpy, puffy feel. I am curious about your decision to use cut pieces of orange tile for the sun rather than broken ones."

"They're not cut. I had a small batch of them custom made. The idea is that because the sun's only going to be half showing over the horizon, by using round-edged, squiggly shapes and leaving a dividing line down the middle, we can make what's clearly a sun suggest a brain as well."

"Because it's a psychologist's office," Rutherford said. "That's really clever!"

Terri said, "Yes, it is."

Rutherford turned. Every construction worker and cop in the room was watching them, having overheard their entire conversation. They all seemed amused. Terri was standing right next to them, and did not.

"May I have a word with my colleague?" Terri asked, then pulled Rutherford away before the designer had a chance to respond.

Rutherford knew he had broken character, and was embarrassed at how little time he'd taken to do it. "Terri," he said quietly, "I'm sorry."

Terri moaned. "Rutherford, don't apologize."

"I really am sorry, though."

Terri hissed, "Rutherford! Silence!" She lowered her voice enough that only Rutherford could hear what she was saying, but everyone else was clear on how she was saying it. *Angrily.* "I told you to act badass, and you screwed up. A public apology isn't going to fix this particular problem! Now, you are going to do exactly as I tell you for the remainder of the time we are in this building. You will not speak unless spoken to. If you are asked a question, you will answer with *yeah, nah,* or *dunno.* Not *yes, no,* or *maybe. Yeah, nah,* or *dunno.* Aside from that, you will stand behind me, and you will look unhappy, like you do right now. Do you understand?"

Rutherford sulked for a few seconds, then muttered, "Yeah."

Terri smiled. "Excellent."

EIGHT

Rutherford was not at all happy to be relegated to standing within sight of his immediate supervisor, but at least he was back near where actual investigation was taking place. He was close enough to Albert to look down and see the 3-D model of Dr. Shaw's office taking shape on his computer.

He decided to risk stepping one foot farther away from Terri so he could peek into the actual crime scene. The late Dr. Arledge was splayed facedown on the carpet. There was surprisingly little blood. Oh, there was blood, just not as much as one would expect at a murder scene, and what there was had soaked into the carpet. Still, one look at the victim's skin tone told Rutherford that he had been dead for quite a while, and a quick glance at the back of his head made it clear that he had probably started being dead before he hit the ground. It looked like the killer had continued hitting him anyway. Whatever weapon had been used against him was heavy, hard, and compact enough to be swung quickly.

Aside from the fact that it was a murder scene, the office was pretty much as the designer had led him to expect. Bland, expensive carpet under a well-made but rather plain wooden desk, surrounded by four walls: two made of exposed brick, and two painted an Easter-egg shade of purple. Across from the desk, there was a large velour couch, a floral wingback chair, and a low-backed leather club chair. The furniture was well worn, meticulously mismatched, and just expensive enough to be considered *expensive enough*. The desk held a lamp, a blotter, a laptop, and a framed photo. Of what, Rutherford couldn't say, as it was turned away from the door. A set of built-in shelves behind the desk held an impressive array of awards, mostly plaques with a few bronze statuettes and Lucite obelisks for good measure.

Rutherford's mental trip to IKEA was interrupted by Albert's squadron of quadcopters buzzing through the air, their rotor noises harmonizing to create a wavering minor chord that made Rutherford's teeth hurt.

Albert shook his head. "Number three has dropped half a note."

The four drones flew to the center of the waiting room and then separated and moved to the corners, near the ceiling.

"Okay, everyone," Albert shouted amiably. "No need to be alarmed. We're just going to scan the reception area now. Please feel free to go about your business. Just refrain from moving or looking directly at the lasers. In fact, you should probably just close your eyes while the lasers are functioning."

While everyone else's attention was fixed on the quadcopters, Max, Sloan, and the man who'd been identified as Dr. Shaw slipped out of the waiting room and headed back into Shaw's office. Terri followed them. Rutherford followed Terri.

"Thank you again for your understanding, Dr. Shaw," Max said, closing the door behind them. "I know this is a difficult time for you, and we certainly aren't making it easier."

"True, but frankly, I'm happy you're asking me these questions," Dr. Shaw said. There was no cheer in his demeanor. Indeed, there shouldn't have been, but there was also no irritation. He just seemed sad, confused, and whenever he glanced at Sloan, momentarily uncomfortable.

"I want to know who did this to Daniel," Shaw said, "and you wouldn't be doing your job properly if you didn't eliminate me first. I assume you'll speak to his wife . . . uh, I mean his widow next."

Max told him he was correct, then changed the subject by introducing the doctor to Terri and Rutherford. He had introduced Sloan earlier, when he introduced himself. Shaw offered everyone a seat. The carpet and paint were identical to Dr. Arledge's office, and the furniture seemed to have been ordered from a cheaper page of the same catalog. Max and Sloan took the couch. Terri took the side chair, leaving Rutherford with no option but to stand.

Max said, "In the interest of, as you say, eliminating you first, you and Dr. Arledge were partners. Now that he has passed away, does his share of the practice revert to his wife, or to you?"

Shaw drew in a deep breath. "That's a complicated question. I don't know what's in his will. I have to assume his share goes to Olivia, but I'd argue that I already own most of the building. I've been slowly buying it from him so that when he retires I'll own it outright."

"And when was he planning to retire?" Max asked.

"In a couple of years. Like I said, I've already paid for most of the building."

"But is it in your name?"

"No, it's in Daniel's name, so I suppose it's Olivia's now, but she knows about our arrangement. I don't think it'll be a problem."

"Good," Max said. He paused for a moment. "We have heard that there is a patient who has expressed displeasure with Dr. Arledge. Do you know anything about that?"

"No, but we didn't really discuss our patients with each other much."

"Understandable. Still, did you see or hear anything to indicate that a patient might be a danger to Dr. Arledge?"

"No," Shaw said. "Nothing. But, I mean, we're therapists. Our patients don't always behave rationally."

Max leaned forward, interested. "I thought he specialized in overstressed businessmen."

"He did. We did. I still do, but he changed his focus in the last year or so. He had a nice nest egg, and retirement was coming fast. In those circumstances, a guy's priorities can shift. I think he wanted to make sure he was remembered as a good psychologist, not just a successful one, if that makes sense. He stopped taking on as many paying clients, started spending his time doing pro bono work studying low-grade social disorders. He hoped to write a book about it. He was trying to use group therapy to identify the point at which an antisocial decision pattern becomes a treatable disorder. Very interesting work."

"So his clientele had changed."

"Very much so."

"Were any of his new patients prone to violence?"

"Possibly."

Max thought for a long moment. "I know that HIPAA confidentiality rules make it difficult to obtain information about a doctor's patients."

"Yes," Shaw said. "I'd never want to be accused of violating the privacy of the clinic's patients. On the other hand, I want very badly to know who killed Daniel. I think I can supply the police with the names, addresses, and broad descriptions of his current patients without divulging any confidential information about their treatment."

Max said, "That would be most helpful." He sat silently for a moment, then he stood up, signaling to everyone in the room that the interview was over. Dr. Shaw stood and started walking toward the door.

As he followed, Max said, "One last quick question, Doctor. We have a specific plan of how we intend to proceed, but you have the advantage of knowing the victim and the people in his life. If you were investigating this, who would you talk to next?"

"Well, as I said, I assume you'll want to talk to Olivia."

"That's the victim's widow, yes? Indeed we will, but do you think it likely that she could be involved?"

"I have a hard time believing it, but you should definitely talk to her. The sooner you eliminate those of us who were close to him, the sooner you'll find the killer."

NINE

As the team was walking back to their cars, Terri grumbled, "We're off to a rough start."

"I don't know about that," Max said. "We don't have any firm leads yet, but we only just got the case."

"I wasn't talking about that," Terri said. "Or to you." She looked back over her shoulder at the people following her until she pinned her gaze on Rutherford.

"Look, I'm sure it's easy for you to go rogue and do whatever you feel like doing, but I'm the one who's going to have to explain your actions to our boss. I don't need him chewing me out because you don't think the rules should apply to you."

"All I did was strike up a conversation."

"A friendly conversation about interior design, in which you came off as a bright, tasteful, professional young man."

"Thank you," Rutherford said.

"Don't thank me, Rutherford. That was criticism. *Withering* criticism!"

Professor Sherwood, who was walking toward the back of the group, asked, "Is that really what we're calling him? *Rutherford?*"

"That is my name," Rutherford said.

"It seems, I don't know, disrespectful," Sherwood said. "Maybe it's a generational thing."

Max said, "Perhaps we should call him *Mr. Rutherford,* or *Detective Rutherford.*"

Sherwood said, "See, and that seems too formal."

Albert said, "We call you *Professor Sherwood.*"

"Yes, but I'm a college professor. The job is inherently formal."

Rutherford asked, "Where do you teach?"

"North Seattle Community College."

Rutherford said, "Huh."

"You've seen it," Albert said. "It's that big concrete building with the floodlights across the freeway from Northgate Mall."

Rutherford said, "Yeah, I know it. I used to think it was a prison."

"In a sense, it is," Max said. "All community colleges are prisons of a sort. People get sent there as punishment for getting bad grades."

Albert said, "Or for having one of their bees sting their university's biggest donor, eh, Professor Sherwood?"

"I should have never told you that story, and I'll repeat, it wasn't my bee, it was just a bee. The dean had always wanted me off his campus. That was his excuse."

"Why'd he have it in for you?" Rutherford asked.

"Because he was allergic to bees, Detective Rutherford."

"Rutherford," Terri said. "We call him Rutherford, because Mr. Capp says that we have to call him Rutherford, which is all the reason we need. Beyond that, *Rutherford* sounds cool and it fits the image he's supposed to be portraying."

"And his first name doesn't sound cool?" Professor Sherwood asked.

"My first name is Sinclair," Rutherford said.

Albert said, "Maybe a nickname. We could call him *Sin*." Everyone considered this in silence for a moment, then Albert, Max, and Sherwood all chuckled for no readily apparent reason.

Terri laughed as well, then said, "*Sin* is a good idea, but it isn't Mr. Capp's idea, so we all know it isn't going to happen." She glanced back over her shoulder, smirking, but her expression changed quickly to confusion. She stopped walking, then stepped to the side to look past the four men who were following her. Max, Rutherford, Albert, and Professor Sherwood all turned too, and saw that Sloan had stopped walking and was standing on the sidewalk, leaning on her cane, looking down an alley. She looked back at the police lines, now nearly a full block behind them, then glanced at the rest of the team.

Max said, "She's right. That alley would make a great place to leave a murder weapon."

"Yes," Terri said. "I suppose it would, and the cops don't seem interested in searching it. You should go check it out. The rest of us will head to the cars and wait for you." She glanced back down the street, her eyes narrowing in on the tall satellite mast of a local TV station news truck. Beneath it, a sleek blonde woman with a microphone was standing in front of bright lights and a camera.

Terri said, "You'd better take Rutherford with you. If something happens and we make the news, Mr. Capp will want him visible. And you'll be in a filthy alley. The risk of him getting lost in a discussion about the decorative arts is minimal."

As Max and Rutherford headed toward the alley together, Max glanced sideways at Rutherford and asked, "Young man, I'm curious. Do you have some problem with your left shoulder?"

"What? No. Why do you ask?"

"You hold your left arm further from your body than the right, and you move that arm less when you walk."

Rutherford said, "Oh, that. That's just the new sidearm Albert gave me. It's larger than my normal weapon."

They reached the opening of the alley. Sloan was silently watching their approach and likely listening to their every word.

"What kind of pistol did Albert have for you?" Max asked.

Rutherford said, "I don't want to pull it out and show it to you here on the street, but it's a replica of a gun the Russians gave to cosmonauts."

"Ah," Max said. "The famous TP-82!" He turned to Sloan. "The breech-loaded gun they were given for fighting off a pack of wolves. You fire your three barrels and kill the first three wolves that attack, then reload while the rest of the pack tears you to ribbons. Even so, I'm sure it would have looked glorious on the cover of *Pravda*."

Rutherford said, "Huh. I guess it was a pretty bad idea."

"What it was, young man, was a pretty bad cover story. They gave their cosmonauts guns and told the public that it was for survival in Siberia, but in reality they wanted the Americans to know their cosmonauts were armed. They were about to launch the Apollo-Soyuz mission and they wanted Deke Slayton to know not to try any funny business."

Rutherford opened his mouth to ask for clarification, but over Max's shoulder he saw Sloan shaking her helmet *no*.

Max looked into the alley. "Yes, I see what you mean, Meg. This would make an excellent place to stash a weapon."

The alley was dark, dank, and cluttered with trash. The odor wafted out and thrust itself up Rutherford's nose. It smelled exactly like a filthy wet alley. Rutherford appreciated the odor's honesty.

Most of the trash was composed of small bits and pieces gathered in the corners and along the walls, but a pile of full trash bags teetered near a building's side entrance.

Max and Sloan entered the alley, Max hugging one side, examining the detritus gathered along the wall. Sloan walked slowly down the middle, helmet swiveling, looking for anything out of place. Without having to be told, Rutherford searched the other side, poking through the trash with his foot as he went.

It occurred to Rutherford that they didn't really know what they were looking for, just an unspecified blunt object. He hadn't seen the victim's remains for long, and if there were any early theories about what the doctor had been bludgeoned with, he hadn't heard them. He looked up from the gutter to ask if Max had any more clues to offer, but got distracted when he saw that Sloan had raised her free right hand to the back of her neck, and was using her ring finger to pull down the turtleneck that usually extended up into her helmet. Her thumb, index, and middle fingers stuck out into the air as she scratched the back of her neck with her pinky finger. The skin's sheen and texture were a textbook example of a severe but well-healed burn scar.

Rutherford looked away, but not before he tripped on the pile of trash bags he'd momentarily forgotten were in his way. He swung his arms wildly, managing to regain his balance just in time for the pile of bags to fly in every direction and reveal the angry homeless man who had been sleeping beneath them, and who was now preparing to assault whoever had kicked him.

Rutherford blurted out, "Oh, Geez, I'm sorry. I didn't know you were in there."

"Yes," Max said. "My friends and I didn't mean to disturb you."

Max had crossed the alley almost instantaneously and was standing next to Rutherford, which was reassuring, but Rutherford thought it would have been more reassuring if Sloan, their protection, wasn't standing behind them.

The homeless man was still bleary from being so rudely awakened, and whatever other issues he had that might have impaired his judgment. He didn't seem to be listening to what

Max and Rutherford were saying, but he obviously saw that he was outnumbered, and the sight of Sloan did nothing to calm him down. He reached into a pocket and pulled out a butterfly knife, whipping the free handle around in a showy blur until it came to a rest with the blade pointed in Max and Rutherford's direction.

"Now, now, my friend," Max said. "Nobody here is threatening you. I don't blame you for wanting to defend yourself, though. Life on the street can be trying. You have a butterfly knife, I see. Those are a lot of fun. May I?" Max reached out and took the knife from the homeless man, who was so surprised and confused that he didn't even think to resist.

Max ran through the wrist-flinging opening and closing routines a few times with no apparent effort while Rutherford and the knife's owner looked on in amazement.

"Yes," Max said. "It certainly looks impressive, but sadly, in this case, I fear it is all for show. Tell me, friend, did you buy this at a smoke shop, or perhaps at a state fair?"

"I stole it from a truck stop," the homeless man said.

"Yes," Max said. "I'm afraid it is a poorly made example." Max took the two hinged handles like a wishbone and twisted. The knife broke into two pieces as easily as if it had been held together with white school glue. "They used low-quality rivets instead of bolts," Max explained, mostly to Rutherford. "Such workmanship would be shameful if it were an accident, but in this case it is deliberate. You have the right to bear arms, so your government floods the domestic market with shoddy weapons like these. That way, if there's ever an armed rebellion, it will at least be poorly equipped."

Max turned his attention back to the homeless man. "I'm afraid you would only get in one good thrust with this knife before it failed, leaving you unarmed with an opponent you'd wounded enough to be angry and desperate."

Max gave the twisted pieces of the butterfly knife back to its owner. "I would tell you to be careful, but that low-grade blade steel can't hold much of an edge anyway."

The homeless man looked at the pieces in his hands, disbelieving.

Max said, "In the future, I suggest that you steal the steak knives from a moderately priced steak house. They're not as showy, but they're designed to be durable and to hold an edge, and besides, you get a steak dinner out of the bargain." Max pulled out and opened his wallet, then turned to Rutherford.

"What do you think? A night at a motel to get cleaned up and a steak dinner for one. I think one hundred dollars would do it, don't you agree?"

Rutherford looked at Max's wallet, then looked at the homeless man. The homeless man was staring at the money. He dropped the ruined pieces of his knife and grabbed for the cash with both hands, but the cash and the wallet it was in had moved, so his hands swiped at empty space. The homeless man's weight pitched forward, and he staggered onto his left foot.

Max said, "Oh, dear!" He reached out with his right hand and grabbed the homeless man's arm, which held him upright while also keeping him off-balance. Max's left hand then shot toward the other man's shoulder, as if to steady him further, but he was holding his wallet in that hand, so instead of grasping the homeless man's shoulder, he struck the heel of his hand against the place where the man's shoulder connected to his neck, causing his arm to twist uncomfortably.

Max said, "Careful, easy now," as the homeless man cried out in pain and slumped forward. Max leaned forward with him, somehow managing to spin the man's body so that he landed gently on his back. By the time the man's weight came to fully rest on the ground, Max was kneeling beside him, one hand planted firmly on his chest, just below his throat.

"Okay," Max said, using his free hand to gently pat the side of the man's face. "It's all right. You're not injured and we're not going to hurt you. Just lie there for a moment and rest. Everything's going to be fine."

The homeless man looked surprised and confused, but Max's soothing tone of voice seemed to be working as intended.

Max said, "Okay, my friend, we are not the police, so please tell me honestly, are there any warrants out for your arrest?"

The man shook his head no.

"Good. You attacked me, so you will be arrested. I will stall until morning, then I will decline to press charges. That way you will get a hot meal, a shower, and a place to sleep tonight."

Max held several twenty-dollar bills in front of the man's face, the money he had been offering just before the attack. "That means you can dispense with the hotel and spend this on new clothes and a steak dinner. It's not as pleasant, of course, but your money will go further this way, yes?" He tucked the cash into the breast pocket of the man's coat. "If the police ask about it, tell them you were saving for a bus trip back to your hometown. They'll sympathize. Good? Okay? We're all fine, aren't we?"

The homeless man nodded. Max smiled and looked up at Rutherford, then repeated the question. "Aren't we?"

Rutherford said, "Yeah, I'm fine," but he was still a bit stunned. Max had just committed the least violent act of violence he had ever seen. He had assaulted and neutralized his attacker so effortlessly that the attacker himself didn't seem to realize he'd been assaulted. Rutherford could only imagine how much training someone would need to make an altercation look that graceful.

Rutherford knelt down and picked up one of the twisted handles of the now-ruined butterfly knife. It wasn't made of aircraft-grade metal or anything, but it felt solid. To make breaking it look so easy, Max had to be alarmingly strong.

Rutherford looked down at Max and asked, "Why on Earth do you need a bodyguard?"

"Bodyguard?" Max said. "I don't need a bodyguard. Why would I need a bodyguard?"

"That's what I'm asking," Rutherford said. "You don't, but Capp said he already had a detective and a head of personal security."

"Yes," Max said. "I'm the head of personal security, and Sloan is the detective."

Rutherford looked at Sloan. Sloan shrugged.

They briefly questioned their would-be assailant before handing him over to the police. He was in a much more helpful mood now that he had a relatively comfortable evening ahead of him and a decisive loss at Max's hands behind him. He said he had been in that alley nonstop since the previous day, not even leaving to use the restroom (which explained some of the nonpertinent evidence Rutherford had discovered). He hadn't seen anybody enter or leave, but it was entirely possible that someone might have come through while he was asleep.

Once the police had taken Max's new best friend away, Rutherford, Max, and Sloan continued with their search.

It would help if we knew what we were looking for, Rutherford thought. *I mean, there are plenty of things here that could be a used to kill a guy. Rocks, bottles, boards, sharp glass. None of it fits the crime though, and all of it has probably been here for weeks. I'm not seeing anything out of place, and I'm definitely not seeing anything that shouts "murder weapon."*

Max shouted, "Murder weapon!"

Max was crouched at the far end of the alley. Soon Rutherford and Sloan were standing beside him. Moments later, Terri, Albert, and Sherwood, who had been summoned over their earpieces, joined them in studying what Max had found.

There, on the filthy pavement, lay a ball-peen hammer. It was not new, but it was also not trash. The wooden handle was worn and the metal head was dirty, but not with the dark, foul-smelling filth characteristic of the rest of the trash in the alley. It was the light coating of dusty particulate matter one finds on a tool at a construction site. There was no sign of blood.

"It was under an old piece of newspaper," Max said, examining the wad of newsprint in his hand. "*The Little Nickel*, if that makes a difference. Maybe the killer is in the market for a new dresser?"

"Hold on to the paper and don't touch anything else," Albert said. "I'll launch the quads to document the site."

Terri said, "Good. Yes. Then I'll call the police over. They'll want to bag the hammer and the paper, and send them for analysis. Maybe they can find some prints."

Sherwood held up his wand and said, "In the meantime, mind if my friends have a sniff?"

Terri nodded, and Sherwood crouched to wave his buzzing wand over the hammer.

"I don't think you're going to find any prints," Rutherford said. "The head of the hammer's dusty, but look at the handle. It's been wiped clean."

Max said, "It could be that the powder came off on the killer's hand."

Rutherford shook his head. "I think it's drywall dust or something, and I'm sorry, but it's been wiped clean all the way up the handle and onto the shaft. Nobody holds a hammer that high when they're using it."

For a moment they all contemplated this while Sherwood's wand buzzed lightly. Max frowned at Sloan, then shrugged, turned to Rutherford, and said, "Yes, I take your point. Very good, young man. It makes sense. If the killer thought to dispose of the weapon, they certainly would have also thought to wipe it down."

"Yes," Sherwood said, squinting at the readout on his wand. "It makes perfect sense, except for one tiny detail. This hammer is definitely not the murder weapon."

"Are you sure?" Terri asked.

Sherwood said, "The bees are."

Terri said, "Well that's something, but I think we'll still document the site and have the police analyze the hammer. I hope you and the bees won't be offended."

"The bees won't be offended," Sherwood said. "They're bees. They only know what they smell."

Terri said, "Good."

"And I won't be offended either," Sherwood added. "I'll just try not to gloat when my bees are proved right."

TEN

If Rutherford had to sum up the widow of the victim in two words, those words would be *distraught* and *suspicious*.

Distraught because she spent almost the entire time he was in her home crying into the steady stream of tissues supplied by Max. *Suspicious* not because she seemed guilty of anything, but rather because what little time she didn't spend sobbing, she spent glancing warily at Sloan—who was sitting silently next to Max, Professor Sherwood—who was wandering around her home waving a buzzing wand at her belongings, and Rutherford—who was dressed like a ruffian and chewing on a toothpick.

The meeting had gotten off to a poor start. Immediately after a round of introductions, Professor Sherwood had produced a small spray bottle from his pocket and asked the widow, "Are you allergic to bee stings?" When she confirmed that she was, he mumbled, "That's unfortunate," and put away the spray bottle.

Rutherford's angry demeanor hadn't done much to improve the situation. Of course, Rutherford wasn't actually angry. In the last hour he had taken in quite a bit of information, but he'd learned almost nothing, leaving him both confused and frustrated. To the casual observer, however, the expressions of anger and confused frustration are almost identical.

The team had split up after finishing in the alley. Terri and Albert had gone back to the office: Albert needed to process and analyze his scans and the long list of chemical compounds Sherwood's bees had detected before he could verify that the item Rutherford was almost certain was the murder weapon was, in fact, not. Terri had to procure and organize as much information as possible about the victim, the crime, and the involved parties. Max, Sloan, Professor Sherwood, and Rutherford had driven off to interview the victim's widow.

Rutherford had hoped to spend the car ride learning more about Max and Sloan—in particular, why Max asked all the questions if Sloan was the detective. While Rutherford drove, Max very readily talked about himself and his background. And then he continued to talk about himself for the entire trip, never once saying a word about Sloan or their work together.

As a young man, Max had entered the Koninklijke Landmacht, the Dutch equivalent of the US Army, and then the Korps Commandotroepen. He showed a certain talent for hand-to-hand combat, and learned everything possible about every fighting system he could. He rose through the ranks until he was recruited to the Dutch Secret Service, the AIVD, which stood for a series of consonant sounds so discordant that Rutherford's ears couldn't parse them as human speech, instead leaving him with the mental impression that Max's tongue and teeth were fighting.

Max spent many years guarding the lives of the very highest-level members of the Dutch government and learning many profound and surprising things about how the world actually works.

"Of course," Max said, "Few of the citizens ever knew who I was, or that I even existed, but in certain circles, I was quite well-known."

"Really?" Rutherford asked. He was genuinely interested, but couldn't manage a more intelligent response because the weather had turned nasty, and he was peering through a rain-soaked windshield at the rain-soaked road, trying not to rear-end the rain-soaked car in front of them.

"Yes. In the security industry, I am known throughout Europe as *the least deadly Dutchman on Earth.*"

Rutherford went over that sentence mentally several times before replying with the question, "And they mean that as a compliment?"

Max laughed. "I understand your confusion, but yes, they do. Even if they didn't, I would take it as one. Any fool can win a fight by using too much force. It's much harder to win a fight using minimal force. The greatest challenge is to defeat an attacker by barely using any force at all, and if you can make your attack seem so passive that an outward observer might think you're trying to help your opponent, well, then you've really accomplished something."

Max went on for the rest of the drive discussing nerve clusters, biomechanical levers, and nonaggressive verbal cues—talking about anything but his arrangement with Sloan.

Now Rutherford was standing behind the couch on which Max and Sloan were seated. This gave him a good view of the victim's widow, Olivia Arledge, who was sitting in a chair opposite them, and the backs of Max and Sloan's heads.

He thought about the brief glimpse of scar tissue he'd seen earlier. He wondered if perhaps Sloan couldn't speak.

Maybe Max asks all of the questions, but she's the one who figures things out, Rutherford thought. *Then she tells him later, using sign language or something. That would work, but if he doesn't ask the questions she wants him to ask, she'd need to signal him somehow. That's why she has to come with him into the field. Otherwise, she could stay in the office and he could report to her. I think I may be on to something here. Of course, I'm not solving the mystery I'm supposed to be solving, but they don't seem to really want my help anyway. Oh well. I'll watch them solve their mystery, and that'll help me solve mine.*

"Mrs. Arledge," Max asked, "did it not strike you as odd when your husband didn't come home last night?"

"No," she sniffed. "He gets caught up in his research and falls asleep at the office all the time. He used to say it was an occupational hazard of being the one kind of doctor who has a couch."

"That's funny," Max said kindly.

"Not really," Mrs. Arledge said. "Other doctors work around beds, so the joke doesn't really work. But he thought it was funny, and I liked seeing him laugh."

At that, a fresh torrent of tears broke loose, absorbed by several more tissues.

Once she'd regained her composure, Mrs. Arledge said, "I wasn't really concerned at all until I woke up and he wasn't here, but I'd slept late. I had a bit more to drink than usual last night. I figured he'd come and gone without waking me."

Max was silent for a moment, then leaned forward a bit. "Please, tell me, you say you drank more than usual last night. May I ask why?"

"Some friends and I go out once a week. Usually somewhere here on the east side, but it was Julie's turn to pick. She wanted to go to Canlis, and that's far enough away that a few of us carpooled, so I wasn't driving."

It's good that we won't have to ask her if she has an alibi, Rutherford thought. *And it's interesting that she has such a good one ready to go, and explained it so fully on the first try.*

Max said, "I hate to pry, but did your husband seem to be under any unusual stress of late?"

"Not that I noticed."

"Any problems with his patients?"

"No. He was finding his work more rewarding than he had in years."

"Because of his work helping people with social disorders."

Mrs. Arledge nodded, and for just an instant Rutherford saw her expression darken, but given the circumstances, who could blame her.

Max asked, "And he wasn't suffering any financial problems?"

The answer was quick and emphatic. "No."

Max pressed the issue. "Is it possible that he was, and chose not to tell you? Husbands do that sometimes."

Mrs. Arledge shook her head. "No, he wouldn't have done that. And he couldn't have anyway. We have equal access to all of our accounts. I handle more of the details than he does. No, money wasn't a problem. We own the house outright. We have plenty set aside for retirement. Our investments are all doing well, and Tyler has almost bought out the practice anyway. I don't know who killed Daniel, but I can't imagine it was over money."

"Can you think of a reason why any of his patients would want him dead?"

"No. He's giving them mental health care for free."

"Did he mention if any of them struck him as dangerous?"

"He wouldn't have been treating them if they did. The whole point of his research was to study harmless, seemingly intelligent people whose attempts to make personal relationships easier made them impossible instead. At least that's what he told me."

Max frowned. "I'm not certain that I understand."

Mrs. Arledge wiped her eyes and said, "I'm not sure I do either, really. He tried to explain it to me more than once. He was tired of working with people from the software business, but he didn't know what else to do. He took on a new client, and the guy talked for the entire first session without ever really saying anything. Dan said it was like he'd created his own language by stringing together quotes from business books, motivational posters, and Francis Ford Coppola movies."

Rutherford knew people like that. *Heck,* he thought, *replace "business books and Coppola movies" with* The Simpsons, *and she's basically describing me and my friends in high school.*

"Dan could have dropped him," she continued. "He wanted to at first. He said it made him uncomfortable the way this guy talked nonstop without seeming to engage mentally, but Dan was intrigued by his own discomfort, so he stuck with it until he got to the bottom of the problem. The guy mostly just quoted things he thought were smart because he worried that if he ever said what he really thought, people would find out that he was dumb."

Max said, "That's sad."

Rutherford thought, *Yeah it is. And, if you replace "dumb" with "not funny," she has now perfectly described me and my friends in high school.*

"Dan said that he started seeing versions of that guy's behavior everywhere, and thought it might be a treatable condition. I'd hate to think that any of his patients had anything to do with this. He really was trying to help them."

Max said, "I think I understand, and you're right, it seems unlikely that the people he was helping for free would wish him ill. Still, did he ever make any mention of *any* patients who made him uncomfortable?"

"No, you still don't get it. They *all* made him uncomfortable. They were there because they made everybody uncomfortable. If one of them was acting particularly hostile or threatening, he'd have seen it as his job to get to the bottom of why."

Max nodded. "Sadly, Mrs. Arledge, it seems possible that he may have done just that."

ELEVEN

It was nearly five o'clock by the time they finished interviewing the widow. They checked in with Terri, who told them to knock off for the night. Rutherford's car was still where he'd left it that morning, parked at the police station that had been his workplace what felt like a year ago. He drove the sedan to the station parking lot, got out, and waved as the others drove off. Then he sat in his Miata, trying to process the events of the day. When it was clear that he wouldn't be done with that particular project any time soon, he drove home.

He immediately took off and laundered his costume pants and shirt. He hadn't done anything to soil them, but the shirt's former owner had, and the very idea of that was enough motivation for Rutherford to use a quarter of a bottle of body wash to scrub his upper torso.

After his shower, he called his sister, Vanessa. She was worried sick about him. So was their mother, now that Vanessa had shown her the video.

"She wanted to call you," Vanessa said, "but I told her to let me. I know how to deal with situations like these."

Rutherford said, "That's true," and he meant it. He'd never met anyone more adept at finding drama, amplifying drama, and placing herself directly in the middle of the drama, all the while declaring that she *doesn't need this drama.*

"I don't need all this drama," Vanessa said.

Rutherford said, "I know."

He listened to her vent for a good long while, then apologized for keeping her, and their mother, in the dark. He told her that he had been offered an exciting new job. She asked to hear all about it. He told her that he couldn't tell her anything. Then he listened to her vent some more.

From the moment he parted with the team until he fell asleep that night, at least half of his brain was continually working on what he'd seen and heard that day. He developed a theory, then slept on it. When he awoke, he was convinced that he had the answer. Not to the murder of Dr. Daniel Arledge, of course—he didn't have nearly enough information for that. He was still convinced that the ball-peen hammer in the alley was probably the weapon, the patient who had left in a huff was interesting, and the widow's ready-made alibi still seemed a bit suspicious. But none of that was solid enough for him to draw a conclusion yet.

However, he thought he had the answer to the Max/ Sloan conundrum, so he shifted his focus to planning the most dramatic possible way to reveal what he'd figured out.

The next morning he drove downtown, fighting his way through the customary gauntlet of confusing one-way streets, clutch-destroying hills, and self-righteous pedestrians who seemed angry at him for stopping in time to not run them over. He didn't have a means of accessing the top-secret garage Terri had shown him, and he couldn't find street parking, so he was forced to pay for a spot in the parking structure that held the secret garage entrance.

The lobby of the building was the domain of a doughy, grim-faced security guard who refused to allow Rutherford upstairs without an ID badge. Albert hadn't given him any credentials, only the ridiculous oversized Russian hand-cannon. Showing it to the guard would almost certainly have gotten him into the elevator, but he decided against it.

When he explained that Mrs. Wells would vouch for him, the guard took another look at Rutherford's leather jacket, ZZ Top shirt, and worn jeans, and shook his head. For just a moment, Rutherford considered showing him the gun after all, but then the guard called Terri and described her "visitor."

Terri said to let Rutherford come up. The guard asked Terri if she was certain and launched into a more detailed description of Rutherford. After he hung up the phone, he very reluctantly allowed Rutherford to board the elevator.

Moments later, Rutherford stepped out into the office. His eyes scanned the room, and his heart sank. It was his first full day on the job and he wanted to make a good impression. He'd been told to report to work at nine. It was eight forty-five, so he was early, but everyone else was already there. When everyone's early the least early person is late, no matter what the clock says.

Albert was the first one to notice that Rutherford had arrived. He was in his office workshop, tinkering away with the door open. He called out, "Hey, Rutherford, good morning!"

Out in the communal area, Max and Sloan were looking at words scrawled on a whiteboard. Professor Sherwood was reading something on a laptop screen. All three of their heads swiveled and locked onto Rutherford's location. Two of them smiled. The door to Terri's office swung open. Her head and shoulders poked out at an altitude and angle that suggested she had rolled to the door in her office chair. A round of *good mornings* were heaved at Rutherford like oddly cheerful rocks.

Rutherford knew from years of bitter experience that whenever a group of people was this happy to see him, something was terribly wrong. He narrowed his eyes at Albert and asked, "What?"

Albert said, "Calm down. It's good news. I've got some new toys for you. It's my favorite part of the job."

Smiling in a disarming manner, Albert walked over and handed Rutherford a credit-card-sized piece of metal with his full name stamped into it like a giant dog tag.

"This is your ID badge. You just carry it in your wallet. The guard station downstairs has a scanner that reads it. It's encoded with your name, all of your biometrics, and several photos. It'll also help us identify you if something happens that makes dental records useless."

"What would do that?" Rutherford asked.

"Nothing you want to think about this early in the morning. The second thing I have for you is this." Albert held up an irregular beige lump that looked like a piece of chewed gum. Rutherford instantly realized it was his new earpiece. Molded from hard plastic, it had a smooth, organic cone on one end, and the other end was flat and perforated with tiny holes.

Rutherford looked at it and asked, "Right ear?"

"That's the one I scanned," Albert said.

"How do I turn it on?"

"It's always on. It only has two settings: on and out of power. I'll give you a wireless charging pad that'll keep a charge on both your earpiece and your phone."

Rutherford inserted the earpiece. It wasn't uncomfortable, but it wasn't quite comfortable either. He doubted he'd ever forget he was wearing it.

Albert asked to see Rutherford's phone. He tapped the screen a few times and Rutherford's earpiece emitted a beep.

Then Albert turned the phone around so that Rutherford could see the screen. There were icons representing every member of the team. With his finger, Albert traced a circle around his own icon and Max's. Albert tapped on his left hip pocket, and across the room Max looked at his phone and said, "Yes?" He said it at normal conversational volume, from at least forty feet away, but Rutherford heard him loud and clear. This wasn't particularly impressive. Everyone knew how an earpiece worked, but the sound quality was much better than he'd expected.

Albert, also in a normal, conversational tone, said, "Just showing Rutherford how the earpiece works. Sorry to bother you."

Max said, "Not at all."

Albert slashed through his and Max's icons, and the call ended.

"You can open a conversation with one, several, or all of us at any time. The people you call are notified by a tone. If you hear the tone, you can answer it discreetly by tapping on your phone, even if it's in your pocket. If you're in a position to look at your phone, it'll tell you who's calling, and who else is listening."

Albert circled all of the icons with his finger. Rutherford watched as the icons grew slightly larger one by one, signifying that everyone had accepted the call.

"Hey, everyone," Albert said. "I just wanted to let you all know that Rutherford's now available on the party line."

Every head in the office turned to look at Rutherford and Albert. Terri, Max, and Professor Sherwood said things that sounded welcoming, but were rendered unintelligible because they were all spoken at the same time. He could hear them distantly through his free ear and clearly through the earpiece.

Rutherford thought, *I have everyone's attention. I wanted a dramatic moment to tell Sloan and Max that I've got them figured out. I probably won't do much better than this.*

Rutherford said, "Thanks, everyone." He turned to Albert and said, "It sounds great. Loud and clear. Will I also get a silent throat mike, like the one Sloan uses to feed Max questions?"

Max laughed out loud. Sloan tucked her cane under her arm and clapped slowly. Rutherford heard an unfamiliar voice in his earpiece. The voice was female, upbeat, and artificial. It was the kind of voice a smartphone uses to tell you to turn left onto the I-5 on-ramp. It said, "Well done. We were hoping you'd figure it out for yourself."

Albert said, "Rutherford, meet Megan Sloan. Sloan, meet Rutherford."

"You are a little off on the details," Sloan's disembodied voice said. "It's not a microphone. It's a set of sensors built into my helmet and my collar that sense the movements of my mouth and trachea. Then it figures out what I'm saying. Albert can explain it to you if you like. He's explained it to me like a hundred times. Also, I don't just use it to talk to Max. I talk to everyone on the team, except you, yesterday."

Rutherford considered asking why this was necessary, but quickly decided against it. Instead he ran through the events of the previous day in his mind. He remembered all the times Max had paused while questioning a witness. Now that he really thought about it, there were other moments that had struck him as odd.

"There were a few times yesterday when everyone seemed to think something was funny, but I couldn't figure out what," Rutherford said.

Sloan nodded. "They were laughing at things I had said . . . about you."

"I'm sure they weren't all about me," Rutherford said.

Sloan shook her head. "You are mistaken." She held up her gloved right hand and extended the index finger. "When you were introduced to me, I nodded because you couldn't hear me. You said it was good to meet me, then you stood there and fidgeted. I asked everyone if I should nod again."

She extended a second finger. "When we were told that the victim had been bludgeoned by an unidentified murder weapon, I suggested that we have you look at it because you might recognize it as another obscure sex toy."

She held up a third finger. "When we were discussing what to call you, someone suggested shortening your first name, Sinclair, to *Sin*. I suggested calling you *Clair*."

Rutherford said, "That's . . ." then trailed off, fishing for the right word. Finally he settled on, "Comprehensive."

"Memory is a detective's most important tool," Sloan's artificial voice said cheerfully. "For what it's worth, I also agreed with you that the hammer's handle had been deliberately wiped down."

"Yes," Sherwood said. "It's a shame it's not the murder weapon."

Sloan ignored him. "Why don't you come over here? We're going over the evidence. Maybe you'll see something we don't."

"Not yet," Albert said. "There's still one more toy to show him, and I saved the best for last."

Sloan struck her helmet with her palm. "Of course, you're right. How could I forget?"

Max said, "Yes, this will be the highlight of the day!" By the time he had finished saying it, the entire team, Terri included, was standing around Rutherford and Albert.

Rutherford looked at the others warily. "What? What is it?"

"A surprise," Terri said.

"Oh," Rutherford said. "And you've all been waiting to check it out until I got here?"

Terri answered, "No, we've seen it."

"Then why are you all so excited?"

Sloan's voice said, "Because now we get to see you see it."

Albert put a hand on Rutherford's shoulder and started to guide him away from the elevator. Rutherford marveled at how much had happened already, when he'd only taken two steps into the office.

Albert said, "I've shown you the basics of using the party line. There's a PDF with the more advanced stuff on the network. For now, let's dispense with the appetizer and move on to the main course."

As they walked, Terri said, "Rutherford, I don't think we need to keep the party line open, since we're all standing right here."

Rutherford started to swipe his hand across the cluster of icons on his smartphone screen, but stopped and asked, "Will this cut off my ability to hear Sloan? If she's going to make fun of me some more, I'd just as soon hear it."

Sloan's voice cut in. "I'm constantly broadcasting to everyone in my presence unless I specifically choose to cut someone out. So rest assured, if I make a joke at your expense, you'll know. Unless I don't want you to."

Rutherford muttered, "Great," as he killed the party-line connection. He looked up from his phone and realized where Albert was leading him—the garage. Once they reached the frosted glass door, Albert opened it and motioned Rutherford through, saying, "Your chariot awaits."

Rutherford stepped into the garage, blinked in disbelief, then said, "Please tell me it's behind that hideous van."

The van was old, but not quite old enough to be called "vintage." The suspension had been raised in the rear and lowered in the front. It looked like a maniac had been given an impact wrench and told to "have at it." The items bolted to the van included a large spoiler on the roof, a chin spoiler, side steps, a tall chrome exhaust stack capped with a hinged flapper, and flared arches on the rear wheel wells (but not the front). Four massive chrome rims held what were ironically referred to as "low profile" tires.

The windows were tinted, including the one set into the sliding side door and the custom window shaped like a bullet that had been installed in the rear quarter panel. The paint was mostly matte black, but as Rutherford walked toward it, he saw that there were highly detailed pinstripe filigrees painted in gloss black that were only visible when the light hit them. There were several small hatches built into the side of the van. They looked as if they were designed to swing open, but they had no exterior handles or keyholes.

Albert said, "One 1992 GMC Vandura, heavily customized. Aside from the obvious aesthetic modifications, it has also been outfitted with Mr. Capp's Stephenson Motors steam-electric drive, so it has crazy acceleration for such a heavy vehicle. It runs on nothing but electricity and will occasionally need to be topped off with water." He pulled the sliding side door open. Inside, the floor and walls were covered in maroon shag carpeting that almost matched the color of the leather captain's chairs. "It has all of the amenities of a modern passenger vehicle, all of the equipment of a police cruiser, and a few other customizations I helped develop specifically to meet our team's needs. The technicians finished it two months ago. Since then it's been in storage. We've added a toy or two while it was on hold, but really, it's just been waiting for the right person to fill the driver's seat."

Sloan's synthetic voice said, "Don't you feel honored?"

Rutherford blinked at Albert, then turned to Terri and said, "So, wait a second, this means that you had all this leather-jacket, bad-boy crap planned way before you even knew I existed."

"Mr. Capp and his marketing team did," Terri said. "I knew what they had in mind, but I wasn't part of the decision-making process."

"So, I'm just some guy they got to wear the costume?"

Terri shook her head. "No, Rutherford. If that were the case, we could have just hired an actor. You were recruited because Mr. Capp saw potential in you, and felt you could provide certain skills the team needed. You're not just some guy they got to wear the costume."

"You're the specialist who they hand-picked to wear the costume," Sloan added.

Rutherford ignored Sloan, remaining focused on Terri. "You expect me to drive this?"

"No, we're *allowing* you to drive it. It's your company car," Terri said. "You should feel lucky. You and I are the only ones who get them. They took back the second sedan when they dropped your van off."

"Well, let someone else have it. I don't need it."

"It's a cool van. It's designed to fit your image."

"I already have a Miata! It's cool. It fits my image."

Terri said, "I take issue with every part of that sentence, but the point I really need to correct you on is that you don't actually own your Miata. When you signed your contract, you agreed to sell it to Mr. Capp for market value plus ten percent."

"Why does he want my Miata?!"

"He doesn't," Terri said. "He just doesn't want you to be seen in it. You're lucky you're renting an apartment. If you'd owned a place, especially if it was a nice place, it would have been in the same deal."

"He wants to dictate where I live?"

"No, Rutherford, he *wanted* to dictate where you live. You signed his contract, and now he has his wish. Don't worry, he's not going to move you until your new place is good and ready. And when you do move, you'll live there rent-free, which in Seattle is a pretty good deal."

"Where?" Rutherford asked.

Terri said, "Seattle, like I said. Where else?"

"No, Terri. Where specifically will I be expected to live?"

"Well, that's up in the air. His brand consultants are still working on it, but they've narrowed it down to two options. A dilapidated houseboat on Lake Union, or an old Airstream trailer parked illegally on a beach on Puget Sound."

"Illegally?"

"Well, not really. One of Mr. Capp's companies would own the land, but it would look like you were squatting to any outside observers. Look, I can see that you're not happy, but I remind you that none of us got you into this. We're just the people you're going to be working with while you're in it."

Rutherford squeezed his eyes shut and silently counted to ten. When he finally opened them, he said, "You're right, of course. It's just, I didn't really know what I was signing on for, and this . . ." He looked down at his clothing and motioned toward the van. "I don't see how any of this could suit me less."

Sloan said, "You haven't seen the back of the van yet."

Terri glared at Sloan. Sloan shrugged. Max smiled in spite of himself.

Rutherford silently walked around to the back of the van.

The spare tire was mounted on the back, and on the tire's vinyl cover there was a painting of Lady Justice. She wore a pair of menacing black sunglasses instead of a blindfold. In one hand she was wielding a sword that would have been far too heavy for a person to hold one-handed, even without the added weight of the blood and gore clinging to its blade. In her other hand she had scales, which were tipped way out of balance. The lighter side of the scale held a chunk of stone with the word "mercy" carved into its side. The heavy side held a similar stone bearing the word "vengeance."

The painting expressed a sentiment that he could relate to now more easily than he could have two days earlier.

TWELVE

Once everyone had been sufficiently entertained by looking at Rutherford looking at the van, they returned to the conference table and whiteboard in the office's communal room to discuss the case.

Terri sat at one end of the table, glancing at her tablet as she listed the known facts about the case. The others looked at their own tablets as they listened.

"Dr. Daniel Arledge was murdered in his own office by means of blunt force trauma sometime around 9:00 p.m. There's no security camera footage, no sign of forced entry, and no sign of a struggle. He was discovered by the practice's receptionist almost thirteen hours later, just before ten in the morning. The receptionist and his wife both have alibis."

"Yes," Sloan said. "His widow pointed out her alibi without being asked."

"I noticed that too," Rutherford said. "It seemed a little too easy."

Terri said, "Be that as it may, the police have looked into it and her alibi checks out."

"That only means she didn't kill him herself," Max said. "She might have sent someone else to do it."

Sloan said, "Max, anybody might have sent someone else to do it. You might have sent someone else to do it."

He laughed. "Don't be silly, Meg. We all know that if I chose to kill someone, I'd do it myself."

Sloan said, "I suppose so."

"And it would look like an accident."

"True."

"And nobody'd ever suspect it was me."

"Probably not."

"And even if someone did have suspicions, talking about it to another living soul would be the worst mistake of their lives."

"Yes," Sloan said. "We all know that, now."

Terri cleared her throat and continued as if she hadn't been interrupted. "The victim's business partner was home alone and has no alibi, but also has no motive. Since he joined the practice, Dr. Shaw has received a greatly reduced salary in exchange for increasing ownership, which would have transferred to him in full upon the victim's retirement. The victim's death puts that in jeopardy. All of the victim's financials are in order, as are those of the practice. There was no obvious murder weapon at the scene, but while searching an alley near the crime scene we found a ball-peen hammer which Professor Sherwood insists is not the murder weapon."

"Even though the handle looks like it was wiped down to remove any prints," Sloan said.

"And a hammer like that would have been easy for the killer to lay hands on, since the clinic was in the middle of a remodel," Rutherford added.

"Both true," Sherwood said, "but neither of those things prove that it's the murder weapon. My bees didn't smell any blood on the hammer, so it can't have been the weapon."

Terri said, "As much as we all trust the opinion of your trained bees, Professor, there is quite a bit of circumstantial evidence. We may have proof soon. The hammer's being examined by CSI this morning, but it has already been identified as belonging to one of the construction workers."

"Which doesn't prove it was used to kill Dr. Arledge," Sherwood insisted.

"And the autopsy shows that Dr. Arledge was killed by repeated blows to the back of the head with a heavy, pointed object, similar to a ball-peen hammer."

"But that does not prove that it was *that* particular hammer," Sherwood said.

Rutherford said, "It seems like quite a coincidence that someone other than the killer would deliberately hide a hammer so close to the scene where a man was beaten to death with a hammer-like object."

"I never said it was a coincidence," Sherwood explained. "I never implied it was hidden by someone other than the killer. I only said that it is not the murder weapon."

Albert said, "You're suggesting that the murderer, who had to dispose of the murder weapon, decided to go ahead and hide the hammer too because he was already hiding stuff anyway?"

"I wasn't suggesting anything," Sherwood said. "All I know is that the hammer is not the murder weapon. If you want me to suggest an explanation, perhaps the killer planted the hammer, which they knew had no physical evidence on it, in the alley in the hopes that we'd find it, assume it was the murder weapon, and stop looking."

Terri said, "But the hammer *does* have physical evidence on it. The medical examiner found traces of a chalky, powdered material, similar to the white powdery residue on the head of the hammer, in the victim's wounds. Residue which was likely transferred to the victim during the assault when the unidentified, powder-covered, hammer-like weapon was used to murder him."

Sherwood frowned for a moment, then said. "Yes, I see your point. That is compelling. It certainly looks as if the hammer is the murder weapon."

Terri said, "Thank you."

Sherwood continued, "Which will make it all the more impressive when the coroner concludes that it couldn't possibly be the weapon due to the total lack of blood on the hammer."

Sloan leaded toward Sherwood. "Professor, what if the murderer found some way to remove the blood from the hammer, such as, for example, cleaning it?" Her artificial voice's tone was friendly. Her body language was less so.

Sherwood leaned in, mirroring her posture. "Detective Sloan, how would one go about cleaning the blood off a hammer without disturbing the coating of dust that the coroner has concluded was there during the assault?"

Sloan leaned in even closer, raised a single finger in Sherwood's face, and said, "That is a very good point, and one which had not occurred to me. Well done, Professor." She settled back into her chair, looking utterly relaxed.

Professor Sherwood laughed and thanked her, but the mood in the room was still fairly heavy. A moment of silence hung over them, then Albert chuckled and turned the tablet he was studying around for the group to see. He had been flicking through old file photos of the victim, and had stopped on a scan of an interview that had run some years ago in the *Seattle Post-Intelligencer*, the paper itself a relic from the past. The photo showed Arledge and his partner, Dr. Shaw, in happier times. They stood in Arledge's office, shaking hands.

"What about it?" Terri asked.

"It's ridiculous," Albert said. "It's just the most stiff, forced, painfully staged picture I've ever seen. I can't believe the photographer got paid for this."

Rutherford could see what he meant. In the photo, Arledge was wearing a tweed jacket with elbow patches; Shaw was wearing a lab coat. Arledge was holding a pipe in his free hand; Shaw had a pocket watch in his. In the background, along the wall, Rutherford could see the sofa, which appeared to have been moved so it would be in frame. On the desk, centered between the two men, there was a card with an inkblot propped up against a small bust of Sigmund Freud. The photo was intended to scream a two-part message to the reader: *These are two successful psychologists who are also good friends.*

Sherwood said, "Freud's head is at the level of their crotches. You know who would have loved that? Freud himself."

"True," Sloan said. "He'd have seen a lot of symbolism in it. He couldn't have missed it. It would have been at eye level."

Albert had turned the tablet back around and was looking at the image again. "Maybe this is only bugging me because of Rutherford's situation, but it's just so . . . obvious. They're psychologists, so of course they'd have all of the stuff you'd picture a psychologist owning displayed out where you can see it. And the bust really is the last straw. What is it with psychologists and classical pianists and their busts? I mean, who does that? I'm in engineering. I don't have a bust of Edison. Sherwood's in Life Sciences, but I don't see a bust of Darwin anywhere. Sloan, you're a detective. Do you own a bust of Sherlock Holmes?"

Sloan said, "No, but Sherlock Holmes is a fictional character." Her synthesized voice gave the words a cheerful cadence.

"So is Sigmund Freud," Max said. "He was actually an MI6 agent, set up with a false identity. Think about it, who better than the most prestigious psychoanalyst in all of Austria to feed useful intelligence back to Queen and country at that point in history? The cream of Germanic society was lining up to tell him their deepest secrets. All of his nonsensical sexual theories were simply a means to steer his clientele in the most compromising directions."

Albert said, "Nonsensical theories? Are you saying that a cigar is never just a cigar?"

"Don't underestimate a cigar, my friend. In the right hands, a cigar can be a powerful weapon, if it's lit."

Terri said, "Hold that thought for later, but right now we should get our minds back on the case."

"Agreed," Sloan said. "Since none of the obvious answers panned out yesterday, it seems like interviewing the doctor's patients would be the next logical step."

"I thought so too," Terri said. "As you know, he had cut back on his workload considerably, and was giving pro bono one-on-one and group therapy to a few select patients as part of a research project. Dr. Shaw has been very cooperative. He clearly wants us to find his partner's killer. Yesterday afternoon he sent us as much information as he could about the patients in the late Dr. Arledge's therapy group without violating their patient privilege. We have names, addresses, and phone numbers. Unofficially, he also gave me a broad idea of why they were being treated."

"We should speak to each of them." Sloan said. "Even if they don't give us any new leads, maybe just meeting them will give us a vibe."

"A vibe?" Rutherford asked.

"Yes, of course," Sloan said. "Evidence is key, but you have instincts for a reason. You shouldn't base a whole investigation on them, but if someone gives you a funny feeling, it's worth looking at them closer."

"And here's who you'll be looking at," Terri said, pulling something up on her tablet. "We have Erin Estabrook, thirty-eight, who finds it difficult to carry on normal conversations due to obsessive tendencies. Derek Sambucci, forty-three, who exhibits irrational hostility. He's the one who stormed out of a group session, which figures. Oscar Loomis, twenty-three, stand-up comedian, self-identifies as *always on*. Dustin O'Reilly, forty-five. He peppers conversation with a constant stream of innuendo and provocative sexual comments. And Molly Belanger, twenty-six, clown. That's all it says. *Clown.*"

"Any of those giving you a funny feeling, Sloan?" Albert asked.

She answered, "All of them, except the comedian. And the clown."

Terri said, "I've set up some appointments already. I've coordinated with Seattle PD, so you shouldn't show up in the same place at the same time as their detectives. First up is Derek Sambucci, *Mr. Hostility.* I figured you'd want to start with him. Then you'll move on to the obsessive and the comedian. If there's time after that, the perv and the clown. You may have to talk to them tomorrow. We'll play it by ear."

Sloan grabbed her cane, stood up, and said, "I guess we should get cracking."

Terri smiled. "Before you do, I'd like to steer us back to the cigar conversation. I have one last gift for Rutherford. Mr. Capp thinks it's important for your image that you smoke, but you don't. I'm not going to order you to pick up a habit that's hazardous to your health, so Albert and I put our heads together and came up with this." She handed Rutherford an object that looked like a half-used stub of a cigar, but he knew from the feel of it that it was plastic.

Albert said, "It's an e-cigar. It has an LED in the tip and puffs out water vapor. I modified it so that it'll run without nicotine, but the smoke and the ember glow will look the same."

Rutherford said, "So, what, I just walk around with this hanging out of my mouth all the time?"

"That's the idea," Terri said.

Albert added, "You activate the LED by inhaling through it. The tip will glow, and smoke will come out of your mouth when you exhale."

"How hot does the ember get?" Max asked.

"Not very," Albert answered. "He can take it directly out of his mouth and stick it in his pocket without burning any paper he has in there."

Max said, "That's a shame. It will be of very limited tactical use then."

Albert scratched his chin. "There's not a lot of empty space inside the housing, but if I use a capacitor, I might be able to build a single-use stun gun into the tip. It wouldn't knock anyone out, but it would hurt."

Terri nodded. "You do that." She turned her attention back to Rutherford. "If anyone notices that it's not a real cigar, you can just tell them that smoking isn't allowed in your office, so your manager is making you use the fake cigar."

"All of which is true," Sloan said.

THIRTEEN

On paper, the Stephenson steam-electric engine was much simpler to operate than a normal car's drivetrain. A patented electric boiler technology almost instantly converted small amounts of water into superheated steam, which powered a steam engine. It produced little noise, ample power, and tremendous torque, meaning that no gear changes were required. In theory, it was like driving a traditional car with an automatic transmission, only it was quieter and caused no air pollution.

In practice, because of the torque, it was like driving an automatic transmission mated to the engine of a Formula One race car.

Rutherford was not prepared for the difference. The very first time he tried to pull out of the office garage, he left thick black stripes of scorched rubber on the floor. He immediately stomped on the brakes and came to a skidding halt beyond the garage door, inches away from the rear bumper of an SUV that had the misfortune of being parked opposite the secret entrance to the Authorities' garage. A deafening screech reverberated throughout the building.

When the squeal died down, he heard his passengers. Sherwood was yelling for him to be careful; Max was chuckling like a department store Santa; and Sloan was doubled over, convulsing. Rutherford worried he had made her ill somehow, but then the synthetic Sloan voice in his ear said, "Laughing. Laughing. Laughing. Laughing. Laughing."

He looked in the rearview mirror. Through the haze of thick, blue, rubber-scented smoke he saw Terri and Albert, still standing in the Authorities' section of the garage, where they'd been waiting to see the van off on its maiden voyage.

Rutherford rolled down his window and shouted, "Sorry about that. I'll be more careful."

Terri shouted back, "You know what? Don't worry about it. It'll cost us a lot in tires, but the burnouts will help sell your image."

In his ear, Rutherford still heard, "Laughing. Laughing. Laughing."

The van had its virtues. The driver's seat had good visibility and a nice high vantage point. The monstrous amount of torque meant that it drove up steep hills without even noticing them, which, when you're driving in downtown Seattle, is a very good thing. The lack of engine noise made it that much easier to hear the squeal of the tires. These bright points did little to balance the van's greatest flaw, which was that Rutherford found every second driving it to be utterly terrifying.

The first few red lights and stop signs had caused a great deal of stress for Rutherford, and for the other drivers on the road. Nobody expected a sinister-looking black van to make fat, smoking "elevensies" across entire intersections when the light turned green. By the time they reached their destination, Rutherford had his throttle technique refined to the point that the rear tires let out a small, comparatively dignified chirp whenever the van set off.

He had been driving for at least fifteen minutes before Max pointed out that the smoke inside the van's cabin was not from his abuse of the tires, but from his abuse of his e-cigar. He'd been concentrating so hard on driving that he'd absentmindedly used the e-cigar like a snorkel, breathing in through the device and exhaling clouds of thin, white, odorless smoke that had steadily filled the van's interior. He maneuvered the cigar to the corner of his mouth. He tried to smile and say *sorry about that,* but with the cigar clenched between his canines, he wasn't smiling so much as gritting his teeth, and the words came out as "shorry abowt dat." To his own ear, he sounded angry, and a bit drunk.

Ironically, my employers would be quite pleased with that.

The first patient on their list, Derek Sambucci, worked at a mini-mart in Ballard. Thankfully, while the mart itself could indeed be described as *mini,* it was attached to a fast-food restaurant and a car wash, so the parking lot was actually quite large. There was ample space along the side of the building for Rutherford to park the van and later, with any luck, pull out again without endangering any lives.

Rutherford carefully pulled the van into a space and turned the key to Off. As he sagged in the driver's seat, his e-cigar dangled decoratively from his lips. It wouldn't have surprised him if it bore permanent teeth marks. The shirt he had just laundered was already drenched with his sweat, which had hydrated and reconstituted the years of dried union-carpenter sweat conserved in the weave of the fabric.

Sloan said, "Well done, Rutherford. Toward the end there, you really seemed to be getting the hang of it. It certainly didn't seem easy. The whole way here, I kept thinking about how grateful I was that I wasn't driving . . . and that this swivel chair has a seat belt." In her computer-generated voice, it was hard to tell if this was genuine support or sarcasm. It all just sounded like a phone tree.

"You shouldn't put too much faith in seat belts," Max said. "They help a little, but they're mostly a scam. Ralph Nader was a lackey for DuPont, the company that made nylon. A set of lap belts for every seat in every car adds up fast. It wasn't enough for them, though. That's why he pushed for shoulder straps and then air bags, which use both nylon and Teflon."

Sloan turned her helmet to look at Max. "Do you know that for a fact?" she asked.

"I can't prove it, if that's what you mean," Max admitted, "but I believe it."

"But you don't really know it's true."

"Sloan, I've learned many things in this life, and one of them is that sometimes believing something is better than knowing it."

Sloan's helmet tilted a bit to one side. "Do you know that, or just believe it?"

Rutherford found Sloan and Max's conversation oddly soothing. If they were calm enough to bicker about Ralph Nader, the drive couldn't really have been that bad. He took slow breaths and watched the wisps of fake cigar smoke vent from his nostrils, waiting for his heart rate to drop to a more manageable level.

From the back of the van, Professor Sherwood said, "Happily, none of those violent starts damaged the hive."

Rutherford, Sloan, and Max all turned in unison to see Professor Sherwood, who was hunched over in the far corner of his seat. There was a cabinet built into the rear passenger side of the van. It was made of a light-colored wood that had been aggressively sanded, strategically scorched, and coated with a layer of glossy shellac almost a centimeter thick. The professor had one of the cabinet's doors open, and was peering inside.

Sherwood said, "I'd worried that the jostling might have broken one of the combs, but they're completely intact."

"Hive?" Rutherford said. "I thought that was storage for equipment or something."

"I assumed it was a wet bar," Sloan said. "A van like this begs for a wet bar."

"Part of it is," Sherwood said. "Storage, I mean, but back here at the very end, there's a small hive."

Now that the cabinet door was open and he wasn't concentrating on piloting a van-sized steam-rocket, Rutherford could hear a faint buzzing. He craned his neck to see, and while the light, angle, and distance all worked against him, he could just make out a sheet of transparent material behind the door Professor Sherwood was holding open. Behind that there was a moving pattern that looked like a yellow-and-black rendering of static on an analog TV.

"How many bees are in there?" Max asked, voicing the question all of them were probably thinking.

"Oh, it's just a small hive. It's nothing compared to the ones I keep on the roof deck back at the office," Professor Sherwood said. "Only ten thousand or so."

"Or so?"

"Max, I'm sure even in Holland you know about the birds and the bees."

Max said, "In Amsterdam, very much so."

Professor Sherwood smiled. "Indeed, yes. Very good! Anyway, it's hard to know exactly how many bees there are, since the hive's population will fluctuate as bees die and reproduce."

"Is it safe to drive that thing around?" Rutherford asked.

"Certainly. Beehives are transported on flatbed trucks all the time for agricultural purposes. It doesn't harm the bees in the slightest."

Sloan's clipped, computer-generated voice said, "I'm pretty sure he meant, is it safe for us?"

"Oh. Yes, I see. Yes, it's safe. The bees are sealed in a reinforced metal casing that's impact resistant, in addition to being heavily soundproofed. There's a system that circulates air in and out so the bees can breathe, but it vents to the outside of the van. If we got into an accident violent enough to rupture the container, the bees would be the last of our worries."

Or the last thing we ever worry about, Rutherford thought.

"And even if the bees did somehow get inside the van with us," Professor Sherwood said, "they would only really pose a threat if they were upset, and as it happens, smoke calms them down. Positioned as they are near the rear tires, they're probably the only ones in the van who find Mr. Rutherford's driving relaxing."

The team walked into the mini-mart. It was the first environment Rutherford had visited with the team where his clothes made him look right at home. Max and Professor Sherwood were the ones who looked out of place. Sloan stood out everywhere she went, but less so here, because aside from her cane, she could have ridden in on a Vespa.

A man who looked to be in his mid to late forties was standing behind the cash register. A tall, beefy man in poor physical condition, he was the human equivalent of a rusted-out Cadillac with a couple of bad pistons and a shot suspension. There was a single customer at the check stand, and the cashier's hands were scanning bar codes, doling out change, and stuffing items into limp plastic bags. The cashier's mouth, however, was having a loud argument with a much younger, much smaller man of indeterminate Middle Eastern descent, who was busy loading food items that were essentially cold beige tubes onto a cooking apparatus that was essentially a rack of hot silver tubes.

"No," the younger man said. "I'm sorry, no! It is something we cannot do."

"Don't be stupid," the cashier said. "It only touched the floor for a second."

"No. I had to throw it out. Derek, we must respect the customer, and you don't serve something dirty to someone you respect." "Is the floor clean? Is it? Yes or no, is the floor clean? If you go to Jenny with your story about me trying to serve dirty food, you'll be telling her that you either wasted a perfectly good taquito or you didn't do a good job mopping." The customer whose items were being bagged didn't seem particularly alarmed by the conversation, possibly because he wasn't buying any taquitos, or more likely because people who buy convenience-store taquitos tend to have fairly flexible cleanliness standards, as a group.

"Pardon me," Max said. "I wonder if you would happen to be Derek Sambucci?"

"Yes," the cashier said, "I would happen to be." He pointed at Rutherford. "Hey, you can't smoke that thing in here."

Keeping the e-cigar clenched in his teeth, Rutherford said, "It'sh not a real shigar."

Derek Sambucci replied, "And I don't really care." Rutherford pulled the cigar out of his mouth and held it in his hand, which seemed to pacify Sambucci.

Sambucci thrust the overstuffed plastic bag of overpriced merchandise at the customer and gave him a perfunctory nod. The customer walked away with the words *I don't really care* ringing in his ears, which was really a more honest farewell than *Have a nice day* or *Please come again* would have been.

"You the guy who wants to talk to me about Dr. Arledge?" Sambucci asked.

Max replied in the affirmative. Sambucci started walking to the end of the counter. As he passed the younger man, he said, "Rashid, I'm gonna go have a word with this guy."

"You're supposed to work the register."

"Which is why you need to cover for me."

"I have my own work."

"So do your work while you're doing mine. You're in America now. You're gonna have to learn to multitask."

As Sambucci crossed the shop to the back door, Rashid yelled, "Your break is at ten thirty."

"Yeah, and that's when I'll take it."

Rutherford, who was following Sambucci with the others, turned and looked at Rashid. Though obviously irritated by the extra work, the guy seemed grateful for a break from his coworker.

The area behind the mini-mart was exactly as glamorous as Rutherford had expected. The dumpster and grease tank behind the fast-food restaurant did not add to the ambiance. Rutherford thought about how deeply the human lust for French fries must run, since the smell of the rancid, used fryer oil was making him hungry.

"Okay," Sloan said. "Let's start with the preliminaries."

Max nodded, but said nothing. Rutherford reminded himself that Sambucci could not hear anything Sloan said. He put the e-cigar back in his mouth and settled in to watch Sloan and Max get to work.

Max said, "Mr. Sambucci, thank you for meeting with us. My name is Max Warmenhoven. You spoke with our associate on the phone. We're investigating the death of Dr. Daniel Arledge. We just want to ask a few questions, then you can get back to work."

Sambucci said, "Yeah, sure. Take your time. I'm in no rush to go back in there. It's a shame about the doctor."

"Yes, it certainly is," Max said.

Professor Sherwood approached Sambucci and asked, "Would you please raise your arms?"

He looked confused, but he did as he was asked. Professor Sherwood's bee wand buzzed faintly as he passed it over and around Derek Sambucci's extremities.

"Hey, what the hell is this?"

"It's perfectly routine, I assure you," Max said.

Sambucci glowered, but kept his arms raised. Looking away from Max, he gave Sloan the once-over. He changed his expression to a nauseating smirk and said, "Hey, sweetheart, aren't you gonna take that helmet off so I can get a look at your face?"

Sloan shook her head. Sambucci went back to glowering.

Professor Sherwood ran the wand over Sambucci's right front pants pocket. He looked at the readout on the wand before running it over the pocket a second time. He held the wand motionless for several seconds, read the readout a final time, then smiled and winked at Derek Sambucci.

Sambucci said, "What? There's nothing in there."

"No," Sherwood said. "I don't believe there is now. But perhaps there was."

"Don't worry, Mr. Sambucci," Max reminded him. "Professor Sherwood is simply running an experiment. He's not an officer of the law. His findings hold no legal weight."

"Yeah, well, that's good," Sambucci said, "because he's wrong. That stupid doohickey of yours doesn't work."

Professor Sherwood kept smiling. "Tell me," he asked, "are you allergic to bee stings?"

"No," Sambucci said.

Professor Sherwood said, "Good," then sprayed him with a small pumper bottle of clear fluid, hitting him mostly on the chin and neck.

Sambucci spat and wiped his mouth with his arm. "Mwhaa! What the hell, old man? You looking to get that chick's cane shoved somewhere?"

Sherwood turned to address the rest of the team. "My work here is done. I'll be in the van."

As Sherwood walked around the end of the building and out of view, Sambucci shouted, "Yeah, that's what I thought! You better get out of here."

Max said, "I promise we will have a long talk with our colleague, Mr. Sambucci."

"Mostly congratulating him," Sloan added through Max and Rutherford's earpieces. "Max, please ask him about his treatment."

Max asked, "How long were you treated by the late Dr. Arledge?"

"About a year."

"Did you find it helpful?"

"It kept my mom off my back."

"She's the one who encouraged you to seek therapy?"

Sambucci sneered. "Yeah, she knows that until I get married and settle down she's not going to get any grandchildren."

"And you don't do so well with the women?" Max asked.

Sambucci's eyes darted again to Sloan. "Oh, I do fine, but I haven't met one that I'd want to start a family with yet."

Max nodded. "The right woman can be elusive."

"You're tellin' me! God knows I've dated plenty of them, but they're all crazy, stupid, or oversensitive."

From Derek Sambucci's point of view, it must have looked like Sloan silently glanced at Rutherford, but Rutherford and Max heard her say, "The ones he thinks are *oversensitive* were probably the ones who got offended when he called them *crazy* or *stupid.*"

Rutherford said, "Yeah."

Sambucci misunderstood whom Rutherford was agreeing with and said, "See, this guy here is cool. He knows what I'm talking about."

Rutherford heard Sloan's voice say, "Laughing."

Max said, "If you don't mind my asking, what, specifically, were you being treated for?"

"That's none of your damned business," Sambucci said through bared teeth.

Max said, "That is true, Mr. Sambucci, but it is my job to ask."

Of course, they knew he had been in treatment for something relating to irrational hostility, but if they hadn't known already, his attitude would have given them a helpful hint.

Max continued. "But the therapy was helping?"

Sambucci shrugged. "Some of it. The one-on-one stuff, yeah. I'd just talk, tell the doctor about all the idiots and jackasses I know, and what it felt like to tell them off. Dr. Arledge listened and sometimes asked me how I felt when I yelled at them, or how I thought they felt."

"And what would you say?"

"That I felt good, and that I hoped they felt bad."

Max said. "Your answer suggests that you found the group therapy less helpful."

"Yeah, it was just stupid. See, if I've got a problem, and I'm not saying that I do, but if I do, it's that I have a low tolerance for idiots and jackasses. So putting me in a room with a bunch of idiots and jackasses is only a good idea if you want me to get used to them, and I don't wanna get used to them. I want them to straighten up!" Sambucci's voice had risen steadily throughout the exchange. He wasn't quite shouting yet, but it seemed he might be soon.

"Ah," Max said. "We heard that you walked out on more than one group therapy session, looking unhappy."

"Those freaks thought they were gonna help me! Like I needed any help from them!" Now he *was* yelling. "It just shows how checked out they really were!"

Sloan's voice cut in, "Okay, this is a good chance to segue into asking if any of the other patients might have done it." Rutherford noticed that the words were delivered faster than usual. They were pronounced at the same speed, but the gaps between them had shortened. He wondered if she had some sort of variable speed control.

Max nodded. "Mr. Sambucci, did any of your fellow patients have a problem with Dr. Arledge?"

"Yeah," Sambucci said, as if it were obvious.

"How many?" Max asked.

Sambucci seemed to calm down, and squinted at Max. "I suppose one or two."

"Enough of a problem that they might have wished him ill?"

"I suppose it's possible."

Max asked, "Would you please elaborate? Which members of the group may have wished him harm?"

"Who did you all say you worked for again?"

"We didn't," Max said. "The name of our employer is irrelevant to the question."

"But you're not a cop."

"No, I'm not."

"And you are getting paid."

Yes," Max said wearily. "All of us are. This is our job, after all."

Sambucci smiled. "How much? You being paid well?"

"That's not relevant, Mr. Sambucci."

"I think it is. I think it's very relevant. I don't know where you're from, buddy, but here in America, we got what's called *the free enterprise system*, and if I'm helping you do a job you're getting paid for, I don't see why I shouldn't get my fair share."

"If you think we're going to receive a reward for finding Dr. Arledge's killer, I promise you, that's not the case," Max explained. "We merely draw a salary."

"I'll take a cut of that," Sambucci said. "I'm not picky."

Sloan said, "This is going south fast." Neither Max nor Rutherford needed to be told that.

"We're not going to pay you for information," Max said.

Sambucci stood a bit taller, leaned toward Max, and said, "Well that's just greedy."

Sloan said, "Rutherford, be ready to chase him."

Rutherford asked, "Why?"

Sambucci, who couldn't hear Sloan, said, "Because you're hoarding all the profit for yourselves when I'm the one who has the information you need."

Sloan, who knew what question Rutherford was really asking, said, "Because that's why you're here. To look mean, chase people, and get attention."

Rutherford frowned, but nodded as he did it. Like it or not, it was true.

Over the earpiece, Professor Sherwood, who was in the van, said, "I'll assist if I can."

"How do you know what's going on?" Rutherford asked.

"Because I was in the therapy sessions and I know all the people involved." Sambucci shouted. "Keep up, dummy!"

Max tried to reason with Sambucci. "We haven't established that you have useful information, and if you do, there are ways to legally compel you to tell us."

"I've been listening in to your audio feeds," Professor Sherwood explained.

Rutherford said, "You can do that?"

Sloan and Sambucci, who were both talking to Rutherford about totally different things, said, "Yes, we all can," and "No, he can't."

Max continued, "Let me clarify. You're right, I personally cannot, but my associate, Mr. Rutherford, the man you recently referred to as *dummy*, is a sworn law enforcement officer. If he has reason to believe you're knowingly obstructing justice, he can hold you in custody until the police arrive."

"And I do," Rutherford said.

"Indeed," Max agreed. "When the police arrive and question you, they'll happily tell us whatever you tell them. We could have them here in a matter of minutes. I wonder if whatever our friend detected traces of in your pants pocket is still in your vehicle, on your coat, or in your bloodstream, for that matter. I also wonder if you can account for your whereabouts at the time of the murder."

Sambucci started to shout something, but clamped down on the words. He looked at Max with wild eyes, started to shout something again, stopped short again, and averted his gaze to Sloan and Rutherford. Then he cleared his throat and took off running around the far end of the building.

Rutherford sighed, but he chased Derek Sambucci as he did it.

Max's voice in his earpiece said, "Chase on. Alert. Chase on."

Rutherford rounded the corner of the building and saw Sambucci running into the parking lot. Despite his head start, he was only about thirty feet away and the gap was closing fast. Rutherford was running smoothly, leaving a trail of e-cigar smoke floating in his wake.

Sambucci was large and bulky, but he was in terrible shape. Rutherford's police training and limited experience told him that men such as these were actually quite dangerous. They had the confidence of a large man, but lacked the skills, experience, or physical capacity to back it up. Doughy men are still men, and all men tend to assume that they're pretty good fighters until it is demonstrated to them that they are not. Unfortunately, physical size does give a fighter an advantage. If a large, inept fighter got lucky and managed to pin you beneath his bulk, you'd be helpless as he slowly and clumsily beat you into submission.

Sambucci was running toward a four-door Toyota parked at the end of the lot, presumably his car. He wasn't halfway there before Rutherford caught up to him and shoved him forward, grabbing a handful of his uniform smock as he did so. He heard a clinking noise that he instantly recognized as his e-cigar hitting the pavement. It had been dislodged from his mouth the moment he hit Sambucci's back. He wasn't sorry to hear it go.

His effort to bring Sambucci down was less successful than he would have liked. Sambucci merely lurched forward, his balance having been upset by Rutherford's shove. Rutherford kept his grip on Sambucci's smock, so he was yanked forward and off-balance himself. The big man staggered to a stop and swung around drunkenly, trying to wrench himself free from Rutherford's grip.

In his earpiece, Rutherford heard the sound of a desk chair rolling quickly across an office floor, followed by Albert's voice saying, "Okay, HQ here. Launching chase-cam."

Sambucci threw a wide, slow punch that would have connected with Rutherford's head if he had been shorter, standing several inches to the right, and not watching. As Rutherford was none of those things, he managed to grab Sambucci's left arm and trap it in his own right armpit. Sambucci was now held in place by his arm and his shirt. He twisted and spun in a bid to tear his shirt free, but he only succeeded in causing the two of them to pirouette in place.

In his peripheral vision, Rutherford saw a dark shape rise over the roof of the van. He didn't tear his focus away from his assailant, but his ears told him that it was one of Albert's quadcopters. He hadn't know that the van concealed drones, but he wasn't particularly surprised to find out. It darted toward him, dropping to a height of about four feet as soon as it was clear of the van.

Sambucci used his free right arm to break Rutherford's grip on his uniform, then threw another poorly aimed, low-velocity punch at Rutherford's face. Rutherford deflected it easily and was able to get a solid grip on the larger man's wrist. Rutherford had Sambucci pretty much immobilized, but was himself stuck in a pose any school child would have immediately recognized as that of a *little teapot*. Sambucci, for his part, was struggling in place with his right arm trapped and his left arm extended as if he were being led by Rutherford in a vigorous if inelegant waltz.

Rutherford caught another brief glimpse of the drone, which hovered unsteadily about ten feet away. An off-the-shelf smartphone hung underneath, held by a bracket mounted beneath the drone's spherical chassis.

Rutherford was distracted for a moment, but his attention was wrested back to the task at hand when he realized that Sambucci had managed to extend his right leg forward, between Rutherford's feet. Fearing for his groin, Rutherford reflexively brought up his left leg to protect that delicate region, but this cost him his leverage. The big man shoved him backward. As he fell, Rutherford released his grip on his adversary's arms in a doomed effort to catch himself.

Rutherford fell and rolled onto his back at Sambucci's feet. Sambucci looked down at him with murder in his eyes. In Rutherford's ear, he heard Terri, who was also listening in from the office, say, "Okay, Professor Sherwood."

Derek Sambucci pulled back his left leg, intending to kick Rutherford, either in the head or the ribs, whichever Rutherford left exposed. Then, cutting through all other sounds and rendering all other thoughts moot, Rutherford and Sambucci both heard Professor Sherwood shout, "Stop, or I'll release the bees!"

Sambucci was confused. Either his mind couldn't comprehend what it had just heard, or it had, and was choosing not to believe it. Either way, he kicked Rutherford halfheartedly and resumed running toward his car.

Professor Sherwood shouted, "Stay down, Rutherford!" Then the air filled with buzzing.

It grew louder. Rutherford saw that one of the hatches in the side of the van had opened, and inside it were what appeared to be untreated wooden slats. He couldn't make out much more detail because his vision was engulfed by a growing cloud of live bees swarming toward him.

Most of the bees passed overhead with enough speed to create a noticeable Doppler effect, but some stopped and massed on Rutherford's arms. His instincts screamed at him to slap at the bees and kill as many as possible in the hopes of scaring the others off, but Professor Sherwood was shouting, "Freeze! Don't move! Stay calm, and they won't sting."

Rutherford chose to listen to Professor Sherwood, though he couldn't take his eyes off the bees crawling over the arms of his jacket.

"Ah," Professor Sherwood said in a quieter voice. "Sorry about this, Rutherford. Some of the scent marker must have rubbed off. He probably touched his neck, then touched you. Please remove your jacket carefully. Keep your motions as slow and deliberate as possible."

Rutherford shimmied out of the jacket as slowly as he could. It certainly seemed to take an eternity to him. He set the jacket on the ground and stepped back with such rapidity he nearly bumped into someone. It was Professor Sherwood, who had accessorized his usual windbreaker-and-Dockers ensemble with a beekeeper's hood and gloves.

Sherwood handed Rutherford a spray bottle. "Please spray this on the bees. I'd do it, but I need to keep an eye on Mr. Sambucci."

Rutherford did as he was told and watched as the bees abandoned his jacket and joined the rest of the hive *subduing* Derek Sambucci, who was silently experiencing a living nightmare while Albert's quadcopter hovered nearby, capturing the moment for posterity.

Rutherford turned to hand the spray bottle back to
Professor Sherwood, and only then noticed that Sherwood had
what looked like a small sniper rifle aimed at Sambucci.

Obviously seeing the confusion on Rutherford's face,
he said, "Relax. It's a dart gun. Epinephrine. He said he wasn't
allergic, but we can't be too careful."

* * *

For the remainder of the interview, Sloan channeled her questions
through Professor Sherwood. He and Sambucci stood in the
parking lot where the fight had come to an abrupt end while the rest
of the team waited in the van, listening to the interrogation over
the party line. The police were present, but were understandably
keeping their distance until Professor Sherwood finished his
business and collected his tiny, buzzing assistants.

"He says he was at work when the murder took place,"
Professor Sherwood said.

"We know," Sloan said. "We heard him, though it was a
bit hard to hear him over the buzzing."

Sherwood said, "Please try to speak up."

"Yes, sir," Sambucci nearly shouted. "I'll try, sir. I'm
just . . . oh, God, I'm just so nervous, sir."

"I know," Sherwood said. "Try to calm down. It's just a
three-pound beard of bees. If memory serves, the world record
is a little under ninety pounds. Can you imagine what that must
have felt like?"

"Oh, God," Sambucci moaned. "Oh, God!"

"Now, now, there's no need to cry. You're in surprisingly
little danger. I'll remove the bees as soon as we're done talking."

Sloan said, "He implied earlier that he knew some
helpful information. Please suggest to Mr. Sambucci that this
would be an excellent time to share it."

Professor Sherwood paraphrased Sloan's words, and Sambucci said, "Yeah, uh, okay. A few months back, the group started acting funny."

"Funny how?" Sherwood asked.

"Uptight. Weird. You know, funky."

"Weren't you all being treated for social problems? Wasn't it normal for them to be uncomfortable in groups?"

"No, not, uh, not always. A few of them would usually be talking when I showed up for a session, but they'd always stop when I came in."

"Why?" Professor Sherwood asked.

"Because they're stuck-up assholes."

"Yeah," Sloan said. "That's one theory."

Sherwood chose not to pass that particular comment along. "But then things changed," he pressed.

"Yeah, I came in one day, and everyone was on edge. Nobody talking. Lots of tension."

"Why?"

"Dunno. They didn't tell me and I didn't care enough to ask."

"Okay, what else can you tell us?"

"That's all I got," Sambucci said.

Sloan said, "Remind him that he told us he had information that would help us."

Professor Sherwood said, "You claimed to have information that would help us. Once you've told us everything, I'll have my colleagues bring me a smoke pot, and I'll scrape off the bees. Not before."

Sloan added, "And try to sound angry."

Professor Sherwood said, "Dammit!"

"I'm sorry! I'm sorry! I don't know anything else. Really! I figured if there was good money in it, I could ask the other patients, you know, since I already know them."

"And if the money wasn't good?" Sherwood asked.

"I figured if I got paid up front it wouldn't matter if I really helped you or not. I'm sorry!"

Sambucci was wailing with fear and regret, not at all responsive to Sherwood's attempts to calm him. Then the wailing suddenly cut off.

"Nghuu! Dare's un in mu mouf!"

"I'm sorry," Sherwood said. "What?"

"A bee ids in mu mouf!"

"Oh! There's a bee in your mouth! I see! That's okay. Be careful. Try not to hurt it."

"I'b nod worried aboud be hurdig da bee!"

"Well, you should be, Mr. Sambucci. How we treat smaller creatures reflects on our character. Also, if that bee's sisters get the feeling that she's in distress, they'll attempt to defend—"

"OH, GOD! OH, GOD!"

"Calm down! Just take a deep breath and gently blow her out. Breathe in through your nose, though. You wouldn't want to inhale her."

Rutherford, Sloan, and Max sat silently in the van, listening to Derek Sambucci sniff and blow heavily while sobbing.

FOURTEEN

"That's all he had?" Terri asked. "They were all weird and tense a few months ago?"

"Yes," Sherwood said.

"And he didn't know why?"

"No."

Max said, "Instead of helping us solve our mystery, he gave us a second smaller mystery."

"And a less interesting one at that," Sloan added.

Rutherford chose not to add anything. The party line made it easy for them to communicate as a team and pass along important information, even though they were driving down the freeway and Terri and Albert were sitting at their desks back at the office. Unfortunately, communicating and receiving information did not help Rutherford drive the van.

He had managed to train his foot not to press too hard on the gas pedal (or steam pedal, in this case), and not to overreact and pull completely off the road when he did press too hard, causing the van to lurch forward as if it had been rear-ended by a meteor. Still, throttle management was taking up a huge amount of his mental bandwidth and most of what was left was occupied with steering the large van through Seattle traffic.

"It wasn't a total loss," Professor Sherwood said. "I'm quite happy with how my bees performed."

"Yes," Max said. "Who knew it would be so useful to have a hive of live bees in the car?"

"I know," Sherwood said. "They've already proved their worth, and they haven't even started producing honey yet! It's the darnedest thing. I'd suspected that they'd be good for detection and maybe pursuit, but their applications for enhanced interrogation simply never occurred to me. It seems so obvious now."

"Yes," Terri said. "It's also obvious that you can never use them that way again. I had a quick call from Mr. Capp's legal counsel. They figure they're going to have to pay Sambucci off to keep this thing out of court."

"Really?" Rutherford moaned. "I hate the idea of that jerk making money off this."

Terri said, "Rutherford, you're the one person in that van who should be happy right now. We sent the cell phone video from the drone over to Mr. Capp and he was very pleased. He already has someone editing it, and once it's uploaded anonymously to YouTube through a dummy account, some of his marketing sock puppets are going to tweet it. He hopes to have it viral by nightfall. If you search *detective saved by bees*, it might already be up."

"Well I'm happy he's getting something usable out of it," Rutherford lied, "because I cracked the screen of my smartphone, and my e-cigar fell in a puddle."

Albert said, "Rutherford, really! Must you be so hard on the equipment?"

"Hey, I'm sorry. I didn't *want* to fall on my phone. That doesn't feel good, you know. It's like falling on your keys, but more expensive."

Albert backpedaled immediately, "Don't worry about it, Rutherford. It's no problem. I have another phone right here. It'll be waiting for you when you get back. I'll figure out a way to clean your cigar."

"Okay. Good," Rutherford said. "Thanks," He was uncomfortable. Albert's mood had done a complete one eighty, and Rutherford had no idea why.

Terri said, "Well, anyway, just because Sambucci didn't know anything doesn't mean that the other patients might not give us some leads. Your next interview is with Erin Estabrook. She's a Caucasian female. Thirty-eight. She is at home with her daughter, Brooke, a nine-year-old whom Mrs. Estabrook homeschools. The daughter is a bright little lady who likes dolls and princesses. She takes gymnastics and violin lessons. She also draws. Mostly horses."

Sloan asked, "Where did you get all of this background on the daughter?"

"Mrs. Estabrook told me, on the phone, when I set up the interview. She was being treated for obsessive tendencies. Now we know what she obsesses about."

A short time later, they made their way through the eastside suburbs to the home of Mrs. Estabrook and her daughter. Unfortunately, reaching the destination also meant parking the van.

The Estabrooks' driveway was completely filled by one SUV. The sides of the streets were lined with parallel-parked cars. There was a space near Mrs. Estabrook's home, but it was only about one-and-a-quarter van lengths with cars on both ends, and nobody thought asking Rutherford to maneuver the van into such a tight space was a good idea, entertaining though it would be to watch. They kept driving and found a much larger opening a block further on.

Max and Sloan exited the van, but as Rutherford started to climb out of the driver's side door, he heard Professor Sherwood call out.

"I'm sorry, I don't think I should accompany you this time. The bees are overstimulated. I'd like to stay behind and keep an eye on them, maybe write up my notes on their performance."

"Sure," Sloan's synthetic voice said. "We'll call you if we need something sniffed or swarmed."

The lawn was a beautifully manicured patch of uniform green, barely wider than the house it surrounded. The house itself was a typical late-nineties northwest suburban palace: a collection of gables, pillars, garage doors, and windows of various sizes held together with light blue clapboard siding. Max rang the doorbell. Almost instantly the door swung open, and they were met by a small, thin, well-groomed woman with intense eyes and a weak smile.

Max greeted the woman, introduced himself, and mentioned that Mrs. Wells had called ahead. Erin Estabrook was welcoming enough when she returned Max's greeting, but she regarded Rutherford's leather jacket and ratty T-shirt with mild panic. Then she saw Sloan, with her helmet and cane, and she stepped up to medium panic. Still, she invited them in.

The interior of the house looked exactly as Rutherford had expected. The coffee table was covered with garish children's books. The matching end tables held an assortment of empty glasses and small electronic devices. The chairs were clean and tastefully upholstered, but there were permanent butt-shaped dents in the cushions. There was a heavy base coat of safe, tasteful decoration sitting beneath a top coat of real life.

At the center of the room, a little girl sat on a large couch, watching a huge TV. She wore pink jeans and a dark gray T-shirt with a repeating pattern of faux spray-painted graffiti hearts. She stared, unmoving, at the TV, where an animated young woman and a snowman were talking.

Max said, "Mrs. Estabrook, these are my associates, Ms. Sloan and Mr. Rutherford. We wanted to ask you a few questions about . . ." He deftly glanced at the little girl, then back to Mrs. Estabrook. "Dr. Arledge," he said casually.

"Yes," Mrs. Estabrook said. "I understand. I'd like to help you but . . ." Now she glanced at the oblivious girl on the couch. "I don't know what I can really say, given the circumstances."

"She can't be worried about upsetting her daughter," Sloan said. "The kid hasn't even noticed that we're here."

Max threw a quick frown Sloan's way. "If you're concerned that we'll *disturb* your daughter, we could talk in a different room. I promise, we'd be discreet."

"Yes," Mrs. Estabrook said, "but then she'd be alone, and she might find that upsetting too."

"We'd only be a room or two away, Mrs. Estabrook."

"Yes, and she'd be in here, alone, while I'm away talking to strangers. It might make her nervous."

Sloan said, "Somehow, I don't think it's the kid who's going to be nervous."

"What if one of my associates stays in here with her?" Max said.

Mrs. Estabrook looked at Rutherford and Sloan and did not seem happy with the idea.

"Offer to wait with her yourself, Max," Sloan said. "You're the least threatening person here. You look like Santa before he let himself go."

"Or," Max said, "I could wait with the young lady."

Mrs. Estabrook looked dubious.

Rutherford said, "Ma'am?"

Erin Estabrook looked at him. He made direct eye contact, hoping that if she was looking at his eyes she couldn't also be looking at his clothes. "I understand," he said. "It's a difficult time, we're perfect strangers, and this was sprung on you with little notice. I don't blame you for being uncomfortable, but we are in law enforcement, here on business. We won't keep you long, and while your daughter is in Mr. Warmenhoven's company she'll probably be safer than she's ever been in her whole life."

Mrs. Estabrook held eye contact with Rutherford's for a moment, then said, "Okay, if it won't take long."

Mrs. Estabrook stepped to the side of the couch, raised her voice about half an octave and a full decibel, and said, "Brooke? Dear? Mommy has to talk to her visitors, but this nice gentleman is going to keep you company."

The little girl kept staring at the TV. "Okay."

Max said, "Hello young lady. My name is Max." He motioned toward one of the chairs. "Do you mind if I sit?"

Without once looking away from the TV, the girl repeated, "Okay."

Max tapped on his phone's screen. To Mrs. Estabrook, it probably looked like he was silencing it, but he was cutting himself off from Rutherford and Sloan's feed. Rutherford understood. If they needed him, they could easily call him, but this way, audio from the living room would not interfere with their interview.

He sat down, looked up at the screen, and said, "Ah, *Frozen*. That's a very good movie."

Brooke said, "Yeah."

Max smiled reassuringly at Mrs. Estabrook, who only seemed slightly more comfortable with the situation.

Rutherford cleared his throat and said, "Ma'am, the sooner we start, the sooner we'll be out of your hair."

Mrs. Estabrook said, "Yes, of course, follow me," and led them toward the hall. Rutherford took up the rear. As he went, he heard Max ask, "Tell me, Brooke, do you know what this film is about?"

Brooke answered, "Being who you are."

"That's what they tell you," Max said, "but do you know what it's really about?"

Mrs. Estabrook led Sloan and Rutherford down a short hall, past a closed door. Rutherford assumed it was the bathroom, as few bedrooms had a hand-painted plaque on the door advising guests on what to do if they "sprinkle when they tinkle."

At the end of the hall, they entered a room that the architects had probably intended to be a bedroom, but Erin Estabrook had other ideas. In the middle of the room, there was a large, empty table with one flimsy rolling office chair. The wall on the right was covered with inexpensive but sturdy shelves. Most of the shelves held plastic bins made of a milky material just transparent enough for you to see that they were full of neatly organized fabrics, papers, and other crafting supplies, but not enough for you to tell what those supplies really looked like.

One shelf, which would be at eye level to a seated person, held a beautifully organized rack of colored pencils. A second rack held equally well-arranged colored pens. A third held a greater variety of scissors than Rutherford would have thought possible. It was a room where one made things for one's daughter, or things about one's daughter, but where one never made things *with* one's daughter, which made the contents of the far wall all the more telling.

Opposite the craft supplies were three shallow shelves affixed to the wall, and on those shelves stood fifteen dolls. Their blank eyes stared out into space. They were all the same height, and came from the same manufacturer, but there were several ethnicities, and each was wearing a different costume. Also, each had a different children's book leaning against the wall behind it.

Mrs. Estabrook closed the door then hotfooted it across the room. She slid the closet door open to reveal more well-organized supplies, a few cheap folding chairs, and a stack of identical pink doll boxes. She pulled out two of the chairs and slid the door closed again.

While Mrs. Estabrook was fussing with the chairs, Sloan told Rutherford, "You're a trained cop. I'll butt in if I think there's something you're missing. Otherwise, just ask the questions that seem important."

Rutherford nodded at Sloan. He settled into his folding chair, looked around the room, and then turned to Mrs. Estabrook, who was sitting in the office chair, radiating tension. "Those are American Girl dolls, aren't they?"

"Yes. Yes, they are. Brooke loves them."

"So did my sister. She didn't have this many, and they weren't in nearly this good shape."

"These wouldn't be either if I let Brooke keep them in her room."

Rutherford nearly laughed. "I bet you're right. It's funny. The outfits and the books are the things that make these dolls special, but in my house they always got destroyed."

For the first time since they'd met her, Erin Estabrook allowed a tiny flash of a genuine smile.

"You seem to have taken quite an interest in your sister's collection," Mrs. Estabrook said.

Rutherford shrugged. "Eh, they were her toys, not mine. I didn't play with them or anything, but I'm secure enough to admit that I always thought they were a neat idea."

Mrs. Estabrook's smile grew stronger. "It's a shame they don't make anything like it for boys."

Rutherford said, "They do, in a way. Dolls that look different, have different outfits, and come with a prewritten backstory. In a sense, action figures are like American Girl dolls for boys. They're just cheaper and more durable, which, boys being boys, is probably smart."

Mrs. Estabrook smiled. "That's a very good point!" Then she swatted Rutherford on the knee, playfully.

Sloan said, "No it isn't. I was a girl and I loved playing with my *Star Wars* action figures. My favorites were Darth Vader and Boba Fett."

Rutherford started to say something, stopped short, squinted at Sloan, then turned back to face Mrs. Estabrook, who was now much more relaxed then when they had come in.

Rutherford said, "Mrs. Estabrook."

"Please call me Erin."

"Thanks, Erin. You can call me Sinclair if you'd like, but . . . everyone calls me Rutherford."

"Thank you, Rutherford."

"Erin, what did you think of Dr. Arledge?"

"He was wonderful. He was always very kind to me."

"We don't know what he was treating you for, and it's none of our business, but was he helping you? Was his treatment successful?"

"Yes, and I don't mind talking about it. In fact, that's the problem. Dr. Arledge was helping me to internalize the fact that Brooke is the center of my universe, but not the center of everyone else's."

"Were the other patients in the group as happy with Dr. Arledge?"

Erin's expression soured. "Some more than others. Are you going to be talking to any of the other patients?"

"We hope to talk to all of them, in time. We just came from speaking with Derek Sambucci."

Erin rolled her eyes. "How'd that go?"

Rutherford smiled, glanced quickly at Sloan, then looked back at Erin and said, "Not smoothly."

Sloan nodded lightly, as if restraining a laugh.

Erin said, "I'm not surprised. Did he tell you anything useful?"

Rutherford took a moment to choose his words. "No. Should he have?"

"No, he probably didn't have anything to say."

Rutherford thought he sensed a little extra spin on the word *he*. "Is there another member of the group who *will* have something to tell us?"

"It's not my place to say," Erin said.

"Anything you could tell us might help us find Dr. Arledge's killer."

"If I thought I knew anything solid, I would have called the police already, Mr. Rutherford. I don't have any facts. What I do have is some juicy gossip. I don't want my little girl to grow into a woman who gossips, so I need to lead by example."

Sloan said, "Constantly telling everyone every detail of her daughter's life probably undermines that."

Rutherford looked at Sloan and muttered, "That's not helpful."

Erin said, "I know it's not helpful, Mr. Rutherford. I'm sorry."

Sloan said, "Laughing."

Rutherford waved his hands apologetically. "No, Erin, I understand. It's good that you have your principles, but there seems to be something you think we should know. Can you point us in the right direction? Just a hint, perhaps?"

"You're going to talk to the other patients from the group?"

"Yes."

"Have you talked to Molly yet?"

"Molly? No, just Mr. Sambucci and you."

"Are you talking to Molly next?"

"I don't think so. Mrs. Wells, the woman who called you, has us meeting with someone else next. Does Molly know something?"

"I'm just suggesting that you talk to all of the patients, including Molly."

Rutherford paused, trying to remember which patient was named Molly. Sensing this, Sloan said, "Molly is the clown."

After a few more standard questions, Rutherford said, "I think we've got everything we need, for now." Erin Estabrook took it as a simple statement, but Sloan understood that it was a question. She confirmed that she had no further questions either, and they all stood. As Erin put the folding chairs away, Sloan looked at the dolls. They stood motionless and emotionless, with blank expressions and colorful clothing.

"Their faces and bodies are just a blank canvas," Sloan said. "It's like you said—they're given personality by an outfit and a fictional story."

She turned to Rutherford and said, "I bet you can relate to that. I know I can."

Erin led them back to the great room, where the movie was still playing, but Brooke was no longer watching. She had turned and was engaged in a lively conversation with Max.

"I'm back, Brooke, honey," Erin said. "Was everything all right while I was gone?"

Brooke said, "Yeah. We've been talking."

"You have a delightful daughter," Max said, rising from his chair.

Brooke said, "Mom, did you know that the movie *Frozen* is really about pooping?"

Mrs. Estabrook said, "What?"

"Yeah," Brooke continued. "See, Elsa makes ice. It just comes from her body naturally. She can't help it. Sometimes it happens by accident. And her parents tell her to never let anyone see it happen."

Rutherford lightly touched Mrs. Estabrook on the shoulder, hoping to distract her. "Erin, thanks for your time. We're going to go now." He kept talking at a fast pace and in a commanding tone of voice while following Max and Sloan out the front door. He said, "You have our number. If you think of anything that might help us, please let us know immediately." But he stopped on her doorstep, looked her in the eye, and made one last attempt to get her to talk.

"Erin, I understand why you don't want to tell us whatever it is that you know, but I promise you, we'd be discreet. Nobody would ever know where the information came from."

She shook her head. "Mr. Rutherford, what I may or may not know probably has nothing to do with what happened to poor Dr. Arledge. I'm sure it's not related. You'll probably figure it out when you talk to Molly. It's just not my place to tell you. It would mean spreading tawdry gossip about other people's personal lives, and only the very worst kind of person would do that."

FIFTEEN

"They were screwing," Oscar Loomis said. He leaned back in his seat and smiled nauseatingly, then made a circle with the fingers of his left hand and used the index finger of his right to demonstrate exactly what he meant.

As soon as they'd left the Estabrook residence, they had called Terri and informed her that they had something that might, if you squinted at it, resemble a lead. She said she'd been putting off the interview with the clown, for obvious reasons, but she'd do her best to set up a meeting as soon as possible. She reminded them that their next appointment was still with Oscar Loomis, a twenty-three-year-old stand-up comedian whom they were meeting at the south end of downtown, which made everyone unhappy.

The day had been scheduled to hopefully give the team plenty of time between appointments to go where the investigation carried them, whether that was back to the crime scene, an impromptu visit to one of the involved parties, or even just back to the office to research things and discuss the case. But due to the respective locations of Mrs. Estabrook and Mr. Sambucci, most of their day had been devoured by Seattle traffic.

People talk about New York and Los Angeles when they discuss terrible traffic, but those people are dilettantes. Any true connoisseur of terrible traffic knows that Seattle is something special. In fact, Rutherford suspected that a big part of the reason there were so many environmentalists in Seattle was that the city itself was designed to make you hate your car.

In a normal city, traffic patterns ebb and flow over the course of the day. In Seattle, everybody appears to be trying to get everywhere at all times. This is the end result of nearly a hundred years of fate playing a game of three-card monte with the civic planners, which the planners always lost.

At first, the planners built roads to make it easy for people to get downtown, where the jobs were. Then Boeing built a big plant to the south, in Renton. Over time, roads were built to bypass downtown and get south.

Then Boeing built a terrifyingly huge factory to the north, in Everett. Planners compensated just in time for Microsoft to take over the world from their campus in Redmond, to the east, putting unanticipated pressure on the two floating bridges that got people over Lake Washington, one of which sank.

Later, Starbucks put its global headquarters at the south end of downtown and Amazon did the same at the north end. Thus, in Seattle, there's always a reason for a large number of people to be driving in any direction.

The only worse place to drive, in Rutherford's opinion, was downtown Portland, Oregon, which was just as congested, but the locals dealt with it by simply continuing to drive at seventy-five miles per hour, despite being bumper-to-bumper with the other cars around them.

The team had lost all possible slack time in their schedule, so Rutherford's only respite from driving and interviews was lunch. Rutherford, Max, and Sherwood ate at a TGI Fridays, which was, alas, the most appealing option available to them at lunchtime. Sloan chose to stay in the van and eat the sack lunch she'd brought with her, but she remained in contact via the party line, and was still an active participant in the conversation, not that she did much talking. Neither did Rutherford, for that matter.

Professor Sherwood spoke at length about Africanized bees. He explained how they had been deliberately brought to the Americas for study, and that if the queen had been kept contained, they never would have spread. The hives that were used for the research had a grate with small openings that allowed the workers to enter and exit, but which were too small for the queen to fit through. It was an elegant solution, and it worked beautifully right up until an assistant saw the grate and thought, *That's stupid. That grate's making it hard for the bees to get through.* He removed it, the queen escaped, and Africanized killer bees had been spreading in the Americas ever since.

Sloan and Rutherford found the story interesting, but Max claimed that it was just a cover story, that Africanized bees were just one volley in a longstanding campaign of biological warfare in which countries tried to sabotage rival states by introducing invasive species. Other notable offensives in this war included kudzu, cane toads, lovebugs, zebra mussels, Argentinian devil ants, and Hermann Goering's über cows.

Their meeting with Oscar Loomis was to take place in Pioneer Square, on the southern edge of downtown Seattle near the sports stadiums—both decent traffic draws in their own rights.

Rutherford eventually managed to find a parking space, and the team made their way to the appointed address, which turned out to be a pizza-by-the-slice joint just off First Avenue.

When they arrived, Oscar Loomis was already sitting alone at a large booth, pounding the keys of an old MacBook that seemed held together by a thick mass of stickers. He was in his early twenties, and he dressed like it. He wore sneakers, jeans, a T-shirt, and a cheap leather jacket. It was essentially the same outfit Rutherford was wearing, but whereas his clothes were deliberately worn and shabby, Loomis's garments looked as if he was trying to keep them clean, and failing.

"I'm sorry we couldn't meet at my condo," Mr. Loomis said, through a mouthful of pizza. "I'm having the carpets steamed. When you throw a lot of parties, the floors take a beating."

Watching Loomis eat, Rutherford doubted that he needed any help making a mess. He also doubted that he owned a condo, or had carpets that were worth steam cleaning.

Professor Sherwood had accompanied them this time, as his bees had enjoyed ample relaxation time in the van. Max asked him if he'd like to scan Mr. Loomis, but Sherwood looked down at the readings on his wand and laughed. "Don't have to. I've already got all I need from this distance."

Loomis had changed his order from a slice of pizza to a pie after Max had communicated that the team would be picking up his tab to thank him for his time. But when Rutherford helped himself to a slice, Loomis still looked at him like he was a thief. Rutherford glared back as he slowly ate the slice with his mouth open. For the first time, he enjoyed playing the lowlife character he'd been assigned.

Max glanced at his smartphone to check his notes. "You say that the late Dr. Arledge and one of his patients, Molly Belanger, were having an affair."

"No, I said they were screwing," Loomis corrected him.

"What's the difference?" Max asked.

"*Screwing* is a funnier way to put it. It has a hard *K* sound in it."

"And was their relationship common knowledge among the other patients?"

"They tried to keep it quiet, but it was pretty obvious from the way they were acting. Of course, I saw right through them. To be a comedian, you have to understand the nuances of people's behavior. They didn't keep it a secret for long. Eventually, the truth came out."

"How did it come out?"

"I told everyone. Derek had just gotten mad and stormed out again. Everyone was all uptight. So I defused the tension by making a joke about the doc screwing the clown."

"Did that really seem appropriate?" Max asked.

Oscar Loomis rolled his eyes. "Look, man, I'm a comedian. I say what other people are thinking. Everyone in the room was thinking about the doc screwing the clown, so I brought it out into the open so we could all laugh about it."

Professor Sherwood asked, "If you were the only person who had it figured out, how could everyone have been thinking about it?"

Loomis said, "Well, they were thinking about it after I told them."

"I'm sure they were," Max said. "And did you all laugh about it?"

Loomis scowled. "Not technically, but I got a reaction. A groan's as good as a laugh."

Sloan's voice in the team's earpieces said, "If that's true, he's gonna be a huge star."

Max nodded almost imperceptibly, then asked, "How did everyone feel about the doctor having an affair with one of his patients?"

Loomis shrugged. "Eh, I dunno. Never really asked. Probably seemed weird to them."

"How did you feel about it?"

"I was stoked! Are you kidding?"

Max looked perplexed. He turned to Rutherford and said, "Stoked?"

"Happy. Excited," Rutherford explained.

Max turned back to Loomis. "Why were you *stoked*?"

Loomis looked amazed. "You have to ask? My therapist was screwing a clown! That's gold! I got, like, five minutes of material out of it! All I had to do was run through all the therapist clichés. *Please lay on this couch. How does that make you feel? What does this stain look like to you? Sorry, time's up for this session.* It writes itself! Then you've got the clown clichés to play with! *Did they do it in her car, and if they did, how many other clowns were in there? They could have a three-way in the glove box. Did she have to redo her makeup to make her O-face? Did any part of her anatomy honk?* It's killer stuff!"

The team looked back at him, stone-faced.

"I word it all much better in the act. Would you like to see?" Loomis opened his MacBook and started sliding his fingers around its touchpad. "It's on my YouTube channel. Here, let me pull it up."

Max said, "No, thank you. That's really not necessary."

"Are you sure? I've got the page up right here."

"Yes," Max assured him. "I'm afraid we're here on business."

Loomis looked down at his computer, dejected. "Yeah, that's cool," he said. "I understand. You can just look at it tonight when you get home." He started to close the computer, but stopped, squinting at the screen. He looked at Rutherford, then back at the screen, then back at Rutherford. Then, again, back at the screen.

"Hey, man, is this you and Derek?" he asked, spinning the computer around on the table. On the screen, Loomis's YouTube start page was displaying videos shared by various feeds he followed, one of which was represented by a freeze-frame of Rutherford and Derek Sambucci, seemingly dancing some sort of demented tango. The text beneath the thumbnail said: "SAVED BY BEES!!!"

"Yes," Rutherford said. "That's me."

Loomis turned the computer back around and jabbed at the touchpad. Tinny grunts of effort played over the laptop's speakers.

On a whim, Rutherford checked his personal phone, which he was still carrying in addition to his new work phone. There was a text from Vanessa. It was three periods in a row. He thought, *It's a bit confusing, but I'll give her a break. It's not easy to text someone an icy silence.*

Oscar Loomis muttered, "Whoever shot this needs to learn to hold their phone sideways when they film stuff."

On the computer, a distant, hollow voice called out, "Stop, or I'll release the bees!" Then there was a buzzing sound, and a look of terror formed on Mr. Loomis's face, both of which intensified as the video progressed.

The buzzing ended abruptly. Loomis said, "Wow."

"The bees helped," Rutherford said, "but I don't know that they saved me. The fight had only just started and I—"

"This says the video was posted today," Loomis interrupted, "and you've already got nearly fifty thousand views."

"Really?" Rutherford asked, wincing.

Loomis said, "Yeah. Hmm. Hey, I can help you make the most of this. You should repost this with a link to one of my videos. I could whip up some bee material. I'll look through my notebook. We can film it here with my phone. It'll take like five minutes, tops. I gotta have something about bees. You throw a *click here* link on your video and I'll do the same back to you. That way we both get something out of it."

"It isn't my account," Rutherford said. "I didn't post the video."

"Oh. That sucks. You should get your own video out there. You gotta use this publicity, man! I could interview you. You—helmet chick—you don't say much anyway. You could film us with the webcam on my computer. I'll do a quick intro, welcome everyone to the Oscar Loomis show, and then I'll ask you questions about how you were getting your ass kicked until the bees saved you."

Rutherford said, "No thanks," in a tone that told Oscar Loomis not to ask again.

"Fine," Loomis said. "Whatever. I don't care. It's your decision. Doesn't matter to me." He glanced at Max as if looking for an ally. "Some people just don't recognize an opportunity when they see it."

Sloan said, "And some people see them where they don't exist."

Max, who was much more accustomed to Sloan's silent commentary than Rutherford was, looked at Sloan and said, "That's true." Loomis thought Max was agreeing with him, when in fact he was joining Sloan in a joke at the comedian's expense. To drive this home, Max winked at Rutherford before turning back to Loomis.

Max asked, "What did you think of Dr. Arledge?"

"He seemed a good guy, for a clown fetishist."

"Were you finding his treatment helpful?"

"Yeah, I did, until he cured me."

Max's eyebrows raised in surprise. "He cured you of your social disorder?"

Loomis rolled his eyes. "I never had a disorder. I just had the wrong idea. I used to try to be *always on*. See, I had this theory that if I just went around constantly making any joke I could think of all the time, at least one out of three of them would be good enough to get a response. That meant that if I made three jokes a minute, I'd make people who met me laugh, or at least smile, once per minute. I figured people would only remember the jokes that worked and they'd think I was the funniest guy they knew."

"But you don't think that anymore," Max said.

"No, the doc showed me that for every one joke that worked, two just made people uncomfortable, and people found the discomfort more memorable than the laughs."

Max nodded. "That must have been a hard lesson to learn."

"Yeah," Loomis said. "But I'm glad I did. It showed me that I can be funny, but my real gift is for making people squirm. I took my act in an edgier direction. I make my audience confront the truths they'd rather hide from. I hold up a mirror and make the audience take a good long look at what I see."

Rutherford said, "You do five minutes of jokes about clowns and therapists having sex."

"That's what I see. Or saw. I didn't really see it. You know what I mean."

Max nodded. "Yes, we understand."

Sloan added, "If he had seen it, you know he would have filmed it and put it on YouTube."

SIXTEEN

Rutherford was physically exhausted after fighting Derek Sambucci in the morning and fighting the van for the rest of the day. The whole team was exhausted mentally after dealing with Oscar Loomis. That said, Sloan, Max, and Rutherford all agreed that the alleged affair between the victim and one of his patients was something they needed to follow up on. It was their first good lead.

"Is it really?" Professor Sherwood asked. "I mean, I know it's juicy and all, but is an affair really a motive for murder? I'm married, and if my wife stepped out on me I'd be angry, but I wouldn't want to kill her."

"That's good for you and your wife," Terri said, her disembodied voice being streamed into their ears via the party line. Rutherford had already gotten used to the idea that when the group was in transit, Max would activate the party line as a matter of course, and any time a team member was on the clock but not involved directly in business, they were expected to participate.

Terri continued, "If my husband messed around on me, I'd at least beat the crap out of him. Or I'd probably have Rutherford do it. It'd be good for his image."

"And not everyone is even as understanding about this as Terri," Sloan said. "Infidelity definitely works as a motive, not just for Mrs. Arledge, but for everyone else involved. Mrs. Arledge could very well have killed him for having an affair, or had someone else kill him. The clown could have killed him for ending the affair. The clown might have a jealous boyfriend. Mrs. Arledge could have an angry friend. Men who cheat seldom only cheat once. Maybe he had another mistress, and that got him killed for any of the reasons I just ran through."

Another thing Rutherford was growing used to was hearing Sloan talk about unpleasant, violent subjects using a cheerful voice that had probably been designed to read web pages to the blind.

Professor Sherwood was a scientist. He understood bees. Sloan and Rutherford had backgrounds in law enforcement, Max was ex-Dutch Secret Service, and Terri had been in corporate management. They all understood motives for murder, so they recognized that Ms. Molly Belanger, aka *the clown*, had one, and had caused several, so even though they were all tired, and would have liked to call it a day, they were not displeased to hear that Terri had managed to set up a meeting with her.

Molly Belanger was twenty-six. She'd graduated with a BA degree in theater from UW. She wasn't married and had no kids. She lived in a pleasant upper-middle-class suburb, on a pleasant upper-middle-class street, with her pleasant upper-middle-class parents, both of whom came to the door when Max rang the bell.

In some climates, homeowners have to work to get plants to grow and be healthy on their property. In Seattle, it is a trick to restrict plant growth to only those species that you want, and to keep them from becoming so robust that they cover the house and blot out the sun. In older suburbs like the one where Molly Belanger lived north of downtown, just beyond the University District, the plants didn't look like decorative items chosen to beautify humanity's artificial habitat. Instead, the neighborhoods looked like small clearings carved with great difficulty into a lush, green forest. The accoutrements of people's lifestyles seemed to have been shoehorned in between the plants wherever there was room. Even the expansion seams in the road stood out, highlighted by a line of bright green flora that was either a very grasslike moss or a particularly mosslike grass.

Rutherford was second in line behind Max as they approached the door, walking single file up several stairs and a steep concrete path across a small lawn clogged with shrubs.

Sloan said, "Hey, Rutherford. Could you please come back here for a minute?"

Rutherford said, "Sure," then stepped aside to let Professor Sherwood pass, which put him in front of Sloan.

"What can I do for you?" he asked as he kept walking.

Sloan said, "Come back here, which you've already done."

"But what do you want?"

Sloan stopped walking and leaned on her cane. "For you to come back here," Sloan replied in her clipped, synthetic voice. She did not look at him as she answered. She was watching Max, who was already ringing the bell. Sherwood stood behind and beside Max. Sloan stepped backward so that she would be behind Rutherford.

Rutherford was confused, but when the door opened, he started to understand. Mr. Belanger answered the door. Mrs. Belanger stood behind him, but only their heads were visible to Rutherford, meaning that only his head, not his scruffy clothing, was visible to them. Standing behind Rutherford, Sloan was practically invisible. To the Belangers, the team was composed of a kind-looking older gentleman with a charming accent, a dignified older black man in a windbreaker, a younger man standing behind them, and maybe someone else.

Unsurprisingly, they were immediately invited inside.

Just as unsurprisingly, the older couple's smiles dimmed as Rutherford passed them and died entirely when Sloan entered. Rutherford was all the more grateful that his e-cigar was too contaminated with puddle water to use.

The living room was the architectural equivalent of the one sweater everyone has that's been worn so much and is so comfortable that you would never consider getting rid of it, even though it's outdated and unattractive. Just looking around the room made Rutherford feel happy and sleepy. A young woman was standing in the center of the room. She had chestnut hair, a pretty face, no makeup, and a dour expression. Mr. Belanger introduced her as his daughter, Molly. She was the person they'd come to see.

Mrs. Belanger offered to take their coats. Max and Sherwood took her up on the offer, but Rutherford, knowing that he had a firearm the size of a tire iron and a small machete strapped to his rib cage, said, "No, thank you."

She turned to Sloan, froze for a moment, watched as Sloan made no effort to remove her jacket or her gloves, then offered, "Can I take your . . . hat?"

Sloan shook her head no.

Mrs. Belanger tried to hide how uncomfortable this made her, but didn't do a very good job. She stammered noncommittally for a moment about how that was okay while she hung Max's wool coat and Professor Sherwood's windbreaker on a coatrack.

Sloan said, "I feel bad, the poor dear. Please be extra nice to the parents. Their daughter may have brought this on herself, but they didn't." Her computer voice was excellent at conveying basic information, but it was as bad at expressing sympathy as it was at sarcasm.

Everyone knew why the team was there, so the clown's parents brought in a couple of extra chairs and then excused themselves. The father glared at Rutherford and Sloan as he left. Molly Belanger sat in a recliner Rutherford suspected was usually the domain of her father. Max and Sloan sat on the sofa and twisted sideways to see her, as the couch and the recliner were at right angles to each other. Rutherford was seated opposite her, so he didn't have to twist, but he and Sherwood were sitting on wooden dining room chairs, which was less than ideal. Sherwood distracted himself from the hardness of his seat by waving his wand in the direction of various items around the room. After a few moments of this, he looked at the readings, turned to Rutherford, and whispered, "It's just as I thought. Potpourri."

After a brief explanation of who they were, what they wanted, and why she shouldn't pay any attention to Professor Sherwood or the buzzing noise she was hearing, Max started the interview. Sloan advised him to start slow, so he did.

"Your parents seem lovely."

"Yeah," Molly said. "They're great."

"I understand you live here with them, yes?"

"Yeah, just until I pay off my student loans. Which, at the rate I'm going, will be five years after I die of old age."

"What did you study?"

"I have a degree in theater."

Max nodded. "And is that where you became interested in clowning?"

"Yes. Before college I was like everyone else. I heard the word *clown*, and I thought of children's parties, kiddy shows, and horror movies. I had no idea the rich history clowning has. You sound like you're from Europe."

"The Netherlands," Max said.

"Then maybe you know, but the traditions of clowning go back hundreds of years. A lifetime could be spent learning about the face paint patterns alone. Clowns use makeup, costume, pantomime, music, props, set decorations, dance, and magic tricks all together at once, and all just to make people laugh at them. A clown is noble. A clown is an artist. And yet their hope is to be seen as a fool. I just can't think of anything more fascinating than that."

"You make it sound wonderful," Max said. "Where do you perform?"

"Mostly at children's parties," she said, sourly. "I tell knock-knock jokes and make balloon animals. It pays the bills."

Max nodded, paused, then said, "Well, Ms. Belanger, I'm certain you know why we're here."

"Yes," she said.

"You were a patient of Dr. Daniel Arledge."

"Yes. And I'm sure you want to ask about our, um, *romantic relationship*," she said with palpable disdain.

"Sadly, I do have to ask."

"I'm sure," she said. "Look, the first thing you have to know is that Dan was a good man. He was. He didn't pursue me. He didn't come on to me. All he did was help me with my problems, then I got carried away."

"And that's how it started," Max said, nodding sagely.

"No, that's not how it started. That's the whole story." Her demeanor had changed quickly from sad to frustrated. She didn't seem angry at Max. She seemed angry at herself for not being able to get her point across. She glanced at Sloan and Rutherford as if looking for assistance, but of course they were as in the dark as Max was.

Max took a deep breath, then said "I know that it's not really anything you want to discuss, but we might understand better if you started at the beginning. I promise, we aren't looking for scandal. We're just trying to figure out what happened to Dr. Arledge."

Molly flopped back in the recliner, sighed, and said, "What the hell. The real story isn't nearly as bad as what everybody thinks anyway. I've been in therapy since I was in high school. My parents worried I might be getting an eating disorder, and they wanted to stop it before it started."

"Did you develop an eating disorder?"

"No, but now we'll never know if I would have or not, which is fine with me. Anyway, I stayed in therapy. In college, I had difficulty connecting with other people. People would show an interest, but they'd always end up pulling away after they got to know me. I was referred to Dr. Arledge because he was studying the kind of problems I was having, and I started the therapy."

"And was it helpful?"

"Very. Particularly group therapy, once I figured out what was going on. After the third session I went to Daniel to complain. I felt like no one else was really opening up. I heard a lot about Erin's kid, and Oscar tried out plenty of material on us, but they never really said anything about themselves. Derek would throw everything back in your face if you asked a question, and even making eye contact with Dustin was a mistake. So Dan . . . Dr. Arledge asked why I thought they might be behaving that way, and I said that they were trying to avoid exposing themselves. He said, 'As if they are hiding behind masks.' I said 'Yeah, exactly.' Then he said, 'Like a clown might.'"

Max slapped his knee and exclaimed, "Ongelofelijk!"

Rutherford looked perplexed.

Sloan said, "I think it's Dutch for *wow.*"

Molly also looked perplexed.

Rutherford said, "It's Dutch for *wow.*"

Molly said, "Thanks."

Sloan said, "You're both welcome."

Max shook his head. "It's not Dutch for *wow*. Dutch for *wow* is *wauw*. Ongelofelijk means something like *incredible*."

"Incredible is right," Molly said. "I realized that I was doing the same thing as them. I wasn't just hiding as a clown . . . I was hiding behind clowning. I didn't think I was interesting, and I wanted people to think that I was, so I'd always steer the conversation toward the most interesting thing I knew about, which was clowning. But I see now that most people don't find clowning interesting. Guys don't strike up a conversation with me because they want to know about clowns. They want to know about me, but all I wanted to talk about was clowns."

"That's quite a realization to have about yourself," Max said.

"And it goes way beyond me. I paid extra attention at group therapy after that and I realized why the other patients' lack of ability to talk about themselves was so off-putting. People don't want to share with someone who won't share back. You don't want to be genuine with someone who's being fake. Oscar in particular gave me the creeps, because he didn't really talk, he just tried out his act and disguised it as conversation."

"That would be unpleasant," Max said.

"And I think that's why no entertainer makes people more uncomfortable than clowns! We clowns try to elicit a genuine reaction from people while showing them nothing but an artificial persona! People find it excruciating! Think about it—the two most famous clowns are known for being sad and being evil."

Sloan nodded and said, "Pagliacci and the Joker."

Rutherford frowned at Sloan, then turned to Molly and said, "Pagliacci and John Wayne Gacy."

Molly blanched, and said, "No, I was referring to the Joker." She did not hear the artificial voice say, "Laughing."

"Really," Molly continued, "Daniel and I agreed that I'd gotten what I needed from group already, but I kept going because it was so interesting. It's a really powerful idea. It could improve the lives of every clown, or it would make for a good thesis if I ever decide to do a doctorate."

"Wouldn't that have interfered with the book he was planning to write?"

"No, he was going for a broader, pop psychology *Why do my relationships fail?* sort of thing. I planned to focus specifically on improving clowning."

"So you continued to attend group meetings for your own research," Max said.

"Yeah, and I'd stay late to compare notes with Daniel."

"And that's when you started getting close?" Max asked.

"He was so wise and kind," she said. "And he was the first man I had really connected with in so long. One night, I got overexcited and I kissed him. He kissed me back for about half a second, then we both realized what we were doing and stopped. I was so embarrassed. I just got out of there."

Professor Sherwood said, "But it grew from there." He had stopped scanning with his wand and was following the conversation intently.

"Oh, now you're interested," Sloan said.

"No, it didn't grow from there. It ended there. That was it! One night I got stupid and kissed an older man. That was the end of it. I came back to group the next week because I thought it would look funny if I didn't, and I was still getting a lot out of it anyway, but Daniel got all uptight when he saw me. That made me act stiff, and that was all it took for the others to figure out that something had happened."

"But if what you say is true, nothing happened," Max said.

"Not nothing," she corrected him. "*Practically* nothing, and that makes a huge difference. Anything we could have said would have sounded like an excuse, so we didn't say anything, and the whole mess gave certain members of the group the thing they wanted most—something other than their feelings to talk about."

"Did Mrs. Arledge ever find out?"

"Yes."

"How?"

"Someone sent her a link to Oscar's YouTube clip. Five minutes of nonstop jokes and occasional laughter, all at our expense."

"Was she angry?"

"I assume she was. Some comic she'd never met was telling the world that her husband was having sex with a clown. Even I know it doesn't get more embarrassing than that."

SEVENTEEN

The consensus was that Molly Belanger was not a suspect. She had no clear motive, and she didn't seem capable of murder. Of course, both of those things could be faked, but she also had one of the greatest alibis in the history of criminal investigation. She had performed at a children's sleepover party in South Tacoma on the night of the murder, and while she'd left the party at a little after 8:45 p.m., there was no way she could have made it to Dr. Arledge's office in time to kill him. The team fed Terri the details and she managed to confirm the alibi before they even made it back to the office. She even sent them photos taken by the parent who'd hired Molly for the event.

"Yes," Max said, looking at his smartphone. "Even with her clown face on, you can tell it's her."

"Still," Professor Sherwood said, "the photos are kind of weird."

"What?" Rutherford asked. "What is it? Do you think they could be faked?" He was unable to look at the photos because he was driving the van.

"No, the photos seem genuine," Max said. "But there is something off-putting about her face."

"It's that she's smiling," Sloan said. "She's got a big toothy grin in every photo, but she's wearing sad clown makeup."

"Yes," Professor Sherwood said. "It's incongruous."

Sloan said, "It warps her painted-on frown into the shape of a bandito moustache."

"And the smile makes the sad-looking eyebrow paint seem more worried," Max added.

Sloan shook her helmet. "She has the ability to make clown makeup even more disturbing. That's a real accomplishment. That should be her doctoral thesis."

"So where does that leave us?" Sherwood asked.

Sloan said, "I still like Olivia Arledge."

Max nodded, and Rutherford said, "Same here."

Sherwood said, "And by *like,* you all mean you think she's the murderer."

Sloan said, "She has a clear motive, and her alibi doesn't rule out the idea that she's involved, just that she did the bludgeoning herself."

"I'm not arguing with any of that," Sherwood said. "I'm just saying that you people's definition of the word *like* seems a bit askew."

Rutherford drove the van into the parking garage and up the ramp. Negotiating the inside of the garage hadn't been fun in a car. In the van, it was far worse. Every beam threatened to scrape the van's roof. Every bumper threatened to crease the van's side. At every landing he was sure the van would grind its undercarriage. When the false wall opened, he nosed the van into the office's attached garage with all the relief of a test pilot who'd been forced to glide to a landing after engine trouble.

"You realize that now you're going to have to back out tomorrow," Sloan said.

"Yes," Rutherford said, "but that's tomorrow. The point is that I didn't have to back in tonight."

They piled out of the van and went into the office. Terri and Albert were already at the conference table, ready to discuss the day's progress while the field team put away their stuff and prepared to go home for the evening.

Terri smiled and asked, "So, Rutherford, how was your first full day on the job?"

"It was interesting. I think it went well."

"You're right," Terri said. "It went very well. *Saved by Bees* has been all over social media this afternoon. Mr. Capp wants you to know that he's very pleased."

"That's, uh, that's great," Rutherford said, "but I was talking about the progress we made on the case."

Terri said, "I know, but that's Sloan's job, not yours. It's good that you're anxious to help, but your main job is to get attention and drive the van, and you got a lot of attention today. How was the van?"

"Terrifying."

"Well, if you're going to crash it, try to do it somewhere it'll be caught on video. Albert, do you think you could rig one of your quadcopters to follow the van at all times?"

"No," Albert said. "The battery life wouldn't allow it. I could put in a dash cam, no problem."

Terri said, "That'll do."

Rutherford said, "Oh, Albert, while you're working on that, I should probably give you these." He reached into a jacket pocket and pulled out his broken phone and the e-cigar he'd been given only that morning. He held the cigar with the tips of two fingers as if it were a dead rodent.

"What exactly happened to it?" Albert asked.

Rutherford shrugged. "It fell out of my mouth while I was chasing Derek Sambucci, and I think one of us may have kicked it."

"We know it landed in a puddle," Max added.

"Next to a garbage can," Sloan said.

Max nodded. "Yes, it was next to a garbage can, but I'm not sure that the puddle was water."

Sherwood moaned. "I wish you'd told me before I set my wand to download the day's chem, GPS, and time-stamp data! I could have given the bees a sniff of it."

Albert furrowed his brow and peered at the scraped and soiled cigar, but he didn't take it just yet. "Really Rutherford, you've only had it a day. Must you destroy every piece of equipment you're issued?"

"I'm sorry, Albert. I really didn't mean for this to happen."

Albert looked chagrined for a moment, then said, "Oh, it's okay Rutherford. Don't worry about it. It's the cheapest piece of equipment we gave you, and it probably only needs to be cleaned."

"Oh. Good," Rutherford said, confused for the second time that day by the sudden shift in Albert's attitude. "Are, um, are you going to take it from me then?"

Still studying the e-cigar, which hung suspended from Rutherford's fingertips, Albert took the broken phone. "Yeah, sure," he said. "Just let me go get some rubber gloves." He got up and disappeared into his lab.

"Professor Sherwood, do you have a moment?" Terri asked as Sherwood strode past, toward the garage.

"I need to transfer the van hive upstairs so the bees can get out and stretch their wings. They've been cooped up most of the day."

"I think they can wait a moment. I have the lab report on the hammer. Wouldn't you like to be here when I tell everyone what it says?"

Sherwood nodded and smiled, but continued toward the garage, saying, "Thanks, but don't wait for me. The bees are my priority. Besides, I know what the lab report will say." He shut the garage door behind him as he left.

"What did the lab find?" Sloan asked.

"Exactly what he said it would. No trace of blood. They agree that the handle looks as if it was deliberately wiped down, but they've ruled out the hammer as the murder weapon."

The door to the garage swung open. Sherwood came in carrying a Plexiglas box festooned with disconnected hoses and big, beefy hinges. The box was also full of live bees. The team regarded him with a mix of respect, resentment, and fear.

"I take your silent stares to mean that the crime lab agreed with my bees. Excellent. I think we can all agree that after ruling out an irrelevant piece of evidence yesterday and saving Rutherford from a public beating today, they've earned their evening's rest." Sherwood hummed "Flight of the Bumblebees" as he ascended the stairs to the roof deck.

The rest of the team chose to move on with business.

"While you all were driving back here, I took the liberty of setting up another interview with Olivia Arledge so you can ask her about her husband and the clown," Terri said. "She's expecting you tomorrow morning at ten. She thinks you have some follow-up questions about her husband's background."

"Good," Sloan said.

Terri said, "I know I don't have to tell you, Sloan, but Rutherford, I'll remind you to be careful of how you approach her. If she's not involved, we don't want to offend the victim's widow, and if she is, we want her to think she's getting away with it."

Rutherford nodded and said, "Yeah, that makes sense."

Albert returned from his office wearing surgical gloves. He handed Rutherford a fresh smartphone and took the soiled e-cigar, which he carried back into his workshop.

"Besides," Rutherford said once this transaction was complete, "Max will do most of the talking anyway. I just have to drive there, which is enough to worry about."

"I'm sure it is," Terri agreed. "But you'll have had more practice by then."

Rutherford said, "Yeah. Wait, what?"

Terri said, "You've still got to drive home tonight and back in tomorrow."

"No," Rutherford said, "I'm taking my Miata home."

Rutherford was so focused on establishing the fate of his Miata that he didn't notice when everyone who wasn't him or Terri walked away from the conversation with feigned nonchalance and great speed. Like anyone who has ever worked in an office environment, they had mastered the skill of staying close enough to an argument to hear it while getting far enough away not to be part of it.

Terri shook her head, looking genuinely sorry. "Rutherford, we talked about this. You don't have a Miata anymore. You agreed to sell it to Mr. Capp for market value plus ten percent."

"Yeah, so you say, but I haven't had time to look it up in the contract."

"Well, sadly for you, Mr. Capp's other employees are a bit more proactive. They came and took the Miata just after lunch."

"What? They can't do that! Not yet! I haven't signed it over! No money has changed hands."

Terri held up her hands in an attempt to get Rutherford to calm down. "Yes," she said, "That's true. They did take a liberty by hauling the car away, and you're right to be upset. But let's calm down and be honest with ourselves. You are going to sign the car over, and we both know it. Even if you were of a mind to cause a fuss about this, you don't want to face the law firm Mr. Capp keeps on retainer. You'd be lucky to get out of it without ending up owing him money. It's just a car, and you're being paid generously for it. I have the title in my office, along with all of your other stuff from the trunk and the glove box. As soon as you sign it, I'll start the paperwork on your payment."

"How long will it take to get my money?" Rutherford asked, slowly shuffling to Terri's office.

"A couple of weeks."

"Great, that part they take their time on."

"It will be paid by direct deposit, so there's that."

"Yeah, but suddenly I feel a lot less comfortable about Capp having my bank information."

Before he walked into Terri's office, Rutherford looked out across the main room. Albert was in his workshop, hopefully boiling the cigar in Lysol. Sherwood was still up on the roof deck. Sloan was seated, hands resting on her cane in front of her. Her head was bobbing slightly, as if she was talking. Max was at his desk, doing some indistinct busywork Rutherford couldn't make out, but his head was nodding, and he was saying, "Yes. Absolutely. I agree." Then Max looked up sharply and made eye contact with Rutherford from across the room. After a moment, the older man smiled and nodded. Rutherford returned the gesture uncertainly, and went into the office.

If Rutherford was being honest, Capp had done him a huge favor by taking the car. It ran fine now, but the head gasket was shot, and he had to feed the car oil to keep it moving. Capp was paying far more for it than it was worth. Still, it was the principle of the thing. When one is tricked into accepting a favor, it feels like a trick, not a favor.

Without Rutherford needing to ask, Terri pulled up a PDF of his contract and highlighted the clause that dealt with the car. He read it, agreed that it seemed ironclad, and requested that she e-mail him a copy, which she did. Then Rutherford signed away his car, picked up the shopping bag full of documents, old sunglasses, greasy pens, and loose change that had inhabited the car's many nooks and crannies, and left Terri's office. When he opened the door, he found Max, Albert, and Professor Sherwood waiting for him.

"Rutherford," Max said, "I'd like to invite you to my house for a little dinner and drinks to welcome you to the team. Sloan can't make it, but Albert and the doctor will be there. You're invited, of course, Terri."

Terri demurred, saying she had to get home to her kids.

Rutherford said, "That's nice of you guys, but I'm really tired."

"We won't be doing anything strenuous, I promise you," Max said. "We're all tired as well, and Professor Sherwood and I are both much older than you. If we have the energy, surely a healthy young man like yourself can make it."

Rutherford mumbled, "I really should spend the evening reading my contract."

"If you didn't read it before you signed it, I hardly see the rush now," Max said.

Rutherford really wanted to go home and rest, but three of his coworkers, people he hadn't even known two days before, and with whom he'd be working for the foreseeable future, were putting themselves out to do something nice for him. His job required him to dress and act like a jerk, but that didn't mean he had to be one.

"Of course I'll come," he said.

Max said, "Wonderful!"

Rutherford glanced at Albert and Professor Sherwood and asked, "Would either of you like to carpool? Looks like I have the van anyway. There's plenty of room."

Albert said no so abruptly that it startled Rutherford.

Sherwood smiled and said, "It's kind of you to offer, but I have to ride in that van with you for work. That's more than enough, thanks."

Rutherford said, "Okay, well I guess I'll see you all tonight."

"Indeed," Max said. "At seven o'clock. I'll e-mail you the address."

Rutherford said, "Great." He stood smiling at the three men, who stood smiling back. Feeling someone's gaze on him, he glanced over his shoulder and saw Terri standing there, looking pleased. Sloan was still sitting in the same chair, but was looking his way.

Rutherford cleared his throat, then said, "Well, um, I guess we should all get our stuff and go home then."

In Rutherford's earpiece, Sloan's voice said, "We will. First, we want to watch you back the van out of the garage."

EIGHTEEN

Rutherford's body was driving to Max's, but his mind kept returning to the case. He agreed with Sloan that following the victim's personal problems could lead them to people who had motives, and in the end, the killer, but he wasn't happy about it. He wanted to be a detective so he could make a difference, protect the weak, and put away evildoers, not because he wanted to paw through people's dirty laundry. If he'd wanted to do that, he could have started a gossip blog.

Rutherford would have preferred to follow a lead arising from good old-fashioned physical evidence, but the crime scene had yielded nothing of use. If they had the murder weapon, it would have probably given them some clues. Even without fingerprints and DNA, the weapon itself might have served as a lead, just as the sex toy had done in the other case. But they didn't know what had been used to kill the doctor. Instead, they had an item that was definitely not the murder weapon, which was just as definitely not useful. If they wanted to find the real murder weapon, they'd have to figure out how the killer had disposed of it.

If we solve the mystery of the weapon's disposal, Rutherford thought, *we can solve the mystery of the weapon. Then, maybe, we can solve the mystery of Dr. Arledge's murder. That's three mysteries deep. No wonder Sloan is investigating his relationships instead.*

Max's home was in north Seattle. Rutherford threaded the massive van through the dark, narrow streets, careful not to hit any of the concrete planters that sat in the middle of intersections, doing the same job as an unsightly four-way stop. The idea, of course, was that drivers would naturally slow down and become more vigilant while steering around the planters. It would have been a much more efficient and attractive arrangement if not for the four bright yellow yield signs that warned drivers not to deliberately plow into the planters or other cars.

Rutherford didn't know what he'd expected Max's home to be like, but he knew that he hadn't expected a medium-sized Victorian on a corner lot. For a moment he doubted that he had the right address, but then he saw Professor Sherwood climbing out of a nondescript champagne-colored sedan. He was wearing a button-down shirt, Dockers, and sensible shoes: the exact same thing he wore to work, except he didn't have his blue B-9 windbreaker. Instead he wore a plaid coat.

Rutherford knew he was supposed to stay in character whenever he was going to be seen in public, but he'd bent the rules, wearing oxford shoes, well-creased slacks, and a nice shirt beneath his leather jacket. He knew Terri and Capp wouldn't be happy with him, but he was on his own time, and if they wanted him to act rebellious, they couldn't be too upset about him bending the rules.

The two men nodded to each other from a distance, then walked toward each other, meeting on the sidewalk in front of Max's house.

Sherwood held up a foil-covered plate with both hands and said, "Brownies. Made with fresh honey."

Rutherford said, "Was there any doubt?" He held up the bottle in his hand and said, "Wine. Red. I didn't know what he was serving, so I took a chance."

"I'm sure it'll be fine," Sherwood said.

"You ever been here before?" Rutherford asked.

"No," Sherwood said. "I found it okay, though. You?"

"Yeah, no problem finding the address. When I got home I ran an extension cord out my window to throw a little more juice into the van, just to be sure I had enough to get here and back. I still don't really know what the range on that thing is."

They looked at the van in silence for a moment, then looked at each other, then at Max's house, then back at each other again.

Finally, Rutherford said, "Shall we?"

They walked up the steps to the porch and rang the bell. Max opened the door. It was a dark, chilly Seattle evening, and the interior of Max's house, which emitted a pleasant, yellowish light and a gust of warm air, was instantly inviting. The sound of big band music and Max's welcoming smile only added to the effect.

Max took their coats and hung them on a coatrack, invited Rutherford and Sherwood to make themselves comfortable in the living room, then took the brownies and the bottle and spirited them away to the kitchen.

Max's living room looked exactly as the outside of the house suggested. Cheerful yellow paint, framed by white sills and moldings. A big, soft-looking couch and a smattering of mismatched chairs. There was no TV visible, but there was a fairly serious-looking stereo on a purpose-built rack.

Albert was already there, crouched on the floor, going through a stack of records. He barely had time to say hello before Max was back. Max offered them drinks: the only alcohol in the house was Rutherford's wine, but he had tea, cocoa, or Sunny D.

Less than five minutes later, Max was back again, everyone had a drink, and they embarked on a pre-dinner tour of the house.

The floorboards groaned as the four men rounded the corner from the living room to the hall. Sherwood tilted his head to one side slightly and bounced up and down a bit, listening to the squeak. "I love these old houses," he said. "You can't fake character like this."

"No," Max said, "And the best alarm system you can have is a creaky old house. Wires can be cut and sensors can be disabled, but everyone has to walk on the floor. If you're alert, that's all the warning you need."

"But what if you're asleep?" Rutherford asked.

Max said, "Just because I'm asleep, doesn't mean I'm not alert. Besides, when the day comes that someone serious decides to eliminate me, there will be no warning. The building I'm in will just explode."

"The whole building?" Sherwood asked.

"Or car," Max answered. "It's easier to make it look like an accident that way. It's ironic, but the more damage is done, the more people want to believe it just happened on its own."

Albert asked, "What about any people who are in the car or building with you at the time?"

Max shrugged. "One would hope that my killers will choose a moment when I'm alone."

Albert nodded, a bit relieved.

"But they probably won't," Max said. "A few innocent bystanders will only make it seem more likely that it was an accident."

Sherwood said, "Well that's…" He trailed off, formulating the end of the sentence, and eventually said, "Terrifying."

Rutherford said, "The scariest part is that you didn't say *if*. You said *when*. Like it's inevitable."

Max shrugged again. "Everybody has to die someday."

"Yes," Rutherford agreed, "and from what you've said, it sounds like we'll be doing it together."

This would have been a good place for Max to say something reassuring. Instead, he said, "This is the TV room. It's also where I keep my computers." Max motioned to a small room with an old couch along one side and a TV mounted on the opposite wall. Beneath the TV, a small desk held three identical laptops.

"Why three computers?" Albert asked.

"I use one to do the things I don't mind the government knowing about. The second uses an encrypted connection. I use it to do the things I want the government to think I don't want them to know about. The third I use to do things I actually don't want the government to know about."

Rutherford asked, "Is it encrypted more securely?"

"No," Max said. "It's not encrypted at all, but it is spoofed so that it appears to belong to someone I don't like. It probably doesn't work, but the NSA respects you more if you make an effort. This way, gentlemen."

He pointed out the bathroom, and they walked past the open door to his bedroom, which looked completely normal. Then he led them upstairs to the attic.

"And this is where I exercise," Max said.

Most of the upper floor had been converted into one large room. The house's roofline caused the walls to slant in at a steep angle, but there was still plenty of room to move around. The floor was padded, but the only physical fitness equipment Rutherford could see was a set of hand weights. He had expected more, somehow.

Albert must have felt the same way, because he asked, "Is this all you use to train? A few weights?"

"I have them and my own body weight for resistance. What more would I need?" Max asked.

"I don't know," Albert said. "I just pictured more stuff."

"You mean like a NordicTrack?" Sherwood asked.

"No," Albert said. "I don't mean like a NordicTrack."

Rutherford said, "I think he means a rack of samurai swords."

"Yes! Thank you! Exactly!" Albert said. "Or one of those wooden dummies you punch and hit with your elbows."

Max laughed. "First of all, I almost never have the opportunity to fight with a sword, so brushing up my kendo skills would be a waste of time and effort. Second, if you think punching a piece of oak will make you a better fighter, you're welcome to try. In my experience, broken fingers and fractured elbows tend to hinder one's effectiveness in a fistfight. I spent a lot of time when I was younger studying different martial arts from Japan, China, Israel, Russia, everywhere. I've trained enough. These days, I mainly stay physically fit, practice my tumbling and some repetitive motions to keep them in muscle memory, and if things turn violent, I do what comes naturally."

Rutherford said, "When things turn violent, what comes naturally for me is to cringe."

Max said, "I've seen you in a violent situation, and that's not true, but if it were, it might be because you have experience cringing. That's what's in your muscle memory."

The room fell silent as Rutherford, Albert, and Sherwood thought about the implications of what Max had just said. Everybody could think of at least one occasion on which they'd acted less brave then they might have liked. The idea that these failings were attributable to a learned response and not an inherent weakness was both empowering and depressing.

Rutherford thought, *Is cowardice a habit? And if it is, am I brave enough to break it?*

Max's words had sent his guests down an introspective rabbit hole, which was probably good for them but bad for his dinner party. Luckily, Max then uttered a single sentence so powerful that just saying it was enough to distract most people, if only momentarily, from most problems.

"So," Max asked, "who's ready for dinner?"

* * *

The four men entered the dining room, which was really just the far end of the living room with a hint of an arch to delineate the two spaces.

The sturdy oak table was surrounded by six chairs, a few of which matched. Four places were set with plates and silverware, none of which matched. A thick manila folder full of papers sat in the middle of the table like a centerpiece.

Max said, "I've got tomato soup and cheese sandwiches for everyone. Albert, if you'll help me finish with the preparations, I'm sure Rutherford and Professor Sherwood will find a way to amuse themselves. By the way, that folder there is Megan Sloan's background information. Help yourselves."

Rutherford couldn't believe his ears. Sherwood seemed equally amazed. They each had a seat and dug into the file, handing each other documents as they finished with them.

The paperwork was arranged in roughly chronological order. It started with a birth notice photocopied from a newspaper called the Modesto Bee. Some quick math told Rutherford that Sloan was thirty-nine. Photocopies from various local and student newspapers showed sixth-grade Sloan placing third in a statewide spelling bee, eighth-grade Sloan being a valuable member of the basketball team, and twelfth-grade Sloan consistently making the honor roll and graduating in the top five percent of her class.

Next there was enrollment paperwork for UCLA, and a transcript of grades that demonstrated a high intelligence but an increasing lack of interest. The college record ended abruptly after a year and a half.

Then there was the entrance paperwork for the police academy. A photo showed a physically fit young woman with black hair cut in a short, easy-to-maintain style, large brown eyes, and an enthusiastic smile. She graduated near the top of her class (much higher than Rutherford had, and his group had been considerably smaller). She worked her way up to detective with astonishing speed. Her evaluations glowed so brightly you could read by them.

The last two items in the folder were newspaper clippings. The second to last was a story about a murder suspect who managed to take two detectives by surprise. The suspect killed one detective immediately and knocked out the other one, whom she restrained and held hostage. The captive detective's name was withheld. A standoff ensued, in which the suspect claimed to have a small amount of high explosives and a huge tank of gasoline that she would use to kill herself, her hostage, and any police who entered the building. The police believed she was bluffing, but they were proven wrong.

The final clipping was a short item about one of the survivors of the ill-fated standoff, the detective who had been taken hostage. They stated that the detective was female, but her name was still being withheld. She had miraculously survived both the initial explosion and the resulting inferno, which had claimed the lives of six of her fellow officers and the perpetrator. She had sustained grave injuries from the fire and flying debris, and was being released from the hospital after countless skin grafts, reconstructive surgeries, and multiple amputations.

Dinner was served while Sherwood and Rutherford were still reading, and it was eaten in silence until they were done. Max also gave them generous glasses of Rutherford's wine without them asking. Rutherford laid down the final clipping, then took a bite of his sandwich as he thought about what he'd read. He glanced at Professor Sherwood and asked, "Did you know any of this?"

"No," Sherwood said. "The team's been together for months, but I joined them less than three weeks ago."

Then he looked at Albert and Max. "But you both knew."

"Yes," Max said. "I don't agree to protect someone unless I know exactly who it is I'm protecting."

Albert said, "I've known a little longer because I helped source and curate her prosthetics."

For the next twenty minutes, Albert described Sloan's various prosthetics, and used his smartphone to demonstrate through photos and videos how they functioned. Cutaway diagrams showed the helmet's silent cooling and anti-fog systems, and the dual microphones that fed binaural sound into her one functioning ear.

He showed them a mockup of what Sloan saw through her helmet's heads-up display. Most of the information that was conveyed on the screen of the team's standard issue smartphone was channeled through Sloan's field of view on one of four floating, semitransparent blocks of text and simple graphics. She navigated through the interface using a joystick and button that were hidden in the decorative details of her cane's silver grip.

Rutherford let out a slow, quiet whistle. "Man, I see what Capp meant about the team developing technology he can sell. If you can market a heads-up display like that, I'd buy one tomorrow."

Albert said, "A heads-up display is the easiest thing in the world to make. Next time you're driving, put your smartphone on the dashboard so you can see the screen reflected in the windshield. That's all a heads-up display is. Of course, it needs to be visible in daylight and impervious to most weather, but that's not hard. Sloan's is made of a few mirrors and cheap screens designed for the fronts of flip phones. The software is the tricky part, and since hers is a simplified phone interface, even that wasn't too difficult. I could make one for you easily, but you'd have to wear a big shield over your eyes all the time. For Sloan, that wasn't a problem."

Moving on, Albert explained the combination of vibration sensors and digital cameras that deduced her speech by monitoring the movements of her damaged vocal cords, her tongue, and her lip.

Rutherford said, "Lip?"

Albert said, "Lip."

He moved on to the legs. He showed that one leg was artificial from just below the knee, and that the ankle joint was computer controlled. It sensed where her balance was and determined whether she was standing or walking. The other foot was a partial rubber sculpture of a foot that slipped over what remained of her original appendage, fulfilling some of a real foot's functions.

Albert had a physical example of the prosthetics used for her hands, so he set the phone down for a moment and showed Rutherford and Sherwood what looked like a minimalist sculpture of a finger. The pads on the finger's gripping surfaces were solid, but the rest of the finger and all of its joints were made from tiny metal struts. At the finger's base, where it would have connected to the rest of the hand, there were two thin metal braces.

"Hers is built into her glove," Albert said. "The remaining portion of the original finger fits into the base of the prosthesis and supplies mechanical force."

He held the braces with one hand. With the other, he grasped the finger between its two lowest joints and gently twisted. All of the other joints flexed as well, causing the finger to curl just like a natural finger would.

"Isn't that cool?" Albert asked.

"Yeah it is," Rutherford said. "Can I see that?"

Albert handed him the apparatus, and Rutherford worked its mechanism several times, marveling at how natural the finger's movement seemed.

"How many of these does Sloan have?" Sherwood asked.

"Several on one hand. A couple of them are tied together because there wasn't enough left of one finger to operate on its own."

Rutherford offered the finger to Sherwood. When he refused, Rutherford handed it back to Albert.

"Here every cop in town thinks she's some sort of kung-fu badass," Rutherford said, "when actually it's amazing that she can walk naturally."

"Yes," Max said. "It is funny in a way. If anyone ever actually hit her, she might fly apart like she's made of Tinkertoys, but just by getting up every morning she proves that she's stronger than any of us."

Sherwood said, "I understand why she needs the voice sensors. I think I do, anyway, but why just feed it to our earpieces? Her not talking throws a lot of people off. Why not play her voice out loud for everyone?"

Albert said, "Do you really think that her robot voice coming from a speaker mounted on her chest would freak people out less?"

"She realizes that she's going to make people uncomfortable no matter what she does," Max said, "so she's decided to do it on her own terms and use the discomfort to her advantage. She put a lot of thought into the look of her clothing and her helmet."

Albert said, "You know how poisonous animals are brightly colored to warn off predators? Some nonpoisonous animals evolve to be the same colors. We've done everything we can to make Sloan look like someone you don't want to mess with because we hope to make people not want to mess with her."

"Of course," Max said, "it has the opposite effect on some people, but that's what I'm here for."

"You really are here just to help and protect Sloan?" Rutherford asked.

Max said, "Yes. We all are. Capp built the team around her. I'm here to help and protect, as you say. Albert's here to maintain her equipment and outfit her team. Terri's here to manage the administrative tasks that would be a waste of her time. You're here to drive her, chase runners, and arrest perpetrators for her, and call attention to her work."

"And me?" Sherwood asked.

"You're here to help in any way you can, and besides, allowing researchers to piggyback on her work means that Capp gets a fat tax deduction, which helps keep the whole thing running."

"That explains why we're all here," Rutherford said. "But why Sloan? Why'd Capp choose her? There are other detectives available who would require less support."

"I've asked that question many times myself," Max said.

"And what's the answer?"

"If one has a satisfactory answer to a question, one usually doesn't ask it *many times*."

Rutherford said, "I see."

"Any more questions?"

Rutherford and Sherwood looked at each other, then Rutherford cleared his throat, looked down at the table, and said, "I kinda have to ask. Can you give us more of an idea what she looks like, you know, now?"

"Sure," Max said. "I have a photo." He pulled out his smartphone and started scrolling through his photos. After a moment, he said, "Ah, here's a good one." He turned his phone around to show the others. Rutherford and Sherwood leaned in close. It was a photo of Max and Sloan standing next to each other. He had his arm around Sloan. She was holding her cane and wearing the same all-black pants suit and full-head helmet she always wore.

"That's what my friend Megan Sloan looks like," Max said. "That's the image she chooses to show the world. As far as I'm concerned, asking to see her without it is the same as asking to see her naked. I'll let it go this time, but if you ever ask me what any of my female friends look like naked again, there will be consequences."

Rutherford mumbled, "I'm sorry," and looked down at the table, avoiding Max's and Albert's eyes.

Max put the phone away. "Don't worry about it," he said. "I would have probably asked in your place. It's natural to be curious. Just don't do it again."

"I won't."

Max said, "Good. Now, are there any more real questions?"

"I have one," Professor Sherwood said. "Why are you telling us all this?"

Albert said, "Because she asked us to."

"She's worked with you for a little while now, Doctor," Max said. He looked at Rutherford, who still felt ashamed, and said, "And she expects to work with you for a long time to come. She wanted you both to know what her situation is. She just didn't want to be there when you were told."

* * *

Max's front door opened, once again draining warmth and light into the chilly dark. Rutherford, Professor Sherwood, and Albert walked out of the door and down the steps. When they reached the bottom, they looked over their shoulders and waved at Max, who waved back and shut the door, cutting off the flow of warmth and light.

Sherwood carried his empty brownie plate like one would carry a Frisbee. Rutherford was empty-handed. There had been wine remaining in the bottle, but he left it with Max, even though Max didn't drink and would likely pour it down the drain. Rutherford was already paranoid about driving the van. It was still prone to the occasional accidental burnout, and with a lack of engine noise it was surprisingly easy to find himself speeding. The last thing he needed was to get pulled over with an open container of alcohol in the car.

The three of them reached the sidewalk. It was still and quiet, the kind of night where the entire world seems to be saying, *Shhhh.*

"Well," Rutherford said, "That was something."

"Yes," Professor Sherwood said. "Something."

Rutherford said, "You know, I had a theory or two about Sloan. I thought she'd been a cop. I figured she'd been burned and there was vocal cord damage or something. It turns out I was right, but there was so much more to it. I feel like . . . I dunno. Like being only a little right is worse than having been totally wrong."

"Yeah," Albert said. "You still don't know the whole story. Neither do I. You never do. Nobody's ever really what you expect, are they? I mean, take Max. He's the closest thing I'll probably ever meet to a real James Bond, and he's nothing like I would have expected."

Rutherford remembered the conversation he'd had with Albert about James Bond and Q. Somewhere in the back of his mind something clicked. Before he could comment, Professor Sherwood spoke.

"Gentlemen, what I'm about to say may sound a bit condescending, but please know that I'm saying it with envy. You're both still young."

The three of them stood in silence for a moment. Rutherford broke the silence, saying, "That's true."

"See, what you just said was meant condescendingly," Sherwood said, "but that's fine. As you get older, you're going to find, as I have, that nobody is ever as cool as you expected them to be." He gestured toward Rutherford and Albert. "Cops, tech whizzes," he pointed at the house, then at himself, "karate men, scientists. Nobody will ever match your expectations. It's easy to become disappointed in the people you meet, but really, you should be disappointed in the quality of your own expectations. Once you learn to let those expectations go, you'll see that while the people you meet are never as cool as you expected them to be, they're actually much cooler than you ever imagined."

NINETEEN

The next morning started with a quick conference call to update Vince Capp on the team's progress.

"So the victim was having an affair with a patient," Capp said. "That's good stuff."

Terri said, "Not really, it turns out, sir."

The team was sitting around the conference table while Capp's image loomed over them from a large flat screen. Capp was wearing a sport coat and a button-down shirt, but behind him there was sparkling water, a white sandy beach, a blue sky dotted with puffy clouds, and thick tropical foliage. Rutherford would have written it off as a fake backdrop if every aspect of the image wasn't moving, and the breeze wasn't occasionally blowing Capp's hair.

Sloan said, "The young woman involved says it wasn't much of an affair. It consisted of one kiss and a whole lot of shame afterward."

Capp muttered, "Been there."

Rutherford hadn't asked, but it was clear that Sloan's voice was tied into the videoconference feed.

Capp shrugged, "So it's a he said-she said. The press loves those."

"As far as we can tell, sir," Terri said, "the victim told the same story, and that's not likely to change now that he's been murdered."

Capp's lips scrunched into a dissatisfied frown. "Hmm. A she said-he's dead." Capp's eyes got wide. "Ohh! *She said. He's dead.* I like that! That'll make a good title for something." He looked to the side of the camera and said, "Capture that."

A distant voice said, "Captured, sir."

Capp looked back at the camera. "Okay. So he at least kissed a patient, which isn't great. Do you think the patient killed him?"

Terri said, "No, sir. She has an alibi."

"How about the wife?"

"We have to assume she was humiliated, if she knew. She may even have feared that her husband was going to leave her. She has motive. And, in a divorce he'd have taken probably over half of their money. With him dead, she only has to pay for his funeral. That said, she does have an alibi," Terri explained. "She could still be involved. We just won't know until we look into it further, so that's what we're going to do."

"Good. That sounds sensible. Glad you guys are on it." Capp was still talking, and his eyes were still locked on the camera, but his mind had obviously started to drift. Now that he had the information he wanted, he was ready to move on to the next important task of the day.

"Let's see, what else? Oh, I'd like to say *well done* to Rutherford and Professor Sherwood. That video of you getting your butt stomped and the bees coming to the rescue was huge for a few hours yesterday. It got a lot of attention. It even got some reflected traffic for that comedian patient of Dr. Arledge's.

He slapped together an interview with the guy the bees attacked and got a few thousand views out of it. Anyway, my marketing wonks have looked over the bee fight and the sex-fist chase, trying to figure out what they have in common."

"They were both embarrassing?" Rutherford said.

Terri started to shoot Rutherford the stink eye for copping an attitude, but stopped when Capp said, "Yeah, that's what they said! Good catch. They say both clips had some extra element that humanized you and made the viewer pity you, the suspect, or both. We're thinking that it's not enough to chase a guy and wrestle him to the ground. If possible, one of you needs to land in dog doo when you do it. I know that you can't really plan these things. People run when they run and they fight when they fight, but if possible I need you to try to make sure these things have a hook. You know what I'm saying?"

Rutherford said, "I think so."

"Good man," Capp said. "We're all pretty happy with how things are going. The marketing team thinks it may be time to go public soon. Also, Professor Sherwood, the Seattle PD has expressed an interest in having you go work with them when your time with us is finished."

"That's great news!" Sherwood said.

"I know. They're particularly interested in using bees for riot suppression."

Max said, "That's nightmarish."

Capp nodded. "Which is why I'm sure it'll work. Moving on: Rutherford, we're getting closer to finding you a more appropriate place to live. Lots of concepts are being thrown around. We're still going back and forth between whether we want to put you in a trailer or a houseboat."

"You could ask me," Rutherford said. "I could break the tie."

"I hope it doesn't come to that, but we'll keep it in mind as an option. We've also put more thought into your name."

"It's Rutherford."

"Yeah, I know," Capp said. "I mean your nickname."

"I don't have one."

"Exactly. We want to change that. *Rutherford* is good and all, but we want to throw something in front of it occasionally to give it some zip, and *Sinclair* won't cut it. We want something classic and a bit nefarious, but relatable. You know what I mean, something like *Wild Bill Rutherford,* or maybe *Blackjack Rutherford.* Any suggestions?"

Rutherford said, "How about *Wild Bill.* Or *Blackjack.*"

Capp smirked joylessly. "I like the instinct, but save the fake bad attitude for the public, Rutherford, not for me. Understand?"

Rutherford mumbled a quick, sincere apology. Even though his attitude had not been fake, he was not a rude person by nature, and felt genuine shame for having been so openly disrespectful to his employer.

Capp said, "Don't worry about it," but much of the joy had drained from his demeanor. "If you come up with any real nickname ideas, we're all ears. The best we've come up with so far is *Iron Fist Rutherford.* I'm not in love with it, though, because the fist you're famous for fighting with wasn't iron, it was chrome, and *Chrome Fist* just doesn't sound as tough. It seems too showy."

The conversation gave Rutherford much to think about as he drove to the widow Arledge's home after the meeting. Aside from his future housing issues and the prospect of having to answer to *Iron Fist* for the rest of his career, his mind was also occupied by driving and the fact that his newly cleaned e-cigar tasted like hand sanitizer. He used the party line to ask Albert why that was. Albert told him that he'd cleaned the device by wiping off all visible material, then slathering it in hand sanitizer and leaving it overnight, which certainly explained the taste. These were the things that felt like problems to Rutherford right up until the moment a warning light appeared on the van's dashboard.

It lit up as the van was entering a tunnel that had no shoulder on which to pull over. The tunnel led to a floating bridge, which also lacked any shoulder. Rutherford had no choice but to keep up with the flow of traffic.

Luckily, Albert was still listening to the party line when Rutherford said, "I've got a warning light! Albert, what's it mean?"

"What does it look like?" Albert asked.

"Is it a picture of an engine?" Sloan asked.

"No. It's not. It's . . ."

He looked down at the dash, then back at the road. "It's two vertical lines and a poofy bit at the top. It's either a chef's hat or a mushroom cloud. Is it a chef's hat, Albert? Please tell me it's a chef's hat."

Albert said, "It's nothing to worry about. It just means you have to descale the boiler."

"Do I have to wear a chef's hat to do it?" Rutherford asked.

"It's not a chef's hat," Albert said. "And it's not a mushroom cloud either."

"Then what is it?"

"It's supposed to look like a plume of high-pressure steam being vented."

Back in the van's second row of seats, Max said, "Megan, I'm sorry, English is not my first language. What is the difference between a cloud and a plume?"

"I think a plume rises more violently," Sloan said. "And I think enough steam would still form a plume that's shaped like a mushroom, so in a sense it is a violent mushroom cloud, but of steam instead of smoke. I don't know if that makes any real difference."

"Oh, it makes a big difference," Professor Sherwood said. "Smoke is only dangerous if you inhale too much of it. Steam can scald you quite badly on contact."

"Not helping!" Rutherford said.

Sloan said, "We know."

Albert's disembodied voice added, "Rutherford, it's nothing. Really. Sometime within the next couple of days, while the van is parked, you just need to set it for a descaling cycle. The van is like anything else that boils water. Minerals will build up and make the boiler less efficient. Descaling just breaks up the minerals into tiny bits and blows them out the smokestack. That's why all Stephenson-drive cars have that big pipe pointing straight up."

Rutherford said, "I thought those were just for show, to remind people of trains."

"Nope," Albert said. "They are functional. They vent the superheated steam in a safe direction. Don't worry about the descaling. It's a quick, perfectly safe procedure."

"Can we do it in the garage when we get back this evening?"

"No! Sorry, uh, yeah, we can't do it indoors. No, tonight you'll have to find an open space, like a parking lot, to do it in."

"But it's perfectly safe."

"Yes, as long as you do it in a large, open space."

So now, on top of everything else, Rutherford had to think of a suitable spot where he could run the van he didn't want through some sort of controlled detonation. He didn't mind, or rather he minded quite a bit, but at least all of his various issues left no room in his mental RAM for the things he'd learned about Sloan.

He'd spent the entire morning in the office using every bit of willpower he possessed to keep from watching her and trying to deduce which ankle was electronic and which fingers were mechanical.

Sloan, for her part, had more or less kept to herself all morning. Rutherford understood that she had wanted the basic information shared to avoid awkward questions, but the silence this morning had felt plenty awkward.

I guess in her situation a certain amount of awkward is unavoidable, Rutherford thought. *The only thing she can control is what kind of awkward she gets, and how much of it.*

It seemed she'd had enough awkward silence for the time being, because she started talking again as they approached the widow Arledge's house.

"I've been thinking," Sloan said in her upbeat, synthesized voice. "I'd like to try something different today. Rutherford, have you ever played Good Cop, Bad Cop?"

"We role-played it at the academy," he said. "They never let me be the bad cop."

Max smiled. "The fact that you needed them to let you might help explain why that is."

Sherwood said, "Wait, are you really talking about doing Good Cop, Bad Cop? Is that a real thing that cops even do? Isn't it kind of obvious?"

"Only if you're obvious about it," Sloan said. "You can put a suspect on the defensive while getting them to open up at the same time. But if you want it to work, you have to tone it way down. It's more like Sympathetic Cop, Suspicious Cop. It takes some acting ability to sell it, usually, but I figure that since the two people who will do most of the talking look like Santa Claus and Serpico, we're already halfway there. Oh, and Rutherford, go heavy on the cigar."

Sloan explained her plan. Max would do most of the talking, with Rutherford adding an occasional follow-up question or statement. She would direct them as necessary. Beyond that, it was just a matter of keeping a certain attitude in mind. She wanted Max to seem as if he believed Mrs. Arledge was innocent in all things, and she wanted Rutherford to seem as if he doubted every word out of her mouth.

When they finally arrived, Max rang the doorbell. Sloan stood behind him. Rutherford, at Sloan's request, brought up the rear. Since Sherwood had already thoroughly scanned the house and his presence would just add another variable, it was decided that he would listen in from the van.

Olivia Arledge answered the door, greeted Max warmly, and invited them in. She showed signs of discomfort at the sight of Sloan, but that was no surprise. Rutherford stopped her dead, or rather, his e-cigar did.

"I'm sorry," she said, not sounding sorry. "You can't smoke in here."

Rutherford fought every natural urge he possessed, and instead of apologizing and telling her that he understood, simply looked her in the eye and said, "I'm not." He sucked in on the e-cigar, making the LED in its tip glow, then exhaled a medium-sized blue-white cloud to punctuate his point.

Mrs. Arledge hadn't expected an outright denial. She tried to hide her annoyance, but she stood her ground. "Yes, you are smoking, sir, and I don't allow it in my house."

"It's not smoke," Rutherford said. "It's a fake cigar. It just puts out water vapor. Think of it as a very small humidifier." He drew another mouthful of vapor and exhaled it through his nose.

Max cleared his throat uncomfortably. Sloan said, "Well done," but of course, Mrs. Arledge couldn't hear that.

"You're welcome to *humidify* outside if you must," she said. "You'll have to stop if you want to stay in here."

Rutherford smiled and said, "Of course." The rest of the team worried that he'd dropped character and reverted to his natural, more apologetic personality. He took the e-cigar from his mouth and said, "It's your house." One's natural expectation would be for Rutherford to grind out the cigar and discard it, but of course it was an electronic cigar, and he could not simply toss it aside. He held the cigar in his hand, as if he could put it back in his mouth at any moment.

Mrs. Arledge said, "Could you please put it away?"

Rutherford said, "No need. It's only activated if I inhale through it. It can't put out any vapor otherwise."

"Well, would you please put it in your pocket?"

Rutherford said, "I'd rather not. It's covered with spit." He held up the mouth end of the cigar so Mrs. Arledge could see. Her eyes narrowed and her voice lowered, but she said, "Just come in."

Max thanked Mrs. Arledge for agreeing to see them again. He promised that they wouldn't take much of her time. She told Max that she was happy to do anything to bring her late husband's killer to justice, but she eyed Rutherford warily as she said it. She led them into the sitting room where they'd questioned her less than forty-eight hours before, and they all had a seat.

"Mrs. Arledge," Max said, "we've been interviewing your husband's patients, and we need to ask you a few questions."

"Yes," Mrs. Arledge said with a sigh. "I suppose you do."

"And I bet you know what we're going to ask about," Rutherford said.

"I assume it's about the clown."

Rutherford nodded.

Mrs. Arledge turned back to Max and asked, "Have you spoken to her?"

"Yes," Max said. "We have."

"What did she say?"

"That she thought a great deal of your husband."

Mrs. Arledge laughed once, humorlessly, through her nose.

Max chose to clarify. "I mean that she admired him and was grateful to him. According to her, what other people have called an affair never went beyond a single kiss, and they both felt terrible about it afterward."

Mrs. Arledge considered this for a long moment, then sighed. "I suppose she doesn't have much reason to lie about it now."

"Quite the contrary," Max said. "If she lied to make it seem more sordid, she could tell the story to the press and perhaps make some money."

"Yeah, that's probably true," Mrs. Arledge said.

In his earpiece, Rutherford heard Sloan say, "Bad cop, ask her why she didn't tell us." He wasn't going to be comfortable asking it, but it was a good question.

"I'm wondering why you didn't mention it, Mrs. Arledge." As he said it, he gestured toward her, thrusting the cigar as if it were a pointer.

"Because it was humiliating! I found out from a bad comedy video that my husband cheated on me. With a clown! She's not even one of those Cirque du Soleil, sexy-unitard clowns, or even a proper circus clown! She does children's parties! What could be worse?"

Sloan said, "A rodeo clown."

Rutherford nodded silently.

Sloan said, "No, say it. *A rodeo clown.*"

Rutherford gritted his teeth and said, "A rodeo clown."

Mrs. Arledge glared at Rutherford until Max drew her attention.

"I'm certain it was very hard for you," Max said. "I don't blame you for not wanting to talk about it, but that was the kind of information we would have liked to know when we were looking for suspects."

"Why? Do you think she killed Dan?"

Max didn't say *no,* but he subtly shook his head while he said, "We're investigating various possible suspects."

Mrs. Arledge muttered, "Investigating possible suspects." She looked Rutherford in the eye and said, "You think I killed my husband, don't you?"

Sloan said, "Soft pedal it."

Rutherford exhaled heavily and said, "We're just trying to follow the logic."

She turned back to face Max. "I couldn't have done it. I was with friends."

Max threw Rutherford a fake reproachful glance, then leaned forward, rested an elbow on his knee, and looked Mrs. Arledge in the eye. "Yes, we know that. We're not saying you weren't. It's just that, logically, you could be involved without having actually committed the crime."

Mrs. Arledge looked more insulted than hurt. She turned away from Max, who had said the thing that insulted her, and rolled her eyes at Rutherford, whom she clearly blamed.

"*Involved*," she said. "Like what? You think I hired a hit man or something?"

Rutherford poked his cigar at her and said, "That's an interesting idea."

Mrs. Arledge said, "Please, I wouldn't even know where to find such a person. Craigslist?" She turned back to Max. "I love . . . loved my husband. I was angry with him, but I didn't want him dead. I'd already punished him. I made him miserable for a couple of weeks, and I may have held it over him in arguments, but that's all."

Sloan said, "Press her on the financial angle."

Rutherford said, "There are other possible reasons." He worked through the angles on the fly as he spoke. "Maybe you thought the clown was just the beginning. If he left you, you would've gotten half of everything at best. If he died after he retired, you would've gotten all of his retirement savings. That's better. But, if he died *before* he retired, before he signed the practice over to Dr. Shaw, then you'd own all of your combined savings, the practice, the building, and all of the money his partner has paid toward it. And that's exactly what has happened, isn't it? Of course, Shaw could sue, but you could throw some money at him to keep it from coming to that. Extortion is usually cheaper than lawyers."

Olivia Arledge shook her head in disgust. "I've already told my attorney to draw up the paperwork to sign the practice over to Tyler." She turned back to Max. "It was the right thing to do. He's already worked so hard and paid so much money."

"That's very fair-minded of you," Max said.

"He offered to keep paying for the two more years he and Dan had agreed on, but that price was based on the value of the practice with Dan at the helm until he retired, not . . ." She trailed off, trying not to lose control of her emotions. When she had her grief back in check, she said, "Not gone. His name was a big part of the draw. Now that things have ended this way, it has to be worth less."

Max said, "I think you're right. You think very highly of Dr. Shaw, don't you?"

She nodded. "Dan did too. He even tried to bring him in on his book. When they published, his name would have been attached as a coauthor."

"He must have been excited about that," Max said.

"I'm sure he was. With Dan retiring, it would have set Tyler up as the working authority on those kinds of low-grade social disorders. But I don't think that will happen now."

"Can't Dr. Shaw pick up where your husband left off?"

"No. I mean, Dan kept good notes, and I'm sure they discussed things, but most of the work was still in Dan's head. He wasted all that time hanging around with weirdoes. It's such a shame."

They asked a few more questions and got clear, direct answers. Eventually, Sloan announced that she'd heard enough. Max said their good-byes. Rutherford slinked out of Mrs. Arledge's house as if he was irritated and embarrassed, which took no acting skill whatsoever.

When they got to the van, Sloan said, "That went well," in her chirpy, computer voice.

"So you think she did it?" Professor Sherwood asked.

Sloan said, "No."

"But you said it went well."

"Yes. We learned things. We learned that she wasn't angry enough to kill, that she didn't see a financial motive, that she went ahead and gave the business to Dr. Shaw, and that Rutherford makes a pretty good ventriloquist's dummy."

"I'm glad you're happy," Rutherford said, pulling the van out of its parking space and into the road. "I looked like a complete A-hole."

Sloan's voice in his ear said, "Laughing. Laughing. Isn't that pretty much your job description?"

Rutherford said, "It isn't that funny."

"I agree," Sloan said. "This thing can't differentiate between a full laugh and an ironic chuckle. Albert's working on it."

TWENTY

The team's next stop, both according to logic and Terri's schedule, was to interview the last member of the late Dr. Arledge's therapy group. They drove to his neighborhood, found his address, parked the van, and interviewed him at length. Now they were walking back to the van in a sullen silence, because every step of that process had gone badly.

Traffic over the lake had been predictably wretched, and maneuvering the van around the narrow, confusing, congested streets of Capitol Hill had been a nightmare.

The van's torque-heavy drivetrain made driving on steep hills quite easy, which should have saved Rutherford a great deal of stress. But he was still surrounded by normal cars that were having difficulty, so he couldn't relax. His ability to hold his position and move forward effortlessly did nothing to prevent the car in front of him from creeping backward into the van, or crawling uphill at a snail's pace. Then he got stuck at a three-way stop that, from above, would have resembled a gothic capital *K*.

The intersection of three roads boasted four stop signs. Four vehicles, one of which was the van, reached the intersection at the same time. All four drivers motioned for one of the other three to go first, and they became mired in an intractable battle of wills. No red-blooded Seattleite is ever going to go first and let some jerk in another car think that he or she is more courteous than they are.

The best parking space Rutherford could find was at the back of a paid lot three blocks away from their goal. As he eyed it, he said, "I think this space is as close as we're going to get. Is everyone cool with walking a few blocks?"

He'd said *everyone,* but it was clear that he meant *Sloan.*

Sloan said, "Yeah, I'm sure we're all fine, thanks."

She'd said *thanks,* but it was clear that she meant *don't ever ask again.*

They abandoned the van and made their way on foot to the third-floor walkup of Mr. Dustin O'Reilly.

Dr. Shaw had implied that Dustin's particular antisocial quirk was that he compulsively made comments of a sexually provocative nature. Sadly, that was accurate. From the moment they entered until the moment they left, every word out of the man's mouth either had a smutty double meaning or a smutty single meaning. Rutherford suspected that even if the interview had taken place in the men's room at his old precinct house, someone would still have asked him to tone it down.

They asked questions and received a mixture of roughly forty percent answers and sixty percent increasingly blatant and profane attempts at sexual humor. Eventually Max did remind him that a lady was present, which was a mistake. Sloan's silence and icy demeanor was off-putting to most men, but that was how all women treated O'Reilly. He saw it neither as an insult nor as a challenge, but simply as par for the course, and he wasn't going to let it stop him.

Talking to O'Reilly was an acutely unpleasant, ultimately fruitless experience. Aside from having a solid alibi, he had taken up a great deal of their time, delivered very little information, and left them all with the vague feeling that they needed a bath.

Rutherford shook his head as they continued their trek toward the van. "Don't guys like that understand that the more they talk about sex, the more certain everybody is that they aren't having any?"

"That's the whole point," Max said. "They never stop talking about it because they don't want anyone—even themselves—to know that they're terrified of sex. It's like politicians who get out of going to war when they're young, then spend their careers trying to start wars."

"That's one of your more plausible theories," Sloan said, "but it doesn't help us with the case at hand. We still have no physical evidence, no murder weapon, and a victim nobody seems to have wanted dead."

Rutherford pulled out his smartphone. "I'm going to call Erin Estabrook to tell her that we know about Dr. Arledge and Ms. Belanger. Maybe that wasn't the juicy gossip she was referring to, and she has some other lead we haven't found."

"That's wishful thinking," Sloan said. "But it's the best idea we have."

She answered after four rings, and seemed happy to hear from Rutherford. In the background, he could hear her daughter Brooke singing. Mrs. Estabrook listened as Rutherford quickly explained the major bullet points of what they'd learned about the victim's so-called *affair*. The whole time he was talking, the girl's singing continued. Rutherford realized the song Brooke was singing in the background was "Let It Go."

Mrs. Estabrook confirmed that the affair was the subject she had been unwilling to discuss. She started to apologize for not being more helpful, but interrupted herself, pulled the phone away from her face, and shouted, "Brooke! Mommy's on the phone! I told you, if you must sing that song, at least to do it quietly to yourself!"

"She's watching *Frozen* again, eh?" Rutherford asked.

"No," Mrs. Estabrook said, with a hint of anger in her tone. "She's in the bathroom. Please be sure to thank your friend Max for entertaining her the other day, will you?"

He promised that he would, and as soon as he hung up, he did. It gave them something to laugh about, which they needed.

Rutherford looked far down the path ahead, trying to estimate their distance from the van. The buildings on one side and the row of trees planted at regular intervals on the other made it look more like a tunnel than a sidewalk. His view was obscured by other pedestrians, but occasionally there would be a gap, and through that open space, Rutherford saw three heavyset men in the distance. They were wearing mostly black, and as they made their approach, they were leaning, slouching, and generally taking up as much space as possible.

Considerate pedestrians share the sidewalk with one another. These guys seemed to be the other kind of pedestrian, who claim a stretch of sidewalk as their own and make it clear that they will only allow other pedestrians through if the trespassers show proper deference.

Rutherford wasn't afraid of them. People who truly feared these types of confrontations might move to the city, but they usually didn't stay long. If you did hang around, you eventually realized the best course of action was to just keep moving and not engage. They might shout at your back as you walked away, but they would rarely bother to follow you.

Rutherford didn't look forward to dealing with them, and his heart sank a bit when he realized that they were probably loitering right in front of the entrance to the lot where the van was parked.

It sank further when one of the loiterers looked down the sidewalk toward Rutherford and said something that caused the entire crew to look, then to roust themselves and start walking toward the team.

Max stopped walking. The rest of the team stopped as well. He turned to Sloan and said, "Please send word to Terri that we're about to be attacked."

Sloan said, "On it," and then fell silent. Rutherford could only assume she had stopped broadcasting to the team so that she could talk to Terri without distracting the others.

Rutherford asked, "Are you sure we're going to be attacked?"

Max smiled. "Aren't you?"

Rutherford looked back up the sidewalk. The large men were closer now, and Rutherford could see that the man walking in the lead had a delighted smile on his face. One of the men laughed as he tapped at his phone and put it away.

"Yeah," Rutherford said, "You're right. We're totally about to be attacked."

Sherwood asked, "Then why are we just standing here?"

"Because instead of meeting them halfway, we're making them come to us. It gives us more time to prepare, and they'll be just a little bit more tired when the fight begins."

Professor Sherwood said, "Okay, I understand all that, but what I was getting at is, why aren't we walking away from them?"

"If we turn around and walk away," Max said, "they'll have to run to catch us. They'll either get to us sooner or we'll have to run to get away. Then we'd be tired, and the attack would come from behind, so we'd be at a disadvantage."

Sloan said, "Terri's sending help, and Albert's launching a camera drone."

Max said, "Please tell him not to."

"Why not?" Rutherford asked.

"The idea is to get film of you fighting, not of me protecting you. Besides, these gentlemen seem like the type who might try to catch the drone and hit us over the head with it."

"Albert heard you," Sloan said. "No drones, but he's recording the sound from our phones."

Max smiled. "Good. Okay, don't worry. There are only three of them. I have it under control. Still, as a contingency, is there any way to get the bees involved?"

"I can't call them like they're Lassie," Professor Sherwood said, "But if I can get to the van, I might be able to send them back."

"Good. Rutherford, try to stick close to Sloan."

"Done," Rutherford said.

Sloan added, "Don't worry, Max, I'll keep him safe."

"Good," Max said. "Everyone stay calm and let me handle this."

Rutherford looked up the sidewalk again. The other pedestrians had all but disappeared, guided by some ancient trouble-avoidance flocking instinct. Rutherford now had an unobstructed view of their future attackers, who were only half a block away. They were all wearing black sport coats over black knit V-neck shirts, with black slacks and expensive sneakers. Rutherford would have taken it for an official uniform if the individual pieces weren't different brands, materials, and cuts on each of the men. Instead of one person who was in charge ordering the others to wear a certain thing, it was probably a case of one person who was in charge wearing something, and the other two choosing to emulate him, which actually made a far more powerful statement of subservience than a forced uniform would.

The man walking in the lead was slightly taller than the other two goons, and judging by the way he carried himself, seemed to be the leader. All three of them had big, dumb smiles on their faces. The kind of smile that said *we both know that you're smarter than me, and more successful, and probably a better person, but we also both know that I don't care.*

The ringleader stopped just in front of Max and smiled down at him.

Max stood his ground and smiled back.

For a moment, everything was quiet. Rutherford was waiting for the alpha bruiser to make a move, throw a punch, use harsh language, anything, but he just stood there smiling.

A giant black SUV squealed to a stop on the street, and two more big guys, these ones wearing mismatched jeans, T-shirts, and heavy jackets, leapt out of the car and dropped in behind the other three men.

Now the alpha bruiser felt ready to speak. "Hey old man," he said. "Are you and your grandkids just going to stand there in the middle of the sidewalk?"

Max said, "Yes."

The goon's smile faded for half a second at the unexpected response, but he regained his swagger quickly. He said, "You're in our way."

Max said, "Oh, pardon us," and stepped to one side. He looked to Sherwood, Rutherford, and Sloan, and motioned for them to step aside, which they did.

None of the other group moved.

Max said, "Your way is clear, gentlemen."

The opposition leader said, "We've decided we like it here."

"Oh, good," Max said. "It is a nice spot. Well, we'll leave you to it."

The goon stepped to the side, directly in front of Max. His associates spread out to block the sidewalk.

The lead bruiser said, "You're not going anywhere until we're done with you. You got that, old man?" As he said *old man* he touched his palm to Max's cheek twice, too firmly to be a pat but not quite hard enough to be a slap.

The meatheads blocking the sidewalk perceived the next ten seconds as the calm before the storm. The team spent it listening to Sloan.

"Okay, there's assault and battery in the space of one sentence. We need a distraction. Rutherford, punch the one who's been doing all the talking."

Sloan's directive only took five seconds. Rutherford looking back at her to see if she was serious, and her nodding toward the leader as if to say *get to it*, took up the next five.

Rutherford knew that she was right, but punching the leader wasn't as easy as she made it sound. It wasn't just Rutherford's wish to avoid being pummeled that was at issue. There were actual logistical problems as well. Rutherford's target and Max were standing nose to nose. The rest of the bullyboys stood behind and to the side of the alpha dog. Rutherford was standing behind Max's right shoulder, next to the window of some random small business. Sherwood was beside him, and Sloan was behind them. Rutherford was surrounded, and he had only a small corridor through which he could reach the target, which he didn't really want to hit to begin with.

Rutherford balled up his right fist and held it at head height. He turned his body so that his left side was toward the lead bruiser. He took two fast, awkward, leaping strides around Max, planted his feet, pivoted, and struck the taller man as hard as he could in the face.

Given the height differential and the ungainly nature of Rutherford's punch, it was not surprising that it only barely managed to get the target's attention.

Rutherford threw six more punches in two seconds. All of them landed with all the force of a BB hitting a moving car. Rutherford's *victim* hauled back his fist, then propelled it forward like a meteor aimed at Rutherford's head.

The punch never landed, because Max surprised everyone involved by saying, "Now, now," and lunging toward

Rutherford, ostensibly to separate him from the man he was attacking. By pushing Rutherford away from the larger man, he also moved him out of the path of the larger man's fist.

Rutherford fell backward, hitting the brick façade to his right, knocking the air out of his lungs and the e-cigar out of his mouth, expelling a noticeable cloud of water vapor in the process.

The brute tipped forward, off balance, as his fist connected with thin air. Max said, "Careful," as he placed his hands on the man's torso for support and jabbed two extended fingers into a soft portion of the larger man's side. The lummox fell to the ground, with Max's *assistance*. He lay there, a crumpled wreck at Rutherford's feet, shrieking in pain.

Sherwood saw his opportunity and took it. He sprayed an unidentified fluid on the man writhing in pain on the sidewalk, then darted to his left, between two parked cars and out into the street.

Sloan's plan worked perfectly. If Sherwood had run for it just a few seconds earlier, at least one of the bruisers would have stopped him, but all four of them were so confused, none even tried. They seemed to think that their fearless leader had tripped somehow, and that Max was just a small obstacle between them and Rutherford, who had thrown the first punch, after all, but Max quickly proved to be a larger obstacle than they'd expected.

After helping guide the leader to the pavement, Max's weight was on his left foot, and his torso was twisted around to his right. As the second bruiser approached, Max kept his feet planted, but shifted his weight and rotated his upper body. He said, "Oh, excuse me," as his left elbow struck the man's cheekbone, then his right fist followed, hitting the exact same spot, causing the beta goon to flop to the ground beside his fallen leader.

The third man lurched to his right in a hasty attempt to step around his comrade.

Max said, "Please watch your step."

As the third man found his footing, he also found Max's hand on his shoulder, pushing him slightly in the direction he was already moving, causing his center of gravity to shift beyond his base of support. He quickly moved his right foot to catch himself, then found his left foot swept out from under him. He heard Max's voice say, "Oh, dear," and felt the heel of Max's hand hit him where his skull met his neck.

The third man spun and fell backward, draping himself gracelessly over the second as if the second were a mattress at the end of a hard day. That left only the two backup bruisers from the SUV. They approached Max cautiously after having watched him dispatch three of their group, apparently by accident.

Rutherford stood still for a moment, stunned by the sight of Max doing what Max does, but then he saw motion in his peripheral vision. He remembered a moment too late that the leader of the goon squad wasn't unconscious, just in pain and very angry. He looked down and saw that the leader had risen to a crouch, surveyed the scene, and spotted Sloan.

Rutherford was leaned back against a wall, and because the lead brute was between him and Sloan, he was in no position to stop any attack. Since the attack took the form of the tip of Sloan's cane hitting the attacker's crotch, this was not a bad thing. The attacker doubled over in pain, but continued moving forward as he did so. He retaliated with a backhand that threw Sloan to the pavement.

The leader smiled and started to advance on Sloan, who was now prone on the sidewalk. But when he glanced down at her, he stopped and a stricken look washed over his face. He stood there just long enough for Rutherford to leap between them and pull his sidearm, the TP-82 Cosmonaut gun.

The bruiser changed his focus from Sloan to the massive, three-barreled pistol that was being pointed at him. Rutherford held it with both hands, his right on the handle and his left gripping the wooden forestock, bracing for the kick. In a perfect world, there would have been time to attach the shoulder stock, but then again, in a perfect world, he wouldn't have been in this fight at all.

The bruiser was trying to figure out if it was a real gun.

Rutherford was trying to remember which barrel was set to discharge first. He wanted to fire the shotgun shell full of rock salt if possible, not the more lethal 9mm round. The tracking dart would be completely inappropriate for the situation.

The bruiser must have seen the doubt on his face and mistaken it for uncertainty as to whether or not he could bring himself to shoot his attacker, instead of confusion as to which barrel he should use for said shooting.

The larger man moved toward Rutherford. Rutherford squeezed the trigger, firing from the hip.

He was ready for the noise and the kick, but it was still not a pleasant experience.

It was much less pleasant for his attacker, who dropped to the ground clutching his right shoulder. He rolled around, cursing and moaning. He would need medical attention, but it could wait. He wasn't going anywhere, which was ironic, since Rutherford was pretty sure he'd shot the poor bastard with the tracking dart.

He looked down to inspect his weapon, wanting to see which barrel was smoking, but his eye was caught by a dark object laying on the ground by his foot.

Sloan's helmet.

He holstered his gun, picked up the helmet, and took a moment to plan his next few actions. Then he turned around.

Sloan had picked herself up from the ground. She was standing like a batter at home plate waiting for a pitch, only instead of a bat she held her cane, and instead of a baseball she'd been preparing to hit their attacker's cranium.

Knowing what he did about Albert's work, Rutherford was not surprised to see bright blue sparks snapping and dancing around the cane's heavy silver head and metal inlay pattern as she gripped the cane by its thinner, lighter, lower end.

Sloan looked at Rutherford. He looked her in the eye, handed her the helmet, nodded once, and asked if he could be of assistance. She shook her head no, so he turned around.

He never discussed the incident, or Sloan's appearance, with her or anybody else.

Quite some time later though, an acquaintance of his bought a motorcycle and got a helmet that offered no face protection.

"Consider how your head is actually constructed," Rutherford told him. "Your neck, the back of your head, your brain pan, that's all pretty solid. There's a lot of dense material packed in there. But when you think about it, your eye sockets are just holes that hold your eyes. Your nasal passages are just a big, empty cavity behind your nose. They're connected to your mouth, which is just another big empty space where your tongue lives. Nobody thinks about it, but your face is like a mask. Behind it there's just a big wet emptiness, both physically, and for some people, spiritually."

Rutherford paused for a moment to make sure he had his friend's attention, which he did.

"So say, hypothetically, that you got in an accident and something hit your unprotected face, say here." Rutherford poked him slightly harder than necessary on the left cheekbone. "And say it did massive damage to your eye and the skin of your face, and that it shattered the bones beneath to powder, which can happen. The good news is that you can survive just fine without large portions of your face. The bad news is that you could end up spending the rest of your life with an unhealable hole in your face large enough to store a couple of golf balls."

Rutherford and his friend sat silently for a moment. His friend asked, "Can that really happen?"

"Yes," Rutherford said, with a certainty that convinced the other man that there was a story behind the statement, and that he did not want to hear it.

His friend bought a full-face helmet the very next day.

Rutherford turned away from Sloan, toward Max. When Rutherford had last seen him, Max was squaring off against two larger assailants. Now one of those assailants was unconscious on the sidewalk, partially draped over the other two unconscious men. Max had the other on his knees and was painfully twisting one of his arms with one hand, and one of his ears with the other.

"Why did you do this?" Max asked. "Why bother us?"

"I was paid to," the man yelped. "It was just a job!"

"Who hired you?"

"He did," the man cried, piteously. With his free hand he pointed at the leader, the man Rutherford had shot, who was still clutching his right side, bleeding and wallowing on the ground. "Kirk! Kirk hired me. He said he had a job and needed backup."

"Both accurate statements, I'm sure," Max said. "How about it, Kirk, who hired you?"

"I got nothing to say to you!" Kirk shouted.

Max paused, listening to the world around them, then smiled and said, "We'll see about that."

Seconds later, a loud buzzing filled the air.

TWENTY-ONE

The entire altercation lasted less than two minutes, and that included the prefight threats. The aftermath lasted well into the afternoon.

First, Professor Sherwood had to placate and remove the bees. He had only started the process when the police arrived and ordered him to stand down. He explained that he was removing the bees. They ordered him to resume posthaste.

Once the bees were removed, the police and paramedics moved in to treat the injured (all of whom were on one side of the fight) and take the stories of those who would talk (all of whom were on the other side of the fight).

As this was the first time the team had been on the foul end of an investigation, it was the Seattle PD's first chance to ask some direct questions and legally demand direct answers. Also, in this case, the police were investigating a disturbance involving the team, not being aided in an investigation by the team, so the officers could not be required to sign the usual nondisclosure agreement.

Representatives of Capp's legal team were present, having arrived after the police but before the paramedics. The lawyers advised the team as to which questions they shouldn't answer, but the SPD still got the team members' full names, which meant the days of Sloan being referred to as the ninja were at an end, as was the illusion that Max was the detective, at least once the background check was complete. It was inevitable that this would happen, but Rutherford was the only one who had experienced the SPD's misconceptions from both sides, so he was sorry to see them go. Now, instead of this bizarre cadre of mysterious, exotic experts, they would be seen, at best, as eccentric colleagues.

Eventually, the police announced that they were free to go. They piled listlessly into the van and drove straight to the office.

When they arrived, the entire team met around the conference table to discuss the events of the day.

Max told Terri and Albert, "The men who attacked us were taken to the hospital."

Albert said, "I know," and held up a tablet displaying a map of Seattle with a blinking red dot over one of the local hospitals. "In fact, if I zoom in, we can see that the guy Rutherford shot is still in surgery." He enlarged the image. The map of the city was replaced with a floor plan, with the dot pulsing away in one of the rooms.

Albert turned the tablet back to look at it himself. "Either that or they removed the tracking dart already and left it behind in the OR. I should be able to follow it all the way to the police evidence locker."

"Good to know," Rutherford said. Today was the first time he had shot his TP-82, the first time he'd shot someone with a tracking dart, and, for that matter, the first time he'd fired any firearm at another human being. It was a lot to process.

Terri said, "All the rest of them are being treated for bone breaks or being observed for concussions. I'm just glad you're all okay."

Sloan said, "Yes, although I could stand to swap out this helmet with my spare. One of my HUD screens is broken."

Albert stood up. "You want to go swap it out now?" Sloan confirmed that she did, and stood up as well.

Before they could leave the table, Rutherford said, "Oh, wait one second." He reached into a pocket and pulled out his e-cigar.

"I'm afraid this needs to be sanitized again. This time it ended up in the gutter."

Albert sighed heavily, rolled his eyes, and said, "Really, Rutherford, must you be so hard on the equipment?"

Instead of apologizing, as he had before, Rutherford smiled and said, "That's what you give it to me for. Besides, if I didn't put a little wear and tear on the toys, you might run out of things to do," Rutherford paused, letting tension build for a moment, then said, "in Q branch."

Albert's face split into a wide grin. He was delighted that someone finally got the joke. In a voice that was just on the verge of becoming a giggle, he said, "Really, Rutherford, you're impossible!" He walked to his office workshop with a jaunty spring in his step. Sloan followed silently, but turned to look at Rutherford as she went.

Changing Sloan's helmet took only slightly longer than it would take for any other person to change helmets, and soon she was back at the conference table. Her spare helmet looked like an earlier iteration. It was larger, with a smaller face shield and obvious holes on the sides for the binaural microphones. Albert stayed in his office, but left the door open so he could hear the conversation while he replaced the newer helmet's heads-up display and slathered the e-cigar in more hand sanitizer.

Sloan took charge of the conversation and steered it in a useful direction.

"The bad news," she said, "is that we have two more questions we need to answer. The good news is that the answer to those questions might help us resolve all our other questions. Our two new questions are: *Why did those guys attack us*, and *why did those guys attack us*?"

Professor Sherwood said, "I'm sorry, I think those were the same question."

Sloan shook her head. "The computer didn't convey my change in inflection. I put more emphasis on the words *those guys* the first time, and the word *us* the second time."

The team took a moment to parse what she meant, then moved on to attempting to answer the questions.

"They couldn't have come after us because we were getting too close to the truth," Max said.

"Yeah," Rutherford agreed. "If we've gotten any closer to the killer, it's just because the circle we've been running in has brought us back around near them again."

Rutherford could tell from the looks on everyone's faces that they didn't appreciate the wisdom of his statement, and, indeed, were trying to figure out what it meant.

Rutherford said, "See, say we've been walking in a circle, and the killer's standing near the circle," his voice grew quieter as he spoke, "we would walk away from them, but then we'd come closer again. I could draw a diagram if you want."

Sloan said, "I don't think that will be necessary."

"No, it won't," Terri said. "Because the police have questioned the guys who attacked you, the ones who are in a position to talk, anyway, and I think you'll find what they said pretty interesting."

"So what were they?" Sherwood asked. "Mob enforcers or something?"

"Or something," Terri said. "They're strip club bouncers."

Rutherford moaned. "Is this really the career I'm going to have?"

Terri ignored him. "The thug in charge rents himself out on the side to accompany prostitutes as protection."

Sloan said, "It's like *who watches the watchmen?* Who escorts the escorts?"

"The answer is: *A bunch of meatheads,*" Terri said. "Seems someone contacted one of the young ladies he protects last night through an ad on Craigslist."

Rutherford and Sloan both said, "Craigslist?" In Sloan's artificial voice, it sounded like a statement. From Rutherford, it sounded like a question.

"Yeah," Terri said. "Why? Is that important?"

Sloan turned to Rutherford and asked, "What do you think? Is it?"

Rutherford said, "Probably not, but Olivia Arledge said that she wouldn't know where to hire a killer, then threw out *Craigslist* as an option."

"Interesting," Terri said, "but the prostitute said that the person who called was a male. They've already questioned her. He didn't want to hire her, but asked her if she used a bodyguard and offered to pay whoever she used very well to do a job for him. Said she'd get a finder's fee for putting them in touch. Once the first guy was hired, he recruited the rest of them."

Max hummed disapprovingly. "What kind of person uses the Internet to hire pimps to beat someone up?"

"Not pimps," Rutherford said, "guys who subcontract to pimps. Subpimps."

"The kind of person who doesn't know where else to find violent men for hire," Sherwood said.

"And," Terri added, "the kind of person who pays for the subpimps with a personal credit card."

"It's probably stolen," Rutherford said.

"From a member of the victim's support group?" Terri asked.

TWENTY-TWO

Max, Rutherford, and Sloan walked down the hall toward Oscar Loomis's apartment. The building appeared to have been built in the forties. Seattle had many buildings from that time period. Developers had bought and renovated a lot of them into condominiums, which offered all of the modern amenities with a dose of retro charm.

Oscar Loomis's building, on the other hand, had not been renovated. It still had what people who sell antiques like to call "a patina," but what most people called "decades of wear, tear, and shoddy repairs." The floors were springy. The air smelled of moisture and mold. The carpet was gray, but didn't look like it had started out that color. As they climbed up the three floors to their destination, it occurred to Rutherford that by using the handrail they were only increasing the likelihood that they would all go down together when it broke away from the wall.

Sherwood had entered the building with them, but the bees in his wand went crazy at the first apartment door they passed. The problem intensified with each passing door, and the bees quickly became overstimulated. The professor handed his spray bottle to Rutherford and returned to the truck, where he'd listen in to see if he could be of use.

Rutherford surveyed the dank surroundings and asked, "Is this how a successful comedian lives?"

"I guess it depends on how he measures success," Max said.

"And if he was telling us the truth," Sloan added. "Which he was not. We know that. For one thing, he said he lived in a condo, and this building's all rental apartments."

"He's better off," Max said. "The governments only incentivize their citizens to buy homes so that they'll be easier to control. It gives them the illusion of having more to lose, you see."

"Don't you own your house?" Sloan asked.

"Yes. I don't want them to know that I'm on to them."

Rutherford snuck a quick peek at his personal cell phone, grimaced, and stuck it back into his pocket.

Max asked, "Is something wrong?"

Rutherford said, "My sister. She's concerned. She saw the videos and wants to know what's going on with me."

"Are you going to tell her?"

"Well, what's going on is that I've been in a fight with strip club bouncers, and I'm currently visiting a flea pit, so probably not."

Max said, "Wise."

Rutherford looked back to the end of the hall and saw the two uniformed police officers awaiting their signal. The cops had every intention of bringing Oscar Loomis, stand-up comedian, patient of the late Dr. Arledge, and Craigslist shopper, in for questioning. Normally they wouldn't have allowed any interference, but Vince Capp had pulled very hard on some rather large strings to get permission for his team to talk to Loomis first. The hope was to get him to confess, not only to having them attacked, but also, perhaps, to the murder of Dr. Arledge.

Capp wanted a confession and an arrest; he wanted both to directly involve his team; and he would have preferred for it to come after a very visible chase, preferably out the window and down the fire escape.

As they approached what they knew to be Loomis's door, they heard the sound of a man yelling. As they drew closer, it became clear that it was Loomis yelling, and that nobody seemed to be yelling back. By the time they reached his door, they could make out most of the words, and Rutherford had to admit, Loomis had a certain creative flair for cursing, which probably served him well in his chosen profession.

Max knocked. The stream of profanities didn't stop. They just changed in tone, from anger at the target of his cursing to confusion over who was interrupting him. The invectives grew louder as Loomis approached the door, and much louder as he flung the door open. He shouted, "God dammit, what do you want, can't you hear . . ." He trailed off to silence at the sight of Max, Sloan, and Rutherford standing in his hall. He was wearing a pair of loose-fitting basketball shorts, socks without shoes, and a black T-shirt with a single-color silkscreen on the front reading, "B.J. Bust-A-Guts: heavy food and light entertainment." There was also a logo that appeared to be a gaping, laughing mouth with a microphone hanging where its uvula should be. His phone was pressed to his ear. It looked like that was where his wrath had been aimed.

He stared at the three of them for a moment. Through the tiny speaker on Loomis's phone, a hopeful-sounding voice squawked, "Sir? Sir? Have you hung up?"

Loomis muttered into the phone, "No, I'm here. One moment." He pressed the palm of his free hand over the phone's microphone and said, "What do you want?"

"To come in and talk."

Loomis looked irritated, not frightened. He said, "Yeah, I guess, whatever. I'll be a minute." He waved them in, stepped away from the door, and resumed shouting into his phone. "Okay, I'm back. Like I told you, I didn't do it, and you can't charge me for it!"

Rutherford looked around the room and reveled at how perfectly the decor suited Oscar Loomis. Not aesthetically. From that point of view it was atrocious, but looking at this room and the things in it told them everything they needed to know about its inhabitant.

The walls were bare. The kitchen was dirty, not from use, but from lack of use. The stovetop was dusty. The sink was full of dishes that had not been washed yet, or perhaps ever. The refrigerator seemed to serve not as a storage place for food, but for the take-out menus that covered it like band flyers coating the light poles in the University District.

In the living space, a pretty nice TV and a state-of-the-art gaming console sat on pressboard shelves so cheap that the manufacturer hadn't even bothered with a proper veneer, instead painting wood grain on in faint brown stripes. The couch and coffee table looked like he'd found them on a street corner. The same beat-to-hell MacBook from the pizza parlor sat on the coffee table, surrounded by soiled paper plates and empty pop cans.

Max and Sloan were also studying the room while they waited. In his earpiece, Rutherford heard Sloan say, "That window leads to the fire escape on the front of the building, just as we'd hoped."

Rutherford wanted to tell her that he knew, he'd noticed, and he hadn't hoped nearly as much as everyone else, but he couldn't. Unlike Sloan, he didn't have the ability to speak to only those he wanted to hear him.

Loomis put his hand back over the phone and said, "Have a seat."

They chose not to.

"Look," he said into the phone, "I have company, so we've gotta wrap this up. I need this credit card to work. I need it to pay for stuff. It's the card I use for my bills. I know exactly how much room there is on it, and there's no way I'd charge five grand to it, especially not at a restaurant. How would you even run up that kind of bill for a meal?"

As a cop, Rutherford knew that an oversized restaurant charge might be camouflage for a payment to a prostitute.

The person on the other end of the phone must have suggested the same thing, because Loomis said, "Do I sound like the kind of person who needs to pay for that? Well, okay, smart guy, you're looking at my account. Do I look like someone who can afford to pay for that? That's right. Especially not five grand's worth of it. What would five grand even buy?"

Rutherford knew the answer to that one as well. Five violent lummoxes at a grand a head, or—more likely—two grand for the leader, a grand for the prostitute for putting them in contact and processing the payment, and five hundred apiece for the other four guys. Any way it split up, it wasn't as much money as Rutherford might have hoped. It was bad enough to have his safety threatened, but he resented having it threatened on a budget.

The worker on the other end of the line must have expressed something resembling sympathy because Loomis stood still and listened for several seconds. Rutherford could hear the person's voice, but couldn't make out what was being said. He thought about the microphones in Sloan's helmet. How sensitive were they? Could she hear both sides of the conversation?

The credit card company stooge said something that, from the inflection, sounded like a question.

Loomis said, "Yes, please do." He covered the microphone again and told Max, "They're putting me through to fraud prevention. I'll try to speed this up."

Max said, "Not at all, Mr. Loomis. Please, take your time."

Rutherford knew without being told that this was more than an example of Max's old-world manners. He was in no hurry to have Loomis hang up the phone because in not talking to the team, he was already answering all of the team's questions, possibly without even realizing it. It was clear that he was going to claim that someone else had used his card to pay for the attack. He would almost certainly tell them that he wouldn't have purposefully maxed out his card to hire the bouncers, particularly if the card was needed for other payments. He would also tell them that using his own card to commission a crime was a stupid move in the first place, because if anything went even the slightest bit wrong, it would immediately draw suspicion his way, which was true.

Of course, this could be an elaborate act to try to shift the blame away from himself. He would have known that even if the beating had occurred as promised, the team would still be alive and looking for whoever was responsible afterward. He had paid to have them beaten up, not killed. He could have deliberately used a credit card that was in his own name, ran it right up to its limit, then strategically used it again later so it would be declined, making him look like he was being incompetently framed for the crime. For all Rutherford knew, Loomis might have been watching out the window for squad cars so he could perfectly time his call to the credit card company.

It was a clever plan, which bugged Rutherford. He hadn't pegged Loomis as being all that clever, or that good an actor, both of which were an issue if he meant to make a living as a comedian. Sloan said, "Rutherford, when we get a chance to talk, lean on him a little bit. We want him to feel some pressure."

Rutherford nodded.

Another burst of high-pitched, modulated noise came from the phone. Loomis said, "What do you mean they aren't answering? I'm busy too. Yeah, you do that. If I don't hear back from you within forty-eight hours I'm taking this to my lawyer. And Twitter! I'm a well-known comedian. Search me on YouTube!"

Loomis ended the call. Before he could say anything, Rutherford said, "You have a lawyer?"

Loomis squinted at him. "Yeah. Uh, yeah I do. Why?"

"I was just thinking you should sic them on whoever you had steaming your carpets when we last met. I'd say they ripped you off, unless these stains are part of some pattern I'm not getting, or this isn't your condo."

Max said, "This might be his office."

"Yeah," Rutherford said. "That makes sense. His condo's probably too luxurious. It makes him lose his edge. He rents this place so he'll have somewhere to make his important business calls to creditors."

"Okay," Loomis snarled. "Fine. You got me. I exaggerated. I don't have a condo. I don't have a lawyer. I'm not doing that well as a comedian yet."

Sloan said, "He's saying what we're all thinking!"

"What else did you lie about?" Rutherford asked.

"Nothing."

"Really?"

"Yes."

"Nothing at all?"

"Yes!"

"Is that another exaggeration?"

"No! Why don't you believe me?"

"Because you lied to us."

Loomis thought for a moment, then scowled at Rutherford and said, "Fair enough. Why are you here anyway?"

Sensing that the *bad cop* portion of the festivities were at an end, Max took over. "We wanted to see if you knew anything further about what happened to Dr. Arledge, or to us."

"Why," Loomis asked. "What happened to you?"

Max said, "We were attacked." He watched Loomis, looking for any flicker of recognition that would tip his hand. "By hired thugs," he continued. "They were hired through a lady of the evening."

Loomis continued to listen, but the look on his face seemed to say that he didn't really understand what Max was telling him, or why he was telling him so slowly.

Max said, "The lady of the evening and the thugs she recruited were paid for with a credit card."

Loomis continued to listen without commenting, as if he were being told a mildly interesting story.

Max looked at Rutherford. They both looked at Sloan. Sloan shrugged at them. They shrugged at each other, then Max told Oscar Loomis, "*Your* credit card."

Loomis looked shocked, then horrified, then embarrassed, then horrified again. It was fairly convincing, and to his credit, the first words out of his mouth were, "None of you were hurt, I hope! Oh man, where's the old black guy? Is he okay?"

Max said, "He's fine. We're all fine. We were able to defend ourselves. But we wanted to come have a talk with you about it."

"You say they were hired through a hooker?"

"Yes."

"Is she hot?"

Max said, "One would assume, by American standards. I don't know if you understand how serious this is. Your card was used to make an illegal contract with criminals to commit a violent felony."

"Against us," Rutherford added.

Loomis looked scared, but not so scared his brain wasn't functioning to some small extent. "But you guys aren't cops. I mean, you can't arrest me, can you?"

Max looked at Rutherford. Sloan said, "You're up."

Before they'd left the office to confront Loomis, Terri had made a quick call to update Vince Capp. That was how he'd known to arrange for the team to go in before the police. Capp had given Rutherford some very specific instructions for what to say if the subject of an arrest came up.

Rutherford said, "I can, but I don't necessarily plan to. I don't have to. The other cops are going to do it for me. The cops who are waiting right outside that door." He glanced over his shoulder, and saw that Sloan was motioning toward the door like a presenter pointing out a new car on a game show.

He frowned at her, then turned back to Loomis and continued. "If you go out there, they're going to take you in for questioning. That shouldn't be a problem, as long as you can prove that it wasn't you who called the hooker and hired the muscle. If you can't prove that, who knows? If we walk out of this room without you, they're going to come in here and take you in for questioning. They have a warrant. Either way, you're going with them."

Rutherford paused, not wanting to continue. In his ear, he heard Sloan say, "Ahem."

"Unless you run," Rutherford said, "through some exit we don't have covered."

Loomis stayed silent for a moment, looking at the floor.

Rutherford thought, *He's not going to take the bait. He can't take the bait. It's too obvious, and he's not that stupid.*

Loomis said, "I see. I see. Say, I feel warm. Maybe I should open a window. Any of you feel warm?"

Sloan nodded enthusiastically.

"Yeah," Loomis said. "I'll just open a window, get some air in here."

He walked over to the window that Rutherford knew led to an ancient fire escape. Knowing what might be in store, he had taken a good long look at it on the way in. It had been affixed to the outside of the building decades before, with the minimum number of bolts code would allow.

Sloan said, "Albert, if you're listening, pursuit will be initiated any second now."

Albert's voice replied, "Thanks. Deploying camera drones now."

Rutherford took his battered fake cigar from his mouth and tucked it in his jacket's inside pocket.

Loomis unlatched the window, then looked nervously over his shoulder at his guests. He heaved upward on the sash, but decades of (probably lead-based) paint were resisting him. No matter how hard he tried, he only managed to open the window a few inches. His shoulders slumped as he looked down at the paltry gap, knowing he could never squeeze through.

Max smiled, winked at Rutherford, then said, "Here, Mr. Loomis, let me help you with that."

Rutherford said, "That's real nice of you, Max."

Max smiled at Rutherford. "Nonsense! It's my pleasure."

Loomis looked doubtful as to whether this jovial, bearded, much older man could be of any assistance, but Rutherford knew that Max was in better condition than most men a third his age. Max grasped the sash with both hands and pushed it upward with little resistance.

Loomis said, "Thanks."

Max said, "You're welcome."

The two of them looked at each other, Loomis uncomfortably, Max expectantly. Max looked at the open window, then back to Loomis, then down at where he was standing. He realized that he was in the perfect spot to stop Loomis from diving through the window, and that Loomis probably recognized that as well.

Max nodded graciously, and returned to where he had been standing, next to Sloan and Rutherford.

Loomis said, "Okay then. I'm just going to get some air." He turned and stuck his head out the window.

Rutherford thought, *Max and Sloan are both having fun with this. I might as well.* He stretched and flexed his arms, then lowered into a runner's crouch, as if waiting for a starter's pistol. In his ear, he heard, "Laughing."

Loomis took a comically deep breath, then another, buying time as he psyched himself up. After the third deep inhale, he scrabbled gracelessly out the window and out of sight down the fire escape.

Rutherford didn't move. Max looked at him quizzically.

"Head start," Rutherford explained. "It won't make a good show if I catch him right away."

Rutherford ran three steps and launched himself through the window, catching himself on the fire escape's railing. The escape shook and flexed unnervingly, but it stayed attached to the wall.

Rutherford looked down. Loomis was on the second floor, trying to lower the ladder to the ground. He couldn't make it budge. When he looked up through the grating and saw Rutherford above him, Loomis panicked and jumped for it, dropping fifteen feet to the ground below. He landed hard, but kept his feet and sprinted down the street, deftly dodging one of the three buzzing camera drones Albert had deployed for the occasion, as well as several pedestrians who were standing on the sidewalk, watching the drone hover at eye level.

Oh, no, Rutherford thought, as he bounded down the steps to the second floor. *He can run! The first time I get cocky and try to play to the cameras and I get a guy who actually has wheels.*

Rutherford knew Loomis couldn't keep his pace up for long, but he wouldn't have to. Even assuming Rutherford didn't turn an ankle or break a leg leaping to the ground, he'd still have to accelerate to Loomis's speed. By then, Loomis would have reached the intersection, and if Rutherford lost sight of him, Loomis had a good chance of ducking around a corner and getting away. Nobody wants to share a video of a man in a leather jacket running to the corner, looking confused, then throwing his hands up and cursing.

Rutherford's brain stuck on the idea of the Internet video. His synapses fired so quickly that his brain couldn't consciously keep up. Thoughts formed and evolved without translating themselves into words, or even fully formed pictures. If asked at that second, he couldn't have coherently explained it, but Rutherford knew that his best move was to shout, as loud as he could, "Stop, or we'll release the bees!"

Loomis's mind was already flooded with adrenaline. The threat of the bees added equal doses of panic and confusion. Rutherford knew Loomis had watched the video of Derek Sambucci being swarmed. He'd probably watched it multiple times, trying to write some snappy bee jokes to throw up on the web and exploit his fellow patient's misfortune. Upon hearing Rutherford shout, Loomis imagined himself being swarmed. It was a vivid image, and one he did not want to become a reality.

The primal part of his brain wanted to keep running, to get as far from the bees as possible. The logical part of his brain wanted to stop so that the bees would never be released. This paralyzing debate within his own brain meant that Oscar Loomis's feet were not getting any clear instructions. They had to decide what to do next on their own. They chose to stumble, making Loomis fall to the pavement, where he slid to a stop on his face, and his back and legs curled up over his head by his own momentum. When his forward motion stopped, he curled into a ball and shouted, "Not the bees!"

The buzzing that filled his ears caused him to repeat the plea several more times. His face was hidden and his eyes were shut. He couldn't know that the buzzing was from one of Albert's camera drones.

Rutherford hung down from the fire escape, dropped gently to his feet, then strolled to where Oscar Loomis was lying on the sidewalk. He assured Loomis that he wouldn't release the bees, then helped him to his feet.

Rutherford shouted, "My fellow officers are going to read you your rights and take you in for questioning. If it was credit card fraud, you'll be fine." He tried his best to sound calm, but the buzzing of the drone forced him to shout, and shouting calmly is not an easy thing to pull off.

Loomis nodded, looking a bit dazed.

Rutherford took Loomis by the arm and led him back to the apartment building. The police met them halfway. As they took Loomis away, the comedian looked over his shoulder at Rutherford and the quadcopter, and asked, "Is that filming? Can I get a copy?"

Rutherford returned to Sloan and Max, who were standing in front of Loomis's apartment building.

Rutherford said, "Either he's way smarter than I ever gave him credit for, or he's not nearly smart enough to have come up with this. I don't know. I'm not sure if he did it or not."

"None of us are," Sloan said. "So now we have to figure out if he really was the one who used the credit card."

"Wonderful," Max said. "Just what we need. Another question."

Rutherford said, "I have a question of my own." He looked at Sloan and said, "How did you clear your throat earlier?"

Sloan said, "I can clear my throat."

"Sure, but when you laugh, I don't hear laughter, I hear the word *laughing*. When you cleared your throat, I didn't hear *throat clearing*. I heard *ahem*."

"Oh, that," Sloan said. "I was trying to get your attention. I didn't actually clear my throat. I said the words *ah* and *hem*. The system's not perfect, so sometimes I have to find a work-around."

TWENTY-THREE

Rutherford entered his apartment with surprising speed for someone who was tired from a long day of work. Before joining the Authorities, Rutherford had made a point of meeting and making a good impression on as many of his neighbors as possible. He hated the idea of them seeing him park his huge, vulgar van, then saunter through the halls in his grubby leather jacket and tattered jeans, so the night before, he had made a point of walking as quickly as he could to minimize the number of neighbors who would see him.

Of course, those who *did* see him saw him speed walking from the van in his grubby clothes, which was even less dignified than sauntering, but Rutherford was trying to err on the side of the least overall embarrassment.

He hadn't forgotten that he needed to descale the van's boiler; the ominous dashboard light made that impossible. He'd been told it was a quick, simple process. He merely had to park the van in an open area, select "descale" from the in-dash electronic feature-management system, and wait thirty seconds while the van ran through the Stephenson Drive's automated descale cycle. Then the red glowing mushroom cloud that haunted Rutherford's peripheral vision while he drove would go away.

He had done a little Internet research, and learned that the boiler descaled by blasting superheated steam directly through the van's internal plumbing and out the smokestack, bypassing the steam engine. This produced a billowing cloud of steam and atomized minerals. Rutherford didn't like the sound of that, so he drove the van to the emptiest, most remote corner of his apartment complex's parking lot before he activated the descale cycle. The screen of the feature-management system went black, then filled with a bright red thirty-second countdown. He watched the numbers decrease until they reached twenty-three, at which point he was severely startled by a loud noise.

He jumped, screamed, looked around, and saw his sister Vanessa, who had just pounded on the driver's-side window, inches from his head.

"Crap," Rutherford shouted. "You scared me!"

"You're scaring us," Vanessa yelled back. In the distance behind her, he saw her Honda sedan. He realized that she must have been staking out his complex, waiting for him to come home so she could ambush him and get answers. "What's with this van? Where's your Miata? You love that car. Why am I seeing videos of you getting into street fights? Mother and I are both worried sick! Sinclair, what's going on?"

Rutherford looked at his sister's bright red face, then looked at the bright red countdown on the van's dashboard, which read twelve seconds. "Vanessa," he said, "You've gotta get away from here!"

"Why," she asked. "Are you in some kind of danger?"

"Please, just get in your car."

"I'm not leaving until we talk."

"You don't have to leave, just get in your car."

"Why, so you can leave?"

"Please, Vanessa, just do what I tell you and get in your car! Now!"

"I will not!"

Rutherford said, "Okay, fine." He threw open the driver's-side door of the van, nearly hitting Vanessa in the process. He scooted to the side so that most of the driver's seat was empty, and said, "Then get in the van, quick!"

Vanessa said, "What?"

Rutherford shouted, "Get in the van!"

"I don't think I should."

The timer reached zero. A deafening hiss filled the air, like God's cat was angry at the world. The superheated steam and fine calcium particles shot straight up into the air. Most of the steam evaporated and all of the remaining moisture and calcium cooled to a safe temperature before it fell back to the ground, but there was an instant, inescapable rise in both the ambient heat and humidity of the parking lot.

For the next twenty minutes, Rutherford and Vanessa sat in the van and talked. Once she had calmed down, he explained that the van, the clothes, and the videos were all part of his new job, which was related to law enforcement, and about which he could tell her nothing further at this time. She was left with the impression that he was working undercover, which, in a sense, he was. He promised not to do anything stupid or dangerous, and she promised to tell their mother that her fears were unjustified, and that her only son hadn't turned into a *crumb-bum*. Then they shared a laugh over their mother's use of the phrase *crumb-bum*. He offered to take her to dinner, but she declined. The humidity from the descale cycle had ruined her makeup and left her feeling like she needed a shower.

Rutherford watched his sister drive away, then walked briskly from the van to his apartment, pausing only to note how many curtains shifted as the neighbors peered out at him.

The descaling instructions said he'd need to top off the water tank, but he decided to do it in the morning. He'd already made enough of a spectacle of himself without stretching a garden hose out to his van.

Once his apartment door was closed behind him, he let out a long, relieved sigh, and went to his kitchen counter to sort through his mail.

For the most part, it was the usual assortment of business enterprises offering to supply goods or services because they wanted his money, and business enterprises asking for his money in exchange for goods or services they had supplied. The only genuinely interesting envelope was addressed simply to his apartment number in a swoopy hand and blue ballpoint ink. It was from the property management company that handled his building. He opened it. A formally worded letter on office stationary told him the good news that he was being let out of his lease several months early, as per his lawyer's request, and that he could move into his new accommodations at the end of the month.

The fact that he had new accommodations was news to him, as were the facts that he'd been trying to get out of his lease and that he had a lawyer.

Rutherford hung his leather jacket on a hook by the door and shoved his fingerless leather gloves in one of the pockets. He brought his shoulder holster and enormous pistol into the bedroom, where he placed them in their assigned spot on top of his dresser. The tail end of his workday had been spent with Albert, examining his TP-82 after its first official use, going over its cleaning procedure, and trading imitation Bond movie banter. As a result, he now understood his weapon much better, and he'd managed to have a few good laughs.

His smartphone and his fake cigar stayed in the pockets of his jacket. Even though the cigar hadn't hit the pavement this time, it still didn't seem quite sanitary enough for his liking. He spent a second trying to imagine a means of sanitizing it every night.

It's a shame it isn't watertight, he thought. *If it were, I could just let it soak overnight in that blue stuff old-timey barbers used to soak their combs in.*

He'd had the e-cigar for two days, and it already looked terribly abused. Rutherford had to admit, it looked like exactly the kind of item the fictional character he was portraying would own, which meant that it was exactly the kind of thing the real Rutherford didn't want in his home, let alone in his mouth.

He took out his earpiece, then peeled off the rest of his costume and deposited it directly in the washing machine so it would be clean when he put it on tomorrow. At least he could just leave the clothes in the dryer when they were done. Wrinkles were not a problem.

He looked forward to the day that the rest of his new wardrobe would arrive. Of course, the idea of a closet full of slightly different distressed jeans and a variety of sweat-stained arena-rock tour T-shirts held little appeal, but it was better than wearing the same jeans and shirt every day.

Having successfully shed his work identity, he took a long, hot shower and put on thick socks, sweatpants, and a clean T-shirt. He grabbed a beer, made a salad, and sat down with his tablet propped up on the table. As he ate, he scrolled through case-related documents, images of the crime scene, and photos of the involved parties.

That's what they are, he thought. *Involved parties. We don't have any suspects. We have a victim, a time of death, a cause of death, and a wife, coworkers, and patients, all of whom seem to have thought well of the doctor. None of whom have an apparent motive for murder. We also have a bunch of bouncers* who were hired to attack us with a credit card from one of the patients, but that doesn't mean he did it. Anyone could have stolen that card: another patient, another comedian, a waiter who took his card. Maybe a server at a comedy club? I bet working in that environment could teach a person to hate.

Rutherford took another bite of his salad and mentally shifted gears. We don't have any physical evidence, a murder weapon, or any witnesses. The one piece of physical evidence we do have has been ruled out as the murder weapon, despite the fact that it seems to have been wiped down and hidden like one. We don't know who used Loomis's credit card, or what they hoped to accomplish by having us attacked. The prostitute who spoke to them only said it was a male with spotty cell phone coverage. If we're getting too close, it's news to us. Anyway, their orders weren't to kill us, just rough us up. Unless it's some kind of distraction, all the perpetrator accomplished was to make himself guilty of another crime. It makes no sense.

Another thing that made no sense was that his jacket, still hanging by the door, seemed to be playing the theme song to *Miami Vice*. He realized that he had never heard his smartphone actually ring before, and that the tone had likely been chosen by Capp's branding specialists. He dug the phone out of a pocket. The screen displayed a photo of Sloan, or at least her helmet. He answered the call.

"Hello? Sloan?"

"Good evening, Rutherford. I hope I'm not disturbing you."

"No," he said, walking back over to his tablet and his salad. "Not at all. What's up?"

"I was hoping you had some time to go over the case with me. Sometimes bouncing things around with someone is more productive than just stewing on them alone."

Rutherford said, "Yeah, of course. Mind if I put you on speakerphone while I finish my salad?"

"Sure," Sloan said. "Live it up."

He activated the speakerphone and sat the phone on the table.

"Who else is in on the call?" he asked.

"Nobody. It's just the two of us, although I suspect that all of our calls on these phones might be recorded for future study and publication."

"Would Capp really do that?"

"Rutherford, Vince Capp would record our calls, run them through auto-tune, and release them over a dance beat if he thought it would turn a profit."

Rutherford noted that hearing Sloan's synthetic voice piped from speakerphone accentuated the sense that he was having an extended conversation with the phone's voice-search feature.

"Yeah," Rutherford said. "You're right. Heck, Max would probably tell us all of our calls are being recorded by the government anyway."

"Yes, and for once, he would probably be telling the truth."

"What do you mean, *for once*?" Rutherford asked.

"Oh, Rutherford. Don't tell me you believe all the things he says."

"No, but I didn't think he was lying. I thought he at least believed it. I guess I thought he was . . . I dunno, truthful, but wrong."

"Yeah," Sloan said. "I can understand that, but I have a theory about Max's theories. A sort of meta-theory, I guess. See, he's not lying about his background, so I figure he has to know a lot of real secrets. But he's retired, and he's getting older, and he likes to talk. I think he's worried that someday he might get sloppy and actually let some sensitive information slip out. So he constantly makes up stuff that sounds just plausible enough that people will hear him out, but just silly enough that they'll disregard it after he's done. That way, if he ever does say something he shouldn't, nobody will take it seriously anyway."

Rutherford swallowed a bite of salad and said, "I like that idea."

Sloan said, "Yeah. It's one of my better theories. It's a shame it's not about the case we're actually supposed to be solving."

"Yeah."

"So, about that, I've been running through things in my head. I'd like a new perspective. How do you see it?"

Rutherford was glad he had just run through all of the known facts for himself. It was relatively easy to rattle off the litany again for Sloan. He finished by saying that the closest thing they had to a lead was the fact that the brute squad had been paid for with the comedian's credit card, which had led to Oscar Loomis being brought in for questioning.

"Yes," Sloan said. "But I don't see any motive for Oscar Loomis. Do you have any ideas?"

He didn't. But Loomis was the only solid lead they had, and they were going to follow it.

"Well," Rutherford said, setting aside his now-empty salad bowl and bringing his tablet forward to take its place, "what would he want that he could gain by killing his analyst?"

"What does he want in general?" Sloan asked. "Attention," she said, answering her own question. "Killers get plenty of that, but only if they get caught. He wouldn't be able to profit from it if he was behind bars."

"Yeah, it would certainly cut down on his touring schedule."

"And fame and a cutting wit are not attributes that set you up for success in a super-max prison."

"No, I bet not," Rutherford said, absently flipping through case-related images as they spoke. "But, I mean, I'm sure he wouldn't have killed Arledge with the expectation of getting caught. He'd assume that he'd get off scot-free, and being so close to a murder could bring him attention. He'd be like that guy from the O.J. Simpson thing way back when. What's his name?"

Sloan's voice processor said, "Gay dough." There was a pause, then she said, "Sorry, his name is not in my word bank. His name was *kay toe*. I have to work around a lot of the less common names. All this time I've been calling our victim *doctor are-ledge*."

"Ah, I see. Anyway, yeah, Kato's the person I was thinking of," Rutherford said. "He was everywhere for a few years there. Of course, Nicole Simpson was a seriously high-profile murder victim. Dr. Arledge isn't."

"It's about a low-to-medium-profile murder right now," Sloan said. "Capp and his marketing team plan to blow it up huge once we find the killer. Loomis is his own marketing team. He might have planned to do the same thing. Maybe put out one of his videos identifying Arledge and Belanger as the psychologist and the clown from his act."

Rutherford looked up from the tablet and thought for a moment. "You know what? That fits. That actually makes sense."

"Yes," Sloan said. "It does, until you factor in the thugs. Why would he send guys to beat us up? Not to kill us, mind you, just to beat us up."

"To discourage us."

"From what? Pursuing him as a suspect? We weren't. We had no reason to suspect him and we hadn't given him any reason to suspect that we might. Maybe he didn't want us investigating it, but that's not likely. His plan calls for drawing attention to the case, and you've gotten more YouTube views by accident than all of his videos combined. The second angle is that he doesn't want the crime to be investigated at all, which again, works against his plan. He'd need it to be investigated, and for the cops to either find an interesting suspect or publically fail to find any."

"Maybe he thought us getting a beating would call more attention to the case."

"And it would," Sloan said, "but then why use his own credit card? All that does is bring attention to himself as a suspect, which is the one kind of attention he wouldn't want."

Rutherford made a quiet, amused snort.

Sloan said, "That wasn't funny. Ironic maybe, but not funny."

Rutherford said, "What? Oh, sorry, yeah, I wasn't laughing at what you said. I'm looking at pictures and stuff, case materials, while we talk. I came across that badly staged picture of Arledge and Shaw in his office with that stupid bust of Freud. It really does seem to be looking at Shaw's crotch."

"Ah, yes. Hey, one second, was that picture in the victim's office or Shaw's?" Sloan asked.

"The victim's."

"What photo is that? Give me the file name. I want to look at it again."

Rutherford read off the string of seemingly random abbreviations and numbers that represented the photo.

When anybody else pauses during a phone call to read or study something, the person on the other end of the call usually hears breathing, rustling, maybe a solid *thunk* when the phone is placed on a table. Because Sloan's voice was synthetic, there was no ambient noise in her line, just silence. After nearly thirty seconds, Rutherford asked, "Are you still there?"

"Yes." Sloan said. "Looking at the photo."

There was more silence.

The computer that spoke for Sloan said, "Laughing."

"What?" Rutherford asked. "What's so funny?"

Sloan said. "That bust, it looks to be what, eight inches tall? What do you figure it's made out of?"

Rutherford zoomed in. "If it were porcelain, it'd be shiny, I think. Some sort of plaster, or that fake stone stuff they make small statues out of for museum gift shops."

"Yeah, and lawn ornaments. That dull white stuff. So it's got to be pretty heavy. Tell me, Rutherford, do you remember what I told you was a detective's most important tool?"

"Their memory."

"Yes. Very good. It would have been really embarrassing if you hadn't remembered that. Your memory is what got you on the team, you know."

"No, having a guy try to clobber me with a sex toy is what got me on the team."

"That's how I sold you to Capp, but your memory put you in a position to fight the three-fisted man, so my point still stands."

"Wait, you talked Capp into hiring me?"

Sloan said, "Yes, because of your memory. You saw the same bruises on the same corpse as the rest of us, but you're the only one who remembered seeing that fist shape on that *MythBusters* episode about punching sharks."

"Well, not everyone saw that show."

"I did. And I remember thinking, *Man, that's one funky looking fist,* but when I looked at the bruise pattern, it didn't ring a bell for me. It did for you."

"You asked Capp to hire me because I remembered one thing you didn't?"

"I thought the team needed a second pair of eyes attached to a brain with investigative training and good memory. Capp thought it needed someone who would draw attention. In you, I saw someone who could do both jobs. And you have."

Rutherford said, "Thanks."

"And the whole experience has made you squirm, which is a lot of fun to watch. Now, back to business. Do you remember seeing that bust in Arledge's office after the murder?"

"No."

"Neither do I. All of the other props in this stupid picture are things that a psychologist would logically keep in their office, but they'd be hidden away in drawers or closets. Not the bust. The only reason to own a bust is to display it. And it was on display in the office at one time, but it isn't there now. It's both small enough for a person to pick up with one hand and heavy enough to kill someone if you hit them in the head with it."

Rutherford said, "If you caught them with the corner of the base, it might even fit the wounds. But that doesn't mean it has to be the murder weapon."

Sloan said, "True. What are some other reasons why it wouldn't be there anymore?"

"Maybe he got tired of it."

"Possible," Sloan said. "But really, it's a bust of Freud. It's not like that goes in and out of style. It's about as timeless as a piece of decoration gets. And it's unlikely that a man who had a bust of Freud in his office ten years ago would change his mind in the time since. It's not like there have been any shocking new revelations about him in that time."

"Unless you believe Max," Rutherford said.

"Which I don't."

Rutherford thought a moment, then said, "Maybe it wasn't in his office. I mean, yes, obviously, we have a photo of it in his office, so it was in there at some point, but maybe it was in Shaw's office and they grabbed it for the photo shoot."

The line was silent for several seconds, then Sloan said, "It wasn't in Shaw's office either."

"You're sure?" Rutherford asked. "You remember Shaw's office that clearly?"

"Albert took scans of Arledge's and Shaw's offices, and they've been loading while we've been talking. I'm looking at Shaw's office right now, and there's no bust."

Sloan studied the scans while Rutherford pulled them up himself. At first, they displayed a three-dimensional wireframe showing the contours of every object in the room. Then the photographic images draped themselves over the objects, giving them their natural colors and textures. Rutherford spun the models and zoomed in on every knickknack, and agreed that the bust was not present in either room.

Sloan said, "Of course, it may have been in the lobby. That was being remodeled, so if it was out there, it would have been put away."

"Even if it was the murder weapon, what does that really tell us?" Rutherford asked. "We don't have it. We can't test it for forensic evidence. We've been to the home of almost everyone we've considered a suspect, and I don't remember any of them having a bust of Freud in their living room."

"True, but if we know what the weapon is, we know what to look for, and we can make some guesses as to how the murderer got rid of it. Also, if we know the weapon, it gives us clues about the murderer and the situation surrounding the murder. Still, you're right. We don't have nearly enough evidence to assume that the bust was the weapon. There are a lot of reasons it could be gone. He could have given it away as a gift. It could have gotten broken. He might have just gotten sick of looking at the thing. Freud was not a handsome man. Having him always staring at you could give someone the creeps. Especially knowing Freud's theories. The idea that he's always watching, listening to everything you say, and inferring things about your childhood and your proclivities. I wouldn't want that around."

There was a long silence.

Sloan said, "Are you still there?"

Rutherford muttered, "Broken."

"What?"

Rutherford said, "You said the bust might have gotten broken. I think the bust is the murder weapon, and I think I know where it is."

"Where?"

"Someplace that's already been thoroughly searched."

"And what are you basing this on?"

Rutherford said, "A discussion I had to pass the time while you were busy doing detective work."

TWENTY-FOUR

Rutherford and Sloan talked for a long time, at a steadily increasing rate.

When putting together a puzzle, finding the corner pieces makes everything else easier.

Destroying a sweater is easy if you find one loose thread along the hem.

The assumption that the missing bust of Freud was the murder weapon led to an educated guess as to how the murderer disposed of it. Asking themselves who would have access to the weapon, the opportunity to use it on the victim, and the ability to then get rid of it in the manner they suspected narrowed down the list of suspects dramatically. Examining the remaining suspects more closely caused them to see a motive they had not thought of earlier. With time and work, they were even able to make sense of the bouncers who'd been hired to rough them up and the hammer in the alley.

Rutherford and Sloan were both sure they knew who had killed Daniel Arledge. Unfortunately, their certainty was not admissible in court.

At a little after one in the morning, Sloan and Rutherford called Terri. They woke her up. She was not happy about it. They told her that they needed her come in to the office a little early the next morning, which did nothing to improve her mood. They explained why. She understood their reasoning. That helped, a little.

The next morning, the three of them came into the office an hour early. Terri immediately started working the phones. Rutherford and Sloan perfected their plan for how to proceed with the case. When Max, Albert, and Sherwood arrived, Rutherford walked them through both the theory and the plan. At 9:58 a.m., the entire team walked into the lobby of the practice that the late Dr. Daniel Arledge had shared with Dr. Tyler Shaw.

The goal was to seem casual at first, so they made a point of being in the middle of a conversation as they entered.

"They were trying to tackle the obesity problem," Max said, holding the door open for the entire team, Terri and Albert included. "The hope was to create a generation of Americans who had a visceral, negative reaction to the idea of snacking. That's why fruit leather combines the flavor of something kids don't want to eat with the texture of something nobody wants to eat."

The lobby remodel was still in progress. The police investigation had interrupted the schedule, but work had resumed. One section of the new terrazzo floor had been poured, and the crew was working quickly but calmly to smooth out the mixture of concrete and stone chips before it cured.

Work on the mosaic mural was nearly complete. A workman stood behind the receptionist's desk taking shards of broken tile from a large tub and mortaring them to the wall. His hands were surprisingly nimble, despite his heavy gloves.

It struck Rutherford that the same workers who had seemed so lazy and shiftless the last time he saw them now looked like a well-oiled machine.

He thought, *Of course, right now they're being paid to get stuff done. Last time I saw them they were being paid to sit around and do nothing. They were just applying the same professionalism to loafing then that they're applying to working now.*

Terri approached the receptionist with her smile cranked up to maximum. "Good morning," she said, pleasantly. "We'd like to see Dr. Shaw."

The receptionist said, "I'm sorry. I'm afraid the doctor is booked solid today. Fridays are busy here."

Terri's smile did not fade. "I understand, but we're here concerning our investigation of the late Dr. Arledge's death. I'm certain he'd be willing to make room in his schedule."

The receptionist looked sympathetic, but shook her head. "I figured that was why you were here, and I'm sorry. I'm sure he'd like to help in any way he can, but he really is booked solid. At most, he might be able to squeeze in five minutes between patients. Would that be enough time?"

Now it was Terri's turn to look sympathetic and shake her head. "No, I'm afraid not. We have quite a few questions only he can clear up. It's going to take longer than five minutes."

The receptionist said, "Perhaps you could meet with him during lunch, or maybe I can cancel someone this afternoon. I'll buzz the doctor and see what we can work out."

"No," Terri said, a little more sharply than expected, stopping the receptionist's hand before it reached the phone. Terri laughed at herself, then said, "I'm sorry, no, I don't want you to bother him prematurely. He's already been so cooperative. Just let me think for a moment. Maybe I can come up with a way to work around his schedule." She looked at her watch and put on her *I'm thinking hard* face.

After a few moments of everyone watching Terri think, the phone rang. The receptionist answered, listened, said that she understood what she was being told in a surprised, delighted tone, and then hung up.

"That was Dr. Shaw's ten o'clock. He says he can't make it today."

Terri had taken a look at the copy of the practice's appointment book that Dr. Shaw had supplied to help the investigation. It had contained nothing incriminating (of course). It did come in handy, though, when she used it to find the name of the patient who was scheduled for ten o'clock and offered him a surprising amount of money to cancel, with a generous bonus if he called at precisely nine fifty-nine. Terri wanted to be there when he called so that she could make sure someone else didn't get moved into his spot, and also because she liked the theatricality of it.

The receptionist called Dr. Shaw. Rutherford heard Shaw's phone ring faintly through the closed door to his office. She explained that the ten o'clock had canceled, but that the team investigating Dr. Arledge's death was there with some follow-up questions. She nodded, said, "Very good," and hung up the phone.

The receptionist said, "He'll be right out." She smiled and started to look down at her computer screen, but out of the corner of her eye she noticed Rutherford's e-cigar. "Sir," she said, "I'm sorry, but you can't smoke in here."

Rutherford said, "I'm not smoking. It isn't real. Technically, I'm water vaporing."

"You still can't do it in the office, I'm afraid."

Rutherford removed the cigar and held it in his hand as a prop. "Tell me," he asked, "If I'd come in chewing on a pen, would you have made me take it from my mouth?"

The receptionist answered in the negative.

Rutherford turned to Albert. "We should look into making an e-cigar that looks like a pen. I bet the boss could make some money off that."

Albert made a note of it on his phone. "Done," he said. "We could also make it not emit any noticeable vapor."

"No," Rutherford said. "It should put out more vapor. It'll be worth it just to make people tell me to stop smoking my pen."

The receptionist started to say something, but was interrupted by her boss emerging from his office.

"Good morning," Shaw said, with a polite but strained smile on his face. "Please, do come in."

Sherwood took the lead, walking briskly toward Dr. Shaw and extending his right hand. Shaw reflexively took his hand and shook it, though he looked somewhat perplexed. He looked far more perplexed when, instead of shaking his hand, Sherwood held it in place and used his free hand to run his sensor wand over Shaw's hand and lower arm. Sherwood looked at the wand's readout, nodded, shook Shaw's hand, and said, "Thank you for your cooperation."

With that, the professor let go and walked back to the reception desk.

Max stepped forward. "Dr. Shaw, we know you're a busy man. We don't want to take up any more of your time than we must."

Shaw was still looking at Sherwood with concern and bewilderment, but he said, "Of course. Do come in."

Max, Sloan, and Rutherford entered Shaw's office. The others stayed behind, and as Shaw closed the door to the lobby, Rutherford heard Terri say, "Sir, pardon me, sir. If you could please stop that for a moment?"

Sloan said, "Okay, remember the plan. Max mostly asks friendly questions. Rutherford mostly makes unfriendly statements. We want him uncomfortable but not alarmed."

Shaw offered his guests seats before settling in behind his desk. Max and Sloan took the couch. Rutherford sat in a chair to the side.

"Thank you for your time, Dr. Shaw." Max said. "We just have a few follow-up questions."

Shaw smiled. "I expected you might."

"I bet," Rutherford said, not smiling. Shaw looked affronted. Rutherford studied the e-cigar in his hand nonchalantly, smiled, and said, "I just mean, you're a smart man. You knew you hadn't seen the last of us."

Shaw looked at Rutherford for a moment before saying, "Yes. It's not easy to catch a killer. It seemed likely that you'd need more information."

Max said, "Indeed! It's just as you say, Dr. Shaw. It's been harder than you may know. Were you aware that we were attacked?"

"No," Shaw said. "That's terrible. Was it the killer?"

"Almost certainly not. No, it was paid hooligans."

Rutherford put the cigar in his mouth and said, "Hired goons." It was a phrase that begged to be said around a cigar.

"Yes," Max agreed. "They were just pawns. Someone else masterminded the attack."

"If you wanna call it that," Rutherford said, "and I don't."

"No?" Shaw asked.

"No," Max said. "The goons, as my friend calls them, were found on Craigslist, and paid for with a personal credit card."

"That sounds easy to trace," Shaw said.

"Yes," Rutherford said, staring at Shaw. "Very easy. Almost as if somebody wanted us to trace it."

Max said, "The card belongs to one of the late Dr. Arledge's patients, but we're not yet at liberty to say which."

Shaw said, "Of course," and exhaled a little too heavily. Continued secrecy suggested continued doubt, which Shaw seemed to find reassuring. "Can I help you find this patient? If I can assist in any way, I will."

"You've already helped us find him," Rutherford said, smirking. "You practically made it impossible not to find him."

"Have I?"

Max chuckled. "Yes, you've been tremendously helpful. The information you gave us about Dr. Arledge's patients was invaluable."

Rutherford said, "Yup. Gave us lots of people to talk to and angles to explore. Kept us nice and busy. We almost had too much information to keep straight. Almost."

"In fact," Max said, "the credit card used to pay the hooligans who attacked us was the very same card this patient used to pay for their treatment at this clinic."

Rutherford said, "You know, a lot of medical professionals keep copies of a patient's credit card information on file, for charging no-show fees and the like. It wouldn't surprise me at all if you have that very credit card number locked up in a filing cabinet somewhere around here."

In his ear, Rutherford heard Sloan say, "Cool it a little. We don't want him to panic. Yet."

Max said, "The patient must be quite desperate. Paying for the hooligans took his credit card over its limit. Of course, that's exactly what the credit card companies want. It keeps the customer paying for years to come. In the end, the goal is to subjugate the citizenry, keep us all docile, and con us into trading our liberty for merchandise. Truman knew all too well what he was doing when he ordered the FTC—"

"You need to cool it too," Sloan interrupted. "We don't want him to think we're nuts."

From Dr. Shaw's point of view, Max had stopped talking midsentence to look at Sloan, who was silently staring back at him. Max laughed at himself to help sell the illusion that he had caught himself getting carried away.

Max said, "My point is that the patient in question was in dire straits and making questionable decisions."

"Clearly," Dr. Shaw said.

"None of Dr. Arledge's current patients are what you'd call *wealthy*, are they?" Rutherford observed.

"No," Shaw said, "I suppose not."

"Means you can't charge them very much, and if they send a friend to see you, that friend's likely to be just as broke as they are."

"What are you getting at?" Shaw asked.

"I'm just saying, it took a lot of heart for Arledge to turn his back on his profitable patients and focus on a group he knew would be much less lucrative. He was a good man."

"Yes," Shaw said. "He was."

Max said, "Of course, Arledge was intending to write a book. Those can bring in some good money, and draw a lot of new business to boot."

"If the book's successful," Rutherford said. "But the vast majority of them aren't. Doesn't seem like the kind of odds you'd want to bet your business on, but it's easy to be selfless and take risks when you already have a nice fat nest egg that isn't in any danger."

The statement hung in the air like a big black balloon for a few seconds before Max punctured it, saying, "Well, enough small talk, I think. You are a busy man, Dr. Shaw. We must get to business. We just have a few questions to ask, then we'll be on our way."

"Yes," Shaw said. "Please do."

Max pulled out his smartphone, opened his notebook app, swiped through a few pages, said, "Okay, here it is, one moment," and started reading to find the right spot.

Sloan said, "Nice. Very *Columbo*."

"Ah," Max said, "Yes, here we are. Dr. Shaw, you said the other day that you've been working at a greatly reduced salary under the understanding that Dr. Arledge would sign over the practice to you when he retired."

"That's right."

"That means that you had a powerful reason to want him to stay alive and healthy until that happened."

"Yes," Shaw said.

Rutherford said, "That and the fact that he was your mentor and a good friend."

"Yes. Of course. That goes without saying."

Rutherford smirked around his e-cigar. "You certainly didn't say it."

Max cut in before Shaw could respond. "We spoke to the widow Arledge. She mentioned that she was going to sign the practice over to you early, because it was what her husband would have wanted."

Rutherford let out a sound that could have been either a cough or a guffaw.

"That's right," Shaw said. He was answering Max, but staring at Rutherford. "She feels that, due to recent events, the value of the practice has been somewhat diminished."

"Sure it has," Rutherford said. He removed the e-cigar from his mouth and gestured back over his shoulder with it, toward the late Dr. Arledge's office. "He made his name treating the wealthy and successful. When he started concentrating on the unsuccessful and shunting his old clientele off to his junior partner, that had to lose the practice some patients and cut into the bottom line."

Shaw gritted his teeth. "That's not what I meant."

Max glared disapprovingly at Rutherford. It was so convincing that Rutherford almost felt real shame.

"Of course that's not what Dr. Shaw meant," Max said. "He was referring, I'm sure, to Dr. Arledge's awful fate and the negative attention it will bring. And sadly, the increased attention still to come if we catch the culprit."

"When," Rutherford said. "When we catch the culprit. And yes, I'm sure you're right. Sorry."

Max smiled and nodded at Rutherford, then smiled and nodded at Shaw, as if to say, *there, we're all friends again.*

Shaw smiled weakly.

Rutherford put his e-cigar back in his mouth, then said in a voice ten percent too loud for the room, "Of course, hypothetically, spending your entire career paying for a practice that caters to the wealthy and successful just to have it shift focus to the poor and unappealing must have been a bitter pill to swallow. Like a bait and switch, played out over a full decade."

Shaw said, "That didn't sound hypothetical."

"No?" Rutherford asked. "Hmm. Maybe I used the wrong word. Do you think *rhetorical* would have worked better?"

"Maybe," Shaw snarled.

Rutherford said, "I wasn't really looking for an answer to that question."

Sloan's voice in Rutherford's ear said, "Laughing. Laughing. You bastard."

Max gave Rutherford a look that was either an angry, disappointed grimace or a restrained laugh. He turned back to Shaw. "On a more pleasant note, we spoke to Mrs. Arledge, several times. She speaks very highly of you. She said that her late husband felt the same way."

"That's good to hear," Shaw said.

Max said, "As with criticism, compliments are often said behind our backs and not often enough told to our faces."

Shaw smiled. "Olivia's always been very supportive. She's a good friend."

"She feels the same about you. The last time we went to her house, my young associate here was a bit abrasive."

Shaw sneered at Rutherford and said, "Really?"

Rutherford smiled brightly and said, "Yes."

"We spoke to her just this morning," Max said. "She tells us that she was upset when we left, and she called you for support."

Shaw's eyes narrowed. He said, "Well, you know, one tries to be there for one's friends, even if all you can do is listen."

"Too true," Max said. "And that's a large part of your job as a therapist, isn't it? Listening and paying close attention."

"Yes. Yes it is."

Rutherford said, "And you listened to Olivia Arledge when she complained about my behavior, which to be honest, was pretty bad. And she told you the joke she'd made about hiring an assassin on Craigslist, which she says you thought was pretty funny."

Before Shaw could respond, Max said, "How has business been, Dr. Shaw? Have you been retaining Dr. Arledge's former clients that have been referred to you?"

"Why do you ask?"

Max said, "No reason."

Rutherford added, "Yes, no reason, since we have the appointment book you sent us, we already know that you've lost nearly half of them. Still, it's not all bad. It made room for the much less lucrative clients Arledge was pushing you to take on."

"Look," Shaw said, on the verge of shouting. "If you're suggesting—"

Max raised his hands in a gesture of nonaggression. "Please, Dr. Shaw, Mr. Rutherford meant nothing by it. Nobody is suggesting anything. Are we?"

Rutherford said, "No. I'm not suggesting anything."

Shaw relaxed a bit.

Rutherford said, "At this time."

Shaw tensed back up.

Max said, "Let's calm down, everyone, please. Nobody's accusing anyone of anything. We all want the same thing here.

Rutherford, I think it might make Dr. Shaw feel better if you said something nice."

Rutherford said, "I love your building."

"Really?" Shaw said, looking dubious.

"Yes, and I think the remodel looks great. I've always had a thing for midcentury modern. The clean lines, the simple, minimalist furniture. I eat it up. I think your designer is doing a great job on this place."

Shaw said, "Thank you."

Rutherford looked around. "Yeah, on *The Brady Bunch*, whenever the father was designing a building, I pictured your new lobby as the kind of thing he was drawing."

Max asked, "You watched *The Brady Bunch*? Wasn't it before your time?"

"My parents watched it. That and *M*A*S*H*."

"You know," Max said, "*The Brady Bunch* was propaganda. Yes, the people of the United States held a grudge about World War Two much longer than the Germans would have liked, so they financed a show about four square-jawed, all-American males living with four beautiful, blonde-haired, blue-eyed . . ." Max trailed off when he realized that Rutherford, Sloan, and Shaw were all staring at him.

Rutherford turned back to Shaw. "Of course, the tricky part of this kind of remodel is making sure that all of the furnishings are appropriate. Means you won't be able to keep any of this mismatched, midnineties, funky coffee shop stuff you have now." Rutherford waved his cigar around as a means of drawing attention to the exposed, distressed brick, the dark wooden schoolteacher desk, the overstuffed velveteen couch on which Sloan and Max were sitting, and the orange, low-backed club chair where he himself was sitting.

Rutherford continued. "A lot of the time, when someone tries to decorate a place of business in such a specific style, someone will bring in an element that doesn't fit, like a high-tech office chair. The beauty of this style is that it's so eclectic it's easier to fit things in. You and your former partner both did a good job of it. Everything goes, but none of it matches. That's hard to pull off."

"Uh, thank you," Shaw said. "Yeah, details were important to Dan. It's part of what made him such a good therapist."

Rutherford smiled and leaned forward in his seat. "And you too, I suspect. You must have an eye for detail as well, 'cause your office is just as well executed. Even the picture frames work."

Shaw said, "Thank you. Yes. I mean, we agreed that the clinic couldn't be too clinical. We aren't giving physicals here. We need people to relax. The goal was to have the place look professional but comfortable."

"And you succeeded," Rutherford said. "I only have one question. What happened to the bust of Freud?" Over the course of the sentence, all of the friendliness had drained out of Rutherford's tone and expression.

At the same time, all of the blood had drained out of Shaw's face. "I . . . what? I don't have one."

"Of course not." Max said. "It would be a bit on the nose, don't you think?"

Rutherford said, "Obvious."

Max said, "The late Dr. Arledge had one though. It's there in old pictures of his office, but it isn't there now. Do you have any idea where it might be?"

"I have no idea what you're talking about," Shaw said.

Max said, "That's not a surprise. It's a silly small detail, really. You wouldn't be too concerned about the knickknacks in your partner's office. You have much more important things on your mind."

"Like the fact that the practice you'd already paid for was becoming less valuable by the day," Rutherford said.

Max said, "We only ask because the murder weapon hasn't been found. If we were to find it, it would give us all sorts of clues about who murdered your friend. Based on the nature of Dr. Arledge's head injury, the bust might just be what we've been looking for. Do you remember it?"

"Yes," Shaw said, carefully. "It seems to me he did have a bust, but I never really gave it much thought."

"That's understandable." Max said. "Do you happen to remember if it was still in his office the day before the murder?"

Shaw thought hard, then said, "I couldn't say."

Rutherford asked, "You don't remember?"

Shaw said, "I couldn't tell you."

"You don't remember?" Rutherford asked again.

Shaw looked at Rutherford, his expression a stone mask barely containing an explosion of panic and rage. He said, "I don't remember."

Rutherford turned to Max, and in a relaxed, conversational tone said, "He doesn't remember."

Max smiled and said, "That's to be expected."

"You're doing great!" Sloan said. "I'm not having to help at all, and I'm going to get all the credit."

Rutherford shot Sloan a dirty look. Of course, Shaw couldn't hear Sloan, so from his point of view, Max had only said, "That's to be expected." Then there had been an uncomfortable silence, followed by Rutherford making some sort of face at Sloan.

Shaw stood up. "Look, I don't appreciate your tone. I've given you more information about my practice than perhaps I should have—"

"That's true," Rutherford interrupted.

Max said, "We're just trying to make sense of this, Dr. Shaw, which is going to be difficult, because the whole thing is so utterly senseless. It looks like the murderer didn't plan to kill Dr. Arledge."

Rutherford said, "We'd call it a crime of passion, but that would be giving the killer too much credit. It seems more like a crime of dumb panic."

Shaw stood behind his desk. His knuckles were white, and his eyes darted frenetically, but his voice was quiet and slow. "I've answered your questions and listened to what I'll charitably refer to as your *ideas*. If you have something provable, I suggest you prove it." He stepped out from behind his desk and started toward the door. "If you don't have this bust you're so worried about, then I suggest checking dumpsters and thrift stores. There's a Value Village on—"

"You know, now that I think of it, there was a trace of a white powdery substance in Dr. Arledge's wound," Rutherford said.

Max said, "But there's no reason for a decorative bust to be covered with white powder."

Rutherford nodded. "True, but if the bust was made of plaster or cast stone, it was effectively made of white powder. Part of it might have rubbed off if it struck the victim's head hard enough, which it did. Repeatedly."

"Or it might even fly off in a cloud if it was struck with something hard enough to shatter the bust," Max said. "Like, say, a hammer."

Rutherford said, "That's interesting, because we did find a hammer that had white, chalky dust on the head, and it had been wiped down to remove any prints."

"And poorly hidden."

"Indeed. Quite poorly. But this is all conjecture unless we find that bust, or the pieces of it."

"Sadly, you're right," Max agreed.

"You know what my favorite part of your remodel is, Dr. Shaw?" Rutherford asked, abruptly changing the subject. "The mural."

Shaw froze, his hand on the doorknob.

"It's a really clever design," Rutherford said. "The sun that looks like a brain, and the sunrise suggests hope and a new beginning. I think the most clever bit is the clouds, the way they're using broken white pottery instead of flat tile to give them a bumpy 3-D texture."

Max said, "Doesn't have to be pottery. They could be using broken statuary as well."

"Yup, no reason why not. You know, if the bust was the murder weapon, the killer might have smashed it with a hammer and put the chunks into the muralist's shard bin." Rutherford paused, then said, "Shard bin. *Shardbin.* Sounds like a Dutch word, doesn't it?"

Max said, "Perhaps to an American who doesn't speak Dutch, and has never heard it spoken."

"Fair enough. Anyway, he takes the bust and smashes it to tiny bits. It gets used as materials for the mural. The killer has gotten rid of the murder weapon by having it permanently glued to the wall of the crime scene. It's a really cool idea."

Max said, "Of course, the killer would have to have access to a hammer and the shard bin, as you call it. I believe any tools or materials left overnight by the construction crew were locked in the storage room, so the killer would have to have access to the key."

"But then why not use the hammer to kill Arledge?" Rutherford asked.

Max said, "Using the bust suggests an impulsive action, not premeditation. Something went terribly wrong."

"Like, I dunno, the senior partner telling the junior partner that he was going to start sending him less affluent patients, forever altering the image and the profitability of the practice that the junior partner was far too invested in to walk away from," Rutherford offered.

"Yes," Max said, "That would do. So, the murderer, he . . . or she, just grabbed whatever was handy and struck the victim without thinking."

"Or maybe he . . . or she, but let's be honest, he, thought a little too much," Rutherford said. "Arledge is unconscious and the killer's looking down at him. He's thinking he can either wait for Arledge to wake up, in which case he'll get arrested and lose everything. Or he can finish the job and maybe keep the practice, complete with Arledge's name, stop treating weirdos, and possibly come out of this ahead."

Max said, "Logic driven by panic is often flawed."

"Shame for the murderer that juries are seldom panicked when they deliberate," Rutherford said.

Max said, "Then, with all of this adrenaline and panic in his system, he had to dispose of the evidence."

Rutherford said, "Someone like that might not have done a very thorough job of cleaning the bust before they smashed it. There'd probably be fingerprints and traces of blood left behind."

"But," Max said, "what about the person making the mural? They'd be leaving fingerprints, and those broken tiles are sharp. Any blood might be theirs."

Rutherford shook his head. "No, the installers have to wear big, thick work gloves when they're working with broken ceramics. The last person to have touched the bust with bare hands would be the murderer."

Max said, "We'll know for sure once we examine the white parts of the mural, but it certainly is an interesting theory, don't you think, Dr. Shaw?"

Max, Sloan, and Rutherford all turned to look at Shaw, who was still standing, silent, in front of the closed office door. He had stood there, paralyzed, listening as his entire plan was unraveled before him.

Shaw gaped at the three of them for a moment, opened his mouth as if to speak, then flung open the door and ran for it.

He made it less than twenty feet.

He had barely entered the lobby when he realized something was terribly wrong. The windows had too many people gathered outside them and there was far too much light streaming in. He stopped abruptly and looked around. The workers who had been pouring the first phase of the terrazzo floor along one side of the room were gone, though their work was only half finished. The mixture of concrete and marble chips had been poured, but not smoothed. Behind the receptionist's desk, Sherwood was waving his wand over the partially completed mural while Albert, Terri, and a forensics technician holding a soft brush and a vial of powder stood by. Sherwood was saying, "I'd start with all of the pieces that have that particular color and texture."

Shaw looked out the bank of windows that made up the front wall of the lobby. As his eyes adjusted, he saw that the people gathered out front appeared to be camera crews from the local TV stations, their lighting rigs burning at full power. Attractive young reporters stood with their backs to the window. All of them seemed to be either broadcasting live or preparing to do so.

Shaw's brain had just enough time to comprehend what it was seeing before a hand grabbed his right wrist and bent it behind his back.

"Okay, Dr. Shaw," Rutherford said. "This'll be over soon." Rutherford took Shaw's left wrist, pulled it behind his back as well, and fastened both with handcuffs.

Outside, the reporters had stepped out from in front of the cameras to give them a clear shot of what was now The Rutherford and Shaw Show.

Rutherford glanced at Terri. She smiled, looked at the camera crews filming them through the windows, then nodded toward the wet terrazzo to Rutherford's right.

Rutherford gave her a look that said *seriously?*

Terri gave him a look that said *oh, yes.*

Capp did want all of my filmed interactions to be embarrassing, Rutherford thought. *At least this time I get to decide who's embarrassed.*

Rutherford started shoving Shaw from side to side while grunting, "Stop resisting. Dr. Shaw. It's over. Stop resisting!"

Shaw was too confused to understand and offered no actual resistance, physical or verbal, aside from surprised grunts and an expression of confused fear.

After a few seconds of *struggle,* Rutherford threw their weight far to the right. Both he and Shaw had to take two large steps into the wet terrazzo. Rutherford managed to stay on his feet. Shaw did not.

Shaw looked up at Rutherford. Half of his face was dripping with wet cement and stone chips. He asked, "Why'd you do that?"

Rutherford said, "Because it's my job. Now let's have a quick conversation about your rights."

TWENTY-FIVE

The team had arrived at Shaw's office a little before ten. Rutherford arrested him not long after. By 1:00 p.m. the same day, the whole team was at a large hotel downtown, sitting in an empty conference room, listening as the crowd's chatter filtered in from the full conference room next door.

That morning, in addition to phoning the police, the victim's widow, and the patient whose appointment they sniped, Terri had also called Vince Capp to tell him that Sloan believed that they knew—and could prove—who the killer was, and that they planned on apprehending him. Capp said that if Sloan was convinced, he was convinced. He was disappointed that Arledge had been killed over money, and that sex wasn't directly involved, but you can't have everything.

After speaking with Terri, Capp made one phone call to his assistant, who made many phone calls to various people, who each in turn made many phone calls of their own. As a result, by the time Capp was finished showering and dressing, his car was waiting to take him to his jet, which was waiting to take him to Seattle, where his UPS truck was waiting to take him to the hotel, where the hotel staff was waiting to take him to the conference center, where chairs and catering had already been arranged for the multitude of reporters who were waiting for him to speak.

It was a testament to what one man could accomplish if he had the will and ambition to pay a bunch of people to accomplish things.

The team would be a key part of Capp's presentation, so they were waiting in an adjacent, equally large conference room, which was being used as a staging area. In the main room, reporters sat in neat rows of chairs, enjoying baked goods and cold drinks. In the side room, Rutherford and Max grabbed enough chairs for everyone off a stack in the far corner and they sat near the door at a round plywood banquet table with no tablecloth, looking at their provided refreshments: a plastic-wrapped case of room-temperature bottled water that had been hastily cut open with a box knife.

"It sounds like a pretty good turnout in there," Terri said.

Sloan said, "The ladies and gentlemen of the press, hard at work, waiting patiently to be told what happened this morning in their own town by someone who was thousands of miles away at the time."

"See, that's what I don't get," Rutherford said. "They know Arledge was murdered. They know Shaw was arrested. They filmed me apprehending him, walking him through the wet cement, and handing him over to the police. What do they think Capp's going to tell them that they don't already know?"

"How Capp's involved," Albert said.

"But they must know that," Rutherford said. "When I was a cop, we knew that you all were working for Capp. At least one cop must have referred to us as *Capp's people* to a reporter. The fact that we work for him can't come as a surprise."

Terri said, "But he hasn't publically admitted it. Even if he just tells them what they already know, the fact that he's telling them is news."

Max said, "If you make yourself interesting enough, everything you do becomes interesting. I'd think you would understand that principle."

"You owe your job to it, after all," Sherwood added.

They passed a few more minutes with small talk. They discussed the weather, the traffic, what descaling the van's boiler was like, what Sherwood would do when his time with the team ran out, and how hard it would be to pick cured terrazzo out of the treads of Rutherford's sneakers.

Finally, the door at the far corner of the room flew open and a smartly dressed woman in her late twenties strode purposefully toward the team, holding a phone to her ear with one hand and a clipboard in front of her with the other. She was saying, "Yes. Yes, of course. Yes. Um, we'll need to discuss that further."

Rutherford suspected that last bit was her version of saying no.

As she approached, Max and Sherwood stood, because that's what men of their generation and upbringing do when a lady approaches. Rutherford and Albert also stood, because that's what men of their generation do when they're reminded what good manners look like. Terri stood too, because she felt silly staying seated. Sloan didn't move a muscle.

As the woman reached their table, she said, "If I can ask you to hold on, I need to brief Mr. Capp's team." She took the phone away from her ear and smiled. "Welcome to the Gaston. I'm Sarah, the event manager. I just thought you'd like to know that Mr. Capp is in the building." She smiled again, put the phone back to her ear, and said, "Okay, I'm back. Yes? Yes. I agree."

Sloan said, "I have to hand it to her. That was brief."

Max offered the woman his seat. She smiled, but refused. Max sat back down, as did the rest of the team. None of them spoke, as to do so in the presence of someone engaged in a phone call would have felt rude.

At one point she put a hand over the phone's mouthpiece and whispered, "Please don't smoke in here," to Rutherford. He had forgotten he even had his e-cigar in his mouth. He started to tell her that he wasn't really smoking, but by then she had returned to her phone call. He shrugged at Terri, who shrugged back, so he tucked the e-cigar in his pocket.

Soon she interrupted her stream of affirmative responses to tell them that Capp was in the elevator, and then that Capp was on their floor.

A few seconds later the door burst open again and Vince Capp entered. He was surrounded by four people in crisp suits. He wore a rumpled suit, no tie, and a shirt undone to the second button. As he entered, he tucked something into his ear. Rutherford suspected it was an earpiece to allow him to converse with Sloan.

The hotel representative greeted Capp and assured him everything was in order, and that his guests were present and being taken care of.

Capp smiled and greeted his team, then asked Rutherford, "Where's your cigar?"

Rutherford said, "She asked me not to smoke."

Capp said, "And you listened to her?"

Rutherford pulled the cigar out of his pocket and stuck it in his mouth. Capp looked happy. The woman who'd asked him to stop smoking did not.

Capp shook her hand, thanked her, and pointed to someone in his well-dressed entourage. "I'd like to introduce you to Lindsay. She's one of my media consultants."

The hotel rep shook Lindsay's hand, then Lindsay hit the woman with a high-speed barrage of information that kept her quite distracted while Capp moved on to the team. He shook everyone's hand and slapped a few shoulders along the way. Rutherford noted that while his tone and demeanor did not change, his grip was much more gentle when he shook Sloan's hand.

As he shook Rutherford's hand, he said, "And you, the new guy, I just couldn't be happier with the work you've done."

Rutherford said, "Yeah, uh, about that. I'd like to have a word with you."

"Sure," Capp said, "we'll have a chance to chat later on." He raised his voice to address the entire team. "Because after the press conference, you're all coming with me. We're going to celebrate, and I have the perfect place all set up."

Everyone reacted positively to this, which seemed to make Capp happy. He turned back to Rutherford and said, "Oh, and there's been a lot of progress on your persona. In fact, we've got the nickname thing cracked."

"Really," Rutherford said, hoping he sounded excited.

Capp said, "Yeah." He was about to continue when another of his suited minions cleared his throat and said, "Sir, the press is waiting."

Capp said, "Of course. Everyone, I'd like to introduce you to John. He's another one of my media consultants."

Everyone nodded or muttered greetings to John, who in return said, "It's a pleasure to meet all of you. Now, in a moment, that door over there is going to open and the press conference is going to begin. When that happens, Mr. Capp will enter first. We'll ask all of you to line up on this side of the door. We'll tell you when to enter."

Rutherford tore his gaze away from John and saw that Capp was already many feet away, next to the door, being fussed over by the two remaining minions.

"There is a raised platform and a podium in front of the press," John said. "There are stairs leading up to it. You are not to go up onto the platform. You'll stand beside the platform, in front of those stairs. Stand up straight, face the audience, and look happy to be here." He paused, glanced at Sloan, stammered for a moment, then continued. "Mr. Capp will do all of the talking. All questions will be directed to him. If a question is directed at one of you, he will answer it. When the conference is over, he'll come back through this door. You will all follow him. Any questions?"

Professor Sherwood said, "I have a question."

John was already looking toward Capp and the other two minions, all of whom were looking back at him. One of the minions pointed at his watch.

John said, "Yes, Stuart," then turned to Professor Sherwood and said, "I'm sorry, but it looks like your question will have to wait until after the press conference."

Sherwood muttered, "What was the point in asking, then?"

John, his eyes bulging, said, "I told you, no question until afterward."

Sherwood said, "That wasn't my question."

John shushed Professor Sherwood, rolled his eyes, and turned away to watch the door.

Sherwood pulled his spray bottle of bee pheromone out of his pocket, eyed the back of John's head, then put the bottle back into his pocket.

Capp walked out the door. The chatter from the crowd in the next room dissolved, replaced by a low muttering and many clicking noises. Capp made some opening remarks that resulted in a chuckle, but Rutherford didn't know what they were. He and the rest of the team were too busy being herded to the door and lined up like soldiers waiting for their marching orders. When they had finally achieved a formation that satisfied the marketing consultants, Rutherford found himself near the middle with Sloan on one side and Albert on the other. Beyond Sloan and Terri, he could see Capp standing at the podium through the open door.

Capp's prepared statement explained that a suspect had been apprehended in the murder of Dr. Daniel Arledge, that substantial physical evidence had been found at the scene, and that said evidence was being carefully chiseled off the wall as he spoke. He confirmed that the suspect was identified by private consultants who had been working with the police, and admitted that the rumors were true, the consultants were bankrolled by him.

He gestured toward the door. In unison, the three marketing minions whispered, "Go! Go! Go!" as they put their hands on the team's shoulders and pushed them through the door.

The team walked to the side of the stage and stopped at the spot they'd been told.

Capp said, "This is my team. They are each an authority in their chosen specialty, so internally we've been calling them the Authorities. They're an elite group of crime-fighting experts, hand assembled by me, working at my direction, with my funding, to solve crimes I deem worthy of their expertise."

Capp continued, enumerating his reasons for starting the group, most of which were variations on the theme of *I wanted to make a difference, and this was a way I could be of service.* All the while, the team stood beside the stage, facing the press and listening.

Rutherford took his e-cigar from his mouth, leaned toward Sloan, and whispered, "I thought you said Max and I had done the work, but you were going to get all the credit. Sounds to me like he's stealing it."

"No, he bought it," Sloan said, her artificial voice loud and clear in his earpiece. "I got the credit from him. Now he's getting his for having hired all of us. That's how credit works. You get a little from me, I get more from him, and he gets a lot from the rest of the world."

"It's almost exactly the same as how the money works," Max said, just loud enough to be heard, "which fits, as they're both forms of compensation."

Rutherford saw the logic in the arrangement, but the part of his brain that was set aside for criticizing his superiors had powered up, and would take a while to coast to a stop.

"I don't know what he's thinking. He lets them see us, but he doesn't tell them our names. He can't possibly think they'll stay secret, can he?"

Sloan said. "He has no intention of hiding our identities. He wants everyone to know who we are."

"Then why isn't he telling the reporters our names?"

"Rutherford, there's a world of difference between failing to volunteer information and hiding it. If he'd told them our names, they'd have jotted them down, put them in their stories, and that's it. By not telling them, he's making them find out the information themselves, and they'll make a much bigger deal out of it when they do."

"Yeah, but then they'll figure out that I'm not really the guy my clothes and car say I am," Rutherford muttered.

"Oh, don't worry about that. Most people live their whole lives without understanding that about themselves, let alone other people. Besides, when those reporters figure out who we are, who do you think will seem the most interesting? The grandfatherly martial artist? The young genius inventor who wears bespoke tweed suits? The woman who uses her talents as a middle manager to fight crime? The disfigured detective? The man who commands the bees to do his bidding? Or a guy in his early twenties whose tastes are evolving? Capp hired you to help draw attention to us in a way that people could easily understand.

You're doing a great job, but his hope is now that we have the press's attention, they'll find us interesting in our own right."

"So I'm not needed anymore."

"No, you're needed more than ever. It's easier to *get* people's attention than it is to *hold* people's attention."

Terri leaned around Sloan to address Rutherford. Her tone of voice was angry and her expression matched, but she whispered, "For example, Mr. Capp is having a hard time holding the reporters' interest because you appear to be mumbling snide comments under your breath. I want them to think I'm chewing you out for it, but this is the kind of thing he pays you for, so well done."

Rutherford grimaced. He looked around, and saw that Capp and all of the reporters were staring at him. In his ear, he heard Sloan say, "Don't apologize. It'll ruin the effect."

Rutherford put his cigar back in his mouth and scowled at the reporters. Capp cleared his throat, smiled, and said, "What can I say, that's *Cement Shoes* Rutherford for you."

The reporters all made a note as if on cue.

Sloan said, "There you go. He mentioned your name. Happy now?"

Eventually, the press conference ended. Capp walked off the stage and out the door. The team followed, the water vapor cloud from Rutherford's cigar trailing behind them like steam from a train.

When they were all back in the prep room, surrounded by Capp's marketing staff and safely separated from the reporters by a flimsy wall and a single door, Capp turned to address his employees, which was everyone in the room.

"Excellent," Capp said. "Good work everyone! I think that all went really well." He laughed and smacked Rutherford on the shoulder playfully. "And you! Mumbling to yourself, disrupting my press conference, genius!"

Rutherford's actual personality surfaced before he could stop it. "It wasn't deliberate, sir. Sorry."

Capp's smile evaporated. The room went silent.

Capp said, "Kid, don't ever embarrass me again, in private or in public, by accident. I pay you to feign disrespect for all authority, not to genuinely disrespect my authority. If you ever behave like that again, you make sure it's on purpose."

Rutherford started to say *yes, sir,* then paused, held up a finger, and said, "Whatever, pops." Rutherford took a drag off his e-cigar and blew the vapor in Capp's face.

Capp laughed, hit Rutherford on the shoulder again, and said, "Well done! I knew I had the right man for the job. Okay, let's get out of here."

TWENTY-SIX

Rutherford followed Capp's UPS truck, as per his instructions. He had asked where they were going, so that he'd still have some chance of getting the team there if he got stuck at a light, but Capp refused to ruin the surprise.

They followed the monorail track north out of downtown for just long enough to half convince the team that they were going to the Space Needle, which, like all iconic structures that define their city for tourists, was usually avoided at all cost by the city's actual citizens.

Eventually, the UPS van led them farther east, around the base of Queen Anne Hill and along the edge of Lake Union. It pulled over and came to a stop, leaving barely enough room for Rutherford to parallel park the van. Conversation inside the van faded into the background for him as he concentrated on maneuvering the behemoth into the available space without damaging the car behind or holding up traffic too much. When the van was finally in place, Rutherford's tunnel vision receded and his other senses filtered back. All he could hear was the sound of the team piling out of the van, and Sloan's voice repeating, "Laughing."

Rutherford looked out the passenger window. He saw slivers of blue-gray water between a large dock and a chaotic multitude of houseboats. The vessels varied in appearance, but fell into one of two basic categories: boats that were being lived in like houses, and houses that were floating on the water like boats. Only one houseboat stood out, despite being situated at the far end of a dock, because it was neither of those things. Also, the fact that Vince Capp was standing in front of it invariably drew some attention.

Rutherford walked down the dock, barely aware of his own actions, and joined the rest of the team, who were staring in fascination at what he knew must be his new home.

A ramshackle aluminum travel trailer sat on one side, almost taking up the entire length of a dilapidated barge, which was little more than a rust-and-tar-colored rectangle. A flimsy garden shed sat at the tail end of the barge so that it and the trailer together formed a big metal L. Capp stood in the remaining empty space, next to three folding lawn chairs and a charcoal grill shaped like a giant Seahawks helmet. He held his arms out and said, "Eh?! Eh?! We couldn't decide between a trailer and a boat, and then we thought, why choose?"

Rutherford carefully walked down the wooden gangplank, followed by the rest of the team.

Capp said, "We bought the barge used, then counter balanced it so you could have the trailer to the side and use this big open space for a deck. Your washer, dryer, and extra storage are in the shed. You have full electricity, cable TV, and high-speed Internet. You're hooked up to municipal water, and a service will come out every week to refill your propane and pump your sewage tank."

Rutherford said, "Good!"

Capp looked over the hybrid trailer-barge and said, "It is, isn't it?"

Terri said, "The view certainly is." Sherwood quickly agreed. Sloan was sticking close to the gangway, holding a corner of the shed for balance, but Sherwood, Terri, and Max had all walked out to the corner of the barge. Rutherford looked around and immediately saw their point.

Queen Anne Hill was behind them, a steep berm of apartment buildings and Victorian suburbia. To the left, butting up to the edge of the lake, was Gas Works Park, then the University District and the towering Ship Canal Bridge. Capitol Hill (Queen Anne's funky brother) was across the lake, and finally, to the right, were the tall buildings of downtown. He had a good view of the Space Needle, and Rutherford knew from experience that on a clear day he would be able to see Mt. Rainier.

While they were standing there, a floatplane came in for a landing on the lake. Rutherford would have suspected that Capp had arranged it if he hadn't already known that they did that at regular intervals all day.

Max asked, "Do you think your family will like this any more than they did the fighting and your van?"

Rutherford said, "The view, absolutely. The trailer, not so much, but the fact that a famous billionaire just told the world I'm working for him should help smooth a lot of ruffled feathers."

Capp said, "Hey, Rutherford, come check out the inside!" He was leaning out of the trailer door and beckoning for him to enter. As Rutherford walked across the deck, he saw a catering crew walk up the dock carrying food, drinks, and all the other things that make a party feel like a party, and not just a bunch of people standing around.

He stepped through the door, expecting the interior to be as well-worn as the exterior, but was shocked to find that it was pristine and surprisingly modern.

"It's a brand new Airstream *Land Yacht*. That's the actual name of the model, *Land Yacht*. Can you believe it? The crew did a bang-up job of weathering the outside. You'd never know this thing came straight off the lot yesterday, would you? I know it's not as roomy as a standard apartment, but you have a king bed in the bedroom, two TVs, a full bathroom and shower, a workable kitchen, and you can't complain about the location. What do you think, Rutherford? Not bad, considering it's rent free, wouldn't you say?"

Rutherford said, "It's so much better than I expected."

Capp said, "I'm glad you like the place."

"Not just the place. The job too, Mr. Capp. It's a mixed bag, but all in all, I think it's going to be a lot better than I expected it to be."

Capp shrugged. "Huh. Okay. Well, I'm glad to hear that."

"Sir, I don't know if you're aware of it, but after you dropped me off with Terri, I was pretty sure I wanted out of this job at any cost. I didn't think I could do it. But I've had more time to think about it now, and I want to stick around and give it a go."

Capp smiled and put a hand on Rutherford's shoulder. "I'm glad to hear that, Sinclair. I really am." He and Rutherford spent a moment just smiling and making eye contact. Then Capp said, "Because you signed a contract, and I wouldn't have enjoyed ordering my lawyers to destroy you. What do you say, shall we go out and join the rest of the team?"

"Yes," Rutherford said. "Let's."

ACKNOWLEDGMENTS

I'd like to thank Steven Carlson; Allison DeCaro; Rodney Sherwood; Ric Schrader; my wife, Missy; and the readers of my comic strip, *Basic Instructions*.

I'd also like to thank Detective Kyle Kizzier and Jeff Guardalabene, PsyD. Any glaring inaccuracies in this book are there despite these men's efforts.

Lastly, I'd also like to thank the gang from Carl's poker night: the least organized poker night of all time, and the birthplace of the game Texas Explain'em. It's been nearly a decade, and I still miss it.

ABOUT THE AUTHOR

Scott Meyer has worked in radio and written for the video game industry. For a long period he made his living as a stand-up comedian, touring extensively throughout the United States and Canada. Scott eventually left the drudgery of professional entertainment for the glitz and glamour of the theme park industry. His comic strip *Basic Instructions* appeared in various weekly newspapers and ran online for over a decade.

Made in the USA
Las Vegas, NV
20 December 2022

63592111R00194